All the Parts of Your Soul

by

Patricia Friedrich
Jen Jensen

All the Parts of Your Soul

Cover Art by *The Wild Rose Press, Inc.*

The Wild Rose Press, Inc.
PO Box 708
Adams Basin, NY 14410-0708
Visit us at www.thewildrosepress.com

Publishing History
First Edition, 2023
Trade Paperback ISBN 978-1-5092-4940-4
Digital ISBN 978-1-5092-4941-1

Published in the United States of America

I was powerfully aware of Pia's presence next to me and shifted so I could feel her shoulder pressed against mine. She leaned into me, welcoming the contact casually, and I looked at her profile, the soft angles of her nose and chin. She turned to smile at me, meeting my gaze, and I wondered how I'd tried to push away a woman with such warm brown eyes. A solo guitarist then began to play Chopin: Etude, Op. 10 No. 6, and I closed my eyes to listen, overwhelmed by the bright blue sky, red dirt of the mesas, and Pia herself.

With my eyes closed, I felt each chord the guitarist strummed, and as the piece continued into its second movement, I also felt Pia's beautiful fingers pull my hand from my lap into hers, where she held it with both hands, her skin warm against mine. She traced the backside of my hand with her finger, while she held it tightly with her other hand. I opened my eyes and turned to her. She sat quietly, looking at our hands in her lap, and then lifted her eyes to mine. She pulled her right hand from mine, lifted her finger, and lightly touched the scar under my right eye, a question in her eyes. I mouthed, "Skateboard when I was nine," and she nodded, returning her hand to her lap, finding my fingers again. The song ended, and I said, with a grin, "I could do that better."

Dedication

For Luiz, guardian of my soul.
~Patricia

For Sarah, my karmic reward.
~Jen

Acknowledgments

The authors would like to thank early readers and family members, who helped make sure this story would resonate with others. Thanks go to Anne Duguid Knol for the early editorial work and *The Wild Rose Press* for believing in this story.

Prologue

Rory
Yorkshire, 1840

I was soaked to the bone when I entered the hackney that would take me away forever, mere months after I had made my way back to my childhood home. The sky cried tears of grief and sorrow the day I left Moorsgrange. The rain now fell from above like thin blades, making it impossible to see at any distance, even as close as the rose garden, a few feet ahead of me. Having succumbed to the urgency of one last stroll across the grounds, I had been exposed to the elements for the better part of an hour, but I did not suffer the cold anymore even as my dress clung to me like a second skin. I was numb to the world, encased in a layer of self-pity so thick that even the voice of the conductor, asking me if I was ready to go, had a hard time reaching me.

When I finally acknowledged him, it was with a simple nod. He looked very sorry, yet unable to find consoling words, and so he stared at the ground, letting the rain slide from his hat, before closing the door. I then buried my face in the crease of my elbow and let sadness overtake me.

My plan was to go to London to spend a few days in a place I knew well enough to settle in and to regain some strength. From there, I would go to Paris and try to put the shreds of my life back together, in what form I did not yet know. I needed to be as far away from Moorsgrange as I possibly could. Once I was established, I would send for my father, whom I had hugged for a long minute at farewell. I did not say goodbye to the lady of the manor, nor to the doctor. Cook looked at me with such pain in her face I could barely stand it. I promised I'd write to her without really knowing if I'd honor my word.

That morning, with her aid and for the first and only time in my life, I had stolen something. I had taken Jules's cravat pin, made of gold and an oddly shaped pearl, one which had belonged to his own father. It was the one thing of him I had, the single object, I would ever have. I planned on making a ring out of it: the only ring I would wear. He would be my spouse. Forever. I solemnly swore this on that day.

Green hills and wet moors rolled out as we made progress toward my destination, the melancholy they provoked sieving through my every pore. I felt no hunger, no thirst. My heart continued to congeal with each mile we crossed, and I welcomed that development because, in that state, it hurt a little less to exist. My pain, at that moment so strong as to take my breath away, might even become tolerable if my heart froze. I never wanted to feel anything again, good or bad—it was all too much to bear.

In the months preceding this winter day, Jules had become my whole life, and now his music, the sounds of the piano, played incessantly in my head, like a fixed idea. Would I ever look at a rose the same way? Would I ever enjoy cake or the chords of a citra by the fire? I doubted I would ever dance again or eat sweets with the same abandon. I should never enjoy a kiss anymore, the warmth of someone's skin against mine, nor experience the joy of being serenaded. All the pleasure in the world had vanished, leaving a trail of longing that could not be quenched.

Jules was dead. That day, except for the maddening symphony of rain and thunder, the music ceased, and one lifetime would not be enough to claim it back.

Part I
Chapter 1

Pia
Sedona, 2019

My feet ache, and I don't care one bit. I'm climbing to the top of Wilson Mountain, overlooking Oak Creek Canyon, because, as stunning as Sedona itself is, I needed the distance of this glorious geography to try and finally bring closure to what has happened to me and to a life I thought I knew. It is September. Below me is a vast expanse of red soil and dark green trees in one of the most beautiful places on earth. The air is dry and cool, and the fragrant breeze in this area smells like something no one has figured out how to bottle. If they ever did, they would be instant millionaires. In a few hours, I will bear witness to the Arizona twilight, with its pinks, blues, and yellows that no camera filter can replicate. If a person does not capture the immenseness of the universe and the depth of the mysteries of creation here, they must be a lost cause. I come to the mountain humbled, having had the good fortune of shaking all of my beliefs about the here and the now, and the finality of everything and everyone. I come here renewed. Do I need to understand the world to be in it? Is that an expectation? I don't know if I should even try.

I have always had self-control. I have also fiercely

believed in science and things I can touch or know. No one was a more unlikely candidate than me for such a sudden acceleration in spiritual growth. If anyone had asked, I would have said I was going about life content, if not completely fulfilled. I took pride in taking care of others, even if deep inside I knew I neglected myself in the process. All of that changed, as my certainties crumbled one by one. It turns out that, as I am faced with the eternity of the mountains, I must also contend with the idea that my life might be like theirs. Endless.

As I put one foot in front of the other and climb higher, I think of the events of the last few months—the visions, the hospital stay, the trip—and how they changed me. Even nature with its acacias, mariolas, and cliffroses looks different to me now. I don't stop to figure things out. I much rather take action and help heal, fix, cure. After all, I'm a nurse. But they turned out to be special circumstances.

I was known to my friends and family as self-reliant, experimental but also very calculating. I once tattooed the name of a lover to my arm, dyed my hair in strands of cobalt blue before asking the hospital where I work if that was all right, and followed another love to China with only two pairs of jeans and a T-shirt in my backpack. I have lived and collected many stories to tell. And tattoos. I've collected quite a few of those too. Yet, for each of these instances of free-spiritedness, I carried a back-up plan lodged in my brain and a little notebook carefully annotated, just in case.

As I continue on this path of red dirt and slightly warm wind, I realize that life caught up with me and my transgressions and taught me a lesson about all I presumed to have mastered. Life asked me, *what if you lost your little notebook?* And at first, I didn't really have an answer. I had never thought to lose it. And yet, I am here, on this mountain, shedding every certainty that shaped who I am, because of her.

They brought her to the hospital one morning in early June, when a big fire destroyed a large part of a condo near the town's touristic center. She had a bad burn in one of her legs and had inhaled quite a bit of smoke. Later, I discovered that she wasn't even in the complex. Instead, she was walking the area, coming back from brunch, when she saw the flames and rushed in. She went inside three times altogether, ignoring the warnings of other passersby, saving a septuagenarian grandmother during the first incursion, a young woman next, and two pups in the end. She is now a local hero.

I first saw her on a gurney, drifting in and out of consciousness because of the smoke inhalation. Something drew me to her corner. She hadn't spoken to me. We hadn't locked eyes. Yet this magnetic pull, this energy, drew me to her side. It was the end of my shift, and I had been counting down the last forty minutes of it, compulsively looking at my watch. Two friends from the East coast were in Sedona for a hiking trip, and I looked forward to lunch with them at a Mexican restaurant in a beautiful piazza, full of art galleries and gift shops. I could have easily left, used the remaining few minutes to tidy things up, but I didn't.

The patients started coming in right then, first in small groups and then in enough numbers to overwhelm our small staff. A young doctor yelled for help. The sound of ambulances was maddening. I offered to stay, and no one opposed me.

We moved her to a slim triage bed, where she

hugged each arm with the opposite hand. When she opened her eyes, they were red and teary, but soon she closed them again. Her rapid breathing told me she needed oxygen right then.

"Hello, I'm Nurse Nowak." I announced, like I always did when I first saw a patient. "Can you speak?"

The question seemed to surprise her, and she struggled to sit up to show me how capable she was. "Yes, I can talk." She squinted with the effort, and I noticed a deep horizontal scar under her right eye, a long-before acquired souvenir of some mishap. It was endearing in a way. "Great. But don't try to move." I eased her back down. Can you tell me your name?"

"It's Rikke. R-i-k-k-e."

"Okay, Rikke. I'll have some questions for you soon, but first, I want to give you some oxygen to help you breathe and clear out your lungs. You're fine with that?"

She nodded.

"Perfect. For now, inhale. I'll listen to your heart." It was surprisingly stable given the circumstances, and its speed was adequate at 70 beats per minute. "It's good. Let me adjust that mask so you get the full benefits of the oxygen."

She nodded again, the mask already better fitted around her nose and mouth. Her breathing slowed, which indicated to me it was panic, more than physical inability, that had caused the breathlessness in the first place. And who could blame her?

"I'm now going to take a look at your leg." I moved toward the end of the bed, and she lifted the sheet to expose her shins. The left one was very badly burned, and she must have been in extreme pain, though she didn't let that show. I wondered if she had ever been told that to cry was a sign of weakness. She looked like that kid who took a fall in school but swallowed the tears they felt they could not shed over their scraped knee.

"On a scale of one to ten, how much does it hurt?"

She shrugged. "Nine?"

She looked very collected for a nine, but the state of the burn was certainly compatible with that assessment. "I'm gonna start cooling and cleaning this wound a bit, and then the doctor will come to see you."

"Thank you, Nurse Nowak." Her voice came out muffled by the mask.

"It's Pia. My name is Pia." I smiled at her, hoping my calmness would be reassuring and somewhat contagious. Secretly, I also wanted her to smile back.

"Thank you, Nurse Nowak, Pia." She closed her eyes and finally relaxed.

When I had a few minutes for myself, I called my friends to let them know a meal together would not happen. Changing plans was a constant in the life of a nurse, so I figured they would understand. Yet, I was rearranging my life for a stranger! It was weird and marvelous and destabilizing all at the same time. When I returned, the doctor let me know that Rikke had been assigned a room, that she would need to be kept under observation all afternoon and overnight, and her bandages would need changing from time to time. She had been given medication to mitigate the pain. Those second-degree burns would make her quite uncomfortable. I hated the thought. It was like the situation was happening to me, to my very skin and my own nerves.

What followed had no logical explanation either. I felt an overwhelming need to protect her, to nurse her back to health, and to ease her pain. Leaving like I did every day, assuming the patients I had seen would be taken care of by my colleagues was not a possibility. I had to make sure, and the only way to guarantee it was to do the job myself, to take control of the situation. Patients' suffering was the reality of my days and nights, and I had learned to balance my compassion with a degree of detachment so that I could do my job. Yet this was different. I was filled with fear. In Rikke's case, the feeling was visceral. The pain was lodged in my body, as much as in hers, and I could not feel good until she did too.

I went to see the head nurse to argue my way out of going home. I'm good at arguing, and we are a small regional hospital, serving Sedona and surrounding towns, and therefore more informal and flexible when it comes to timetables and schedules. Yes, it felt a little wrong to compromise my professional position, but my need to protect this person, for whatever reason my brain had imposed, seemed to trump all my good sense. I put it down to extreme ethical commitment. Whatever is needed to support the patients, we do, I told myself. Deep down I knew that my controlling part and my free-spirited side were having a fight, and that to move forward I would have to count on both.

Nurse Warren, a large woman in her late fifties, with greying hair and deep brown eyes, looked at me and raised an eyebrow. "Why stay?" She asked, hands on her hips in defiance. My powers of persuasion were always tested by Nurse Warren.

I took my time restyling my ponytail. "It's obvious,

isn't it? This fire. Lots of people. I can be here. It's not an inconvenience." Certainly, I sounded too eager.

She examined me up and down, her trained mind scanning for the untold story like she did with patients who tried to diminish the seriousness of their own conditions or check out before it was safe. "I don't know. Something's fishy here."

I feigned ignorance and went for humor. "Must be the cod they fried in the cafeteria today."

"Don't be fresh with me, Nurse Nowak. I don't like this one bit."

"Look, if I promise to go and have a lie down for a few hours, will you let me stay?"

She X-rayed me with her eyes one more time.

"Fine. But make sure you sleep. You have been here too long. No point in staying if you are going to make mistakes out of tiredness. We need fully functioning nurses."

"Thank you!" I joined my hands together as if in prayer.

I had already turned to leave when she completed the thought. "And get something to eat. Perhaps a bit of that smelly cafeteria cod if you will?"

Touché. I turned again and winked at her. She was all right if you knew how to handle her, my dislike for fish notwithstanding.

In the nurses' quarters, after a bowl of soup, I washed and then went to grab a clean blanket. Though I would have inexplicably preferred to be with Rikke, I recognized how tired I was. Lying down on the cold bed sheets, I waited for the warmth of my own body to heat up the clean-scented fabric. At first, I thought sleep would elude me, but when it quickly came to swathe my tired limbs, I let it hold me, as in an embrace, and carry me away. I was out before I could devise a plan for what was to come, which would have been my preference. That was when everything changed. In my dreams, I was walking the streets searching for someone, stopping at every store and peeking inside, trying to call out a name though no voice came out. Ice-cold doorknobs hurt my hands. I was wet and scared. Then the scene changed, and a young man offered me a red rose, which I smelled and put on top of a piano. I looked down and realized I had my feet, all the way to my ankles, immersed in water. The water was cold and sparkly because of the sun. I had a teacup in my hands, and it shattered.

I didn't usually dream, or if I did, I never remembered. Nights and naps were like blackouts. And they were restful but not necessarily insightful. To see so much detail, to smell and hold, and shout were new experiences to me. If dreams were meant to provide wisdom and to reboot our brains, I was definitely missing out on something important.

I woke up with another nurse tapping on my shoulder. I had been asleep for over three hours, and it was well into the afternoon. One of my legs was asleep too, and my neck hurt.

"Nurse Warren thought it was best to wake you up." She said by way of an apology.

"Sure." I replied, trying to get my bearings and keep my eyes open. I stretched my arms and rubbed my hands together. "Are there more patients from the fire?"

"Only the ones who needed extra treatment or overnight observation. Most have gone home."

In front of the mirror, I refreshed my ponytail and

brushed my teeth. Some of the blue strands framed my face, contrasting with the dark brunette of the other locks. I decided the lines around my eyes were soft and added personality rather than age, and I was happy for my arched eyebrows. Instinctively, I turned sideways to catch a good look at my profile. More so than in the last year, when work was all that I had focused on, I now wanted to look pretty. I tucked in my stomach, a little too pudgy in the middle. Things looked different when a person was approaching forty. I made a mental note to go to the gym more often. I flexed my left arm and touched my bicep with the opposite hand to still find good muscle tone.

My thoughts reverted to Rikke, I had, with a slightly more rested mind, concocted a plan to go to the second floor and find out how she was doing. I needed to get past Nurse Warren and her uncanny capacity for lie detection. The good news was that her shift had to be almost over, since it was already late. If I was patient, I might be able to avoid the problem altogether. Night-shift head nurses were a lot easier to handle and certainly no match for me.

It turned out that Nurse Warren actually helped the cause without knowing. When she saw me down the corridor of the staff quarters, she stomped in my direction, yelling my name. "Nurse Nowak, I need to ask you for a favor since you are now rested. I stayed as long as I could, but I have to go home now." She didn't wait for me to agree. "I'd like for you to go upstairs and do the rounds to check on the fire victims. Make sure none of them still needs to communicate with a family member that hasn't yet been notified. If you discover someone has not been helped, do it yourself."

"Yes, Nurse Warren."

"Go home after you're done."

"I will."

On the second floor, I realized that five patients remained. Each was given a private room, starting with a man in his fifties, who had been napping when the fire started. One of his neighbors decided to go back and bang on the door, and how lucky it was that he did because the guy had escaped with only a few superficial burns to his arms and a bad sore throat.

The next patient was a woman, and she was very upset about staying in hospital overnight. She kept pulling on her strawberry blond hair. "I hate hospitals," she said. "I want to go home."

I didn't know if she still had a home but convincing them to do what I knew to be best was one of my specialties. "We want to be certain that you're well. It's only a night after all. Would you like to watch some TV until dinner or until you can fall asleep? I could also bring you some jelly or a cup of fruit if that would help." The offer of fruit made her smile like a child. I grabbed some peaches in syrup from the pantry and turned the television to a rerun of a trivia show. She seemed quite content after that.

The very next room was Rikke's, so I skipped it and went to take care of the last two patients. One was snoring and the other quite the curmudgeon. I was done in less than five minutes. I had checked on patients so many times in my years at the hospital that those rooms were very familiar. In them, I was the best version of myself—helpful and self-assured. But those skills had come at a steep cost. They were the result of my taking care of both my parents, on separate occasions, when they were ill, and I was much too young. In their subsequent absence, I had also taken care of my brother. It had become what I did—take care of people, and I knew, though I often denied it even to myself, that I healed others to the detriment of my own needs and my own health, physical and otherwise.

I had feathers tickling my stomach when I prepared to cross the threshold of Rikke's room. I didn't know why I was so nervous. There was no reason other than the thumping of my heart telling me I should be. She was looking at the garden of succulents, outside her window, one hand holding the curtain to take it out of the way. In the low light of the room, her arms were slender and muscular, her profile angular and strong. The short, spiky haircut revealed a lovely long neck, and I must have blushed at the thought of kissing it lightly, a notion that invaded my brain without my permission.

She hummed a tune. It seemed to be classical music, but it could have been country or folk as well. When she saw me, she sat on the bed and issued a faint, nervous smile, the kind of noncommittal expression fit for every possible occasion. I noticed the row of perfect teeth and immediately wanted to say something smart, so I could get a flash of that grin again. Of course, nothing witty occurred to me.

"I know I should be resting, but my mind has been traveling a mile a minute."

"It's common," I said. "I mean, after a traumatic event. The mind starts wondering about what could have been. It's still on high alert. If it doesn't go away in a few days, that edginess, we can direct you to a counselor who can help."

14

Her eyebrows came together at the center, and her body stiffened. "I don't think that's warranted. I don't need a therapist."

"If it's not, then no worries. But it's always good to know the service exists. How are your lungs?"

She touched her chest below where her collar bone was. "They hurt when I breathe. Like I am very tired, and they have turned heavy all of a sudden. Like a blanket immersed in water. And I'm still coughing."

"I could have a listen?"

"I'm okay."

"Is there anyone you would like us to contact? Maybe to drive you home tomorrow?"

"No," she said a little too quickly. "I have only been in Sedona a short while, and I don't want to worry my family, with their being away and all. I don't want to disrupt the routine of the few friends I have made here either. I keep to myself." She looked down and brought a hand to the back of her neck.

"Fair enough. We'll figure it out tomorrow. I think you should go to bed, though, and try to sleep."

She fluffed her pillow and lay down, staring at the ceiling. "Great. Thank you. Good night."

I had the clear impression that her words and movement were a hint that I should go, but my feet stuck to the ground. A force I could not explain compelled me to take care of Rikke, as if my own life depended on it. I simply couldn't leave. She was my responsibility, in the most intense way.

"I thought I would stay here a bit and monitor your progress. Make sure your breathing is regular. Would that be all right? I could sit and read…"

She thought for a second, as if unsure of what her

options were. It was not that I wanted to get in trouble or anything, but it was as if I had been given a task by a higher power, and I was not about to fail.

"S-sure." She moved her head enough to meet my eyes.

I noticed that when I pulled my thermal shirt up toward my elbows, she looked intently at the snake tattoo in my inner arm. Self-consciously, I pulled the sleeves down again. I had never been embarrassed about my ink before. Or my nose ring. Much less my blue highlights. She had caused me to consider all three in the space of a few seconds.

I told her I would go get a novel that I had in my bag and would come right back. When I returned, breathless for having dashed down the hall, she was half asleep, and I tiptoed to the armchair, afraid to awaken her.

The story couldn't hold my attention for more than a few minutes at a time. A pressure in the pit of my stomach kept robbing my peace. As I looked at Rikke, and she tossed about in her sleep, the certainty that I had met her before descended upon me. There was no chance she was a stranger. *That's it! I know her. That's why I feel so strongly about taking care of her. She must be the sister of a friend. Someone I knew when I was younger. Someone who moved away from Sedona and now is back. She only said she didn't know many people here now. Nothing about the past.* I was so relieved to have a logical explanation that I actually made an effort to concentrate on the story in the book, an intriguing thriller full of twists.

Outside, as twilight replaced the afternoon, light rain had started to fall, and a few bolts of lightning illuminated the room. Rikke's breathing appeared regular. I eased myself into the chair, a hand propping my chin up, and the other holding the book, until sleep came to take me away again, this time for the whole night.

In the morning, Nurse Warren was livid to find out I was still at the hospital. I had sneaked out of Rikke's room at first light while she slept. I was helping a man who had a broken arm when she saw me, and she could barely contain her displeasure in front of the patient. Her face was beet red, and her eyes looked ready to jump from their orbits. I braced myself. She motioned for us to step away for a bit.

"What in the world?"

"I was about to leave when I was called to help that patient. He's got osteoporosis, you know?"

"And you're gonna get a talking to if you don't leave this minute!" She pressed her lips together to show me how upset she was.

"I'm going, I'm going. Jeez."

I imagined she followed me with her eyes when I went to pick up my bag. I was notorious in the hospital for the size of the purse I carried and the fact that, in it, you could find almost anything you might want. Once, during a party, people kept calling out items, challenging me to find them inside.

"A comb! A Band-Aid! Old movie tickets! A mug! She can't possibly have a mug in there, can she?" Sure as the day is long, I had all of them.

A child was crying somewhere in the infirmary. I waved at Nurse Warren, and she engaged her attention elsewhere. As soon as I was out of her field of vision, I took the elevator upstairs to see how Rikke was doing. I felt Christmas-morning excitement at the thought of being near her. I found her searching her room.

"Hi, you should be in bed."

She didn't say hello. "Did you by any chance see my cell phone?"

"I'm sorry, I did not. Everything we had that was yours—small backpack, glasses, umbrella—we gave back to you."

"I don't remember having it since I checked my email a few minutes before seeing the fire. I think I lost it."

"I'm sorry. Losing a phone is a real drag." I took a breath and then went into a completely different conversation. "I am here to check on your bandages. After that, I'm going home."

She sat on the bed and straightened her leg. The wound oozed a bit, and the bandage was damp. "Yeah, it needs changing." I went to the pharmacy a couple of doors down and, waving at the pharmacist, asked for fresh supplies. When I made my way back to Rikke's room, I worked quickly because I didn't want to get caught. "There. This should last a while. I know it looks angry, but it's actually healing properly. The pain is tolerable?"

She nodded. I assumed she was being tough through it.

I didn't think I was going to see her again, so I lingered there stupidly, not knowing what to say. Rikke messed up her blond hair with her hand and something stirred in my chest. She moved about to test the new bandage, grabbing onto the footboard for support. Her body looked fit and strong, the body of someone who would enter a burning building. When the silence became too awkward, she was the one to break it.

"Thank you very much Nurse Nowak, Pia, for your help and care. I really appreciate it."

"Goodbye, Rikke. It was nice meeting you." I turned around and left, alarmed by the teardrop wetting my face. I couldn't fathom what was happening to me.

I drove around for a while, unsure of what I wanted to do next. I was very hungry, so when I saw the Red Rose Bakery atop the hill, I made a turn and stopped there. The overwhelming smell of breads, rolls and pie travelled to my nostrils. I had a chocolate croissant, fruit, and a latte, and then I had an idea.

I rushed back into the car, a glimmer of hope clouding my judgement, and drove to the semi-destroyed apartment complex that had been the spot of Rikke's heroics. It wasn't far. Most places are not far in Sedona.

When I arrived, the desolate scene made my heart heavy with sorrow for the people who had lost their belongings and their home. Luckily, and in part because of Rikke, I had heard earlier that no one had lost their life.

The left front face of the building was completely destroyed. The top corner of the construction was missing, and soot covered the part that remained. It was a cloudy and foggy day, and the humidity from the rain that had fallen the night before only added to the derelict atmosphere of the place. It had become our own castle ruin.

Jumping into action and leaving that piercing empathy locked in my heart, I searched every square inch of the grass below me. I wasn't dressed—or shod—for the occasion, and my feet were wet within a few minutes. I covered the whole area in front of the building up until the part where police tape told the curious to stay out. I considered what to do. How big of an infraction would it really be to cross the police line to look for a phone? Yeah, it sounded bad. Begrudgingly, I stayed back and started to walk toward my car, but only because a young woman was taking photos nearby and had noticed me.

That's when I saw it, under a tree of immense proportions, turned with its screen to the ground. A phone with its black back camouflaged against the dark soil but still unmistakable. Its position and the tree's canopy had protected it from the rain. I picked it up and turned it around, and when I pressed the button on the side, Rikke smiled at me from the screen. I had found her phone.

In the car I called my phone from hers. I thought I should tell her about the importance of password protecting the cell. With her number in hand, I composed a text, asking how she would like me to return her phone. I did not want to return to the hospital, lest I got one of Nurse Warren's famous talking-tos. My hope was that Rikke had a text messenger connected to her computer and would be able to read the text once she got home.

I put the phone in my all-containing bag, and finally started on my way back.

****

James, my brother, was waiting for me when I got to the cottage at mid-morning. I'd been at the hospital for almost thirty hours. He sat on one of the steps of the patio, throwing a tennis ball to Orlando, his Labrador, who bounded across the lawn to pick it up every time.

He strutted to the passenger window, which I rolled down, and peeked inside. His winter trademark look of flannel shirt under a knit sweater had been swapped for a simple buttoned-down green shirt, and his side-parted, light-brown hair, worn like that in all seasons, was as familiar as it was comforting. So was the five o'clock shadow he wore with style.

"Where have you been? I was so worried I came here to look for you." While he spoke, Orlando pranced to the window too and stood on his hind legs and extended a paw in my direction

"Hospital. Did you not hear about the big fire?"

"What fire?"

"Do you ever know what's going on? Like watch the news or something?"

He shrugged. "I'd rather be coding or walking Orlando." He petted the dog on the head.

I offered him the keys. "Take Orlando inside. I'm gonna park." Having a younger brother means you get to boss him around even when you are close to forty and he is past thirty-five.

The cottage felt very hot when I got in. The air-conditioner had been turned off for almost two days because of my extended work at the hospital. Quickly, I turned the thermostat down to seventy-six degrees and grabbed a bandana from a hook on the wall to tie my hair.

"It's like the tropics in here. I think it's much hotter than outside." James offered as he sat on the couch and wiped his brow with the back of his hand. Orlando went to sit next to him.

"Already took care of it. You want coffee?" I suggested.

"If you're making it anyway."

I went through the motions of preparing it while James observed me.

"You look tired," he said, rubbing Orlando's head once more. The dog was half lying on his lap and occupied a great amount of space.

"Jeez, thanks." I found the sugar and the little spoons.

"I mean it. You work too hard."

I ignored him and continued my preparations. "James, do you remember any Rikke from when we were growing up?"

"No. Who is he?"

"She. Someone who came to the hospital, and I'm sure I've met her before. Thought it might be the sister of a friend." I readied the tray.

"Nope. Can't think of anyone." He stretched his arms above his head.

"Never mind. Here's your coffee."

We sat in silence, sipping our hot drink. Then I walked toward him and touched the tips of his hair.

"You need a haircut."

He scoffed and shook his head.

"What?" I asked him, confused.

"You. Always wanting to take care of me. To take care of people. You are a 24-hour-a-day nurse."

"I'm not. For a nurse, I'm actually quite tame." I thought of Rikke.

"Liar!"

"Whatever, James. Drink your coffee." I loved him too much to argue, though I insisted even to myself that he didn't have a point.

"Can I hang out a bit? Me and Orlando? I finished

22

a large project for a tech company and am ready for a nap."

"So am I." I said, finally realizing how utterly exhausted I was.

"Okay, Orlando and I will be here on the couch if you need us to defend you or something." James said, already easing himself into a comfortable position. "But we'll be sleeping so…"

"So I better fend for myself, huh?"

"Yep, something like that." He yawned.

In the silence of the cottage, I took a moment to appreciate how much I loved my home. From the smell of the wood of the wall panels, to the planters in every window and the comfy, well-loved furniture, I had created a world of calm that few were invited to share, and I liked it just like that. James and Orlando were always welcome. I considered it their home too. Ever since our parents had passed, first our mom and then our dad, James had become a big part of my world. He and that adorable dog were my family.

Lunch time came and went, and the light changed like it does in the afternoon. With James and Orlando keeping me company, I felt at peace, finally able to rest a bit and heal from the absurdity of the last two days. I went up the ladder to the loft area that contained my large bed, and, in the span of half an hour, started to feel like myself again. Rikke faded a bit in the background, like dreams do when they get disrupted by the arrival of the first rays of sun. Maybe she was only that—a moment of fancy, a figment of my imagination. She had stirred up emotions that bewildered me, but now, in the safety of my home, they seemed less startling. I let myself drift away into heavy sleep, the weight of the eiderdown pleasurable against my shoulders, until I was completely out.

I woke up to the chime of my cell phone and the quiet of a semi-dark room. No rays of sun there. It had turned into an overcast afternoon and my heavy curtains shielded the bed from the bit of light that tried to peek in. Instead, on the bedside table, the screen glowed, illuminating the ceiling, and I knew whose message it was before I even read it. Rikke's text had only her address and a quick thank you for finding her phone, but it was all the information I needed to get moving. My heart was ready to explode in my chest. So much for the feelings having mellowed.

"Where are you going? You just got here." James complained when he saw me reach for the keys and a coat. "You didn't even change out of your scrubs. Eww."

I looked down, realizing he was right. I felt a little disgusted myself. "Fine. I'll jump in the shower but then I'll go. Help yourself to some lasagna. There are treats for Orlando, as always."

Twenty minutes later, I was stopping at the Red Rose Bakery again, to buy some breads and a piece of cake. Another ten and I rang the bell at Rikke's apartment taking deep breaths to calm me down.

A young woman opened the door. "Hi, you're looking for Rikke?"

"I am. I'm Pia, from the hospital? I wanted to return her phone."

"I'm her neighbor. Paula. She's sleeping. I came to help her a bit when I heard what had happened. Terrible business."

"It sure is." We smiled at each other, the

awkwardness of being strangers showing.

"Would you like to give me the phone?" she asked extending a hand.

"Oh, yeah, sure. Here it is." I reached inside my back pocket. "These are for her too. Some stuff from the bakery. In case she's hungry."

"Right. I'll let her know."

I wanted to linger and was very disappointed not to be able to see Rikke but found no way to intervene.

Paula moved to close the door, but I was still able to catch the "Who is it?" coming from further inside. The familiarity of the voice startled me but not as much as the certainty that I would soon be back and that we must be somehow very well acquainted.

Chapter 2

Rikke

I went into the hospital with second degree burns and smoke inhalation and left with a stalker.

My friend Kate said I was overreacting, but it didn't feel like I was. Nurse Nowak, Pia, my stalker, wouldn't leave me alone. During my overnight stay, she sat by my bed all night, fussed over my oxygen mask, and insisted on changing my bandages. I wanted to touch the bright blue streaks in her hair, to see if they felt as strange as they looked, but I didn't. She worried the small ring in her nose as she watched me try to sleep. When she pushed up the long sleeve thermals she wore under her scrubs to the middle of her arms, I saw tattoos on her forearms and wrists. It was not bright enough for me to see all the details of the tattoos then, but later I would learn that one was to commemorate a trip to China, and the other was for a lover with whom she was sure she'd spend eternity. The latter is a source of some consternation, even now. So much for forever. I pretended to sleep so I could watch her to make sure she didn't smother me.

"This woman won't leave me alone. She texts me to check how I'm feeling, stops by my house. She brings me food. She went and dug around the fire site to find my phone and return it to me. Do you think that a normal person would do something like that?"

Kate sat on my couch as I conveyed this. After what seemed like calculated silence she said, "Rikke, does it occur to you that perhaps she likes you?"

"Likes me?" I asked, perplexed. "Like how?"

"Like, likes you likes you. Like wants to get to know you, is smitten, in love, etc.?" Kate was a massage therapist. It's how we met. I hurt my shoulder moving the couch into my apartment when I arrived in Sedona a few months before. I found her in the phone book left on the counter by the previous tenant. I didn't think people used phone books anymore, or took ads in them, but I was grateful I was wrong. Within a few months, I'd realized Kate was much better with people than I was.

I considered the possibility that Nurse Nowak, Pia, liked me. It had not occurred to me that she might be interested. But then, it never did occur to me that a woman liked me. While other people learned how to read flirting and social cues during adolescence, like any awkward, gender non-conforming, queer kid, I mostly internalized the idea that there was something wrong with me, and then spent the next decade unravelling that notion in therapy. Certain automatic reactions, like dismissing the possibility that someone was interested in me, still happened from time to time.

"Really?" I asked Kate. From the blue hair to the tattoos, to the nose ring and god knows what else hid beneath her clothes, I was not interested. Was I? I was thinking about what was under her clothes. That's an awful lot to notice if you're not interested, I silently acknowledged.

I said all this to Kate, in a more conversational and succinct way, and she seemed to accept it. She said,

"Well, watch next time." Then she left for work, and I was alone in my apartment.

My lungs felt better than they had in days, and I was finally able to move around without tightness in my chest and labored breathing. The burns on my legs still ached, but the pain retreated a meaningful distance from my consciousness with over-the-counter painkillers. I was healing from my heroics, which I still didn't quite understand.

My reaction to the fire had been instinctual, primitive. In a second, I had queried up all genetic survival material from my DNA, and a moment later, it overtook my logical senses. I run regularly, keep in shape, and consider myself healthy, but I moved like an Olympic athlete that day, jumping over couches and chairs, lifting the elderly, young, and dogs. For a moment, I believed I was a superhero. I wish I could tell you how it happened, but I honestly have no idea. I've always worried about taking more than I give. As a result, I live a solitary life. Yet, I've never acted out of such altruism before.

The knock on the door shocked me from this musing, where I'd returned many times since that night. I stood to peer out the peephole, and there was Nurse Nowak, Pia, holding a plate of food, her massive purse, and what looked like a latte from a coffee shop. Whether it was for her or me, I didn't know.

I bottled my anxiety and opened the door. I intended to tell her to leave me alone, that I was not interested in her, but then I saw the brownies on the plate, and noticed a paper bag from the Indian restaurant down the street inside her purse, and I caught the words before they left my mouth. What could it possibly hurt that someone brought me food? I'd learned my impeccable manners from my mother, the debutante and trust-fund baby of a Texas oil baron and could submerge my feelings beneath social expectations of tact when the occasion, or food, called for it. As I recall this, I realize it sounds callous and shallow and I was lying to myself. Perhaps there was another reason I invited her in, rather than sending her away. At the time, I could only attribute it to manners. Looking back, I think it was because the light caught Pia's profile in the entry way, and I thought her beautiful.

"Come in, Nurse Nowak, Pia," I said.

She laughed at me, her smile wide, her dark brown eyes alive with amusement. "Why do you insist on calling me Nurse Nowak, Pia?"

"It got stuck in my brain that way."

"Well, if it's stuck, I suppose it will do." She gestured with a nod into the apartment, as if to be sure I was sure. I pushed the door back further to make my point. She entered the room, and I swear her smile was triumphant. I'd surrendered to a stalker, I thought with alarm, but then I remembered the brownies and Indian food. Pia sat the brownies and food down on the table. I watched in awe as she pulled the whole bag of Indian food from her purse. She wore scrubs and comfortable shoes. I looked at her back and neck and wondered how I might describe her to someone.

She was not thin, but she was healthy, and as she lifted food from the bags, I noted the swell of her breasts and slight roundness of her stomach. She caught me looking, and, with a cough, I jerked my gaze up to her eyes. She stared back with an arched eyebrow. I think I blushed, so I turned away.

"Will you stay and eat with me?" I asked, surprising myself. I stopped in front of the microwave, waiting for her response and looking at my own reflection. I'd dyed my short dark brown hair platinum blonde a month or so before and needed a haircut and touch-up. My hair stood up straight from my head, without any product, and the roots were in dark contrast against the blond tips. I touched the deep scar below my right eye lightly, a nervous habit. I earned it riding my skateboard over Christmas break at home, and despite plastic surgery, it remained haggard and angry. As an adolescent, I worried about it and my square jaw, boyish mannerisms, and crooked grin, but then I'd worried after everything about myself then. Now, I only worried about the new wrinkles around my eyes. I'd grown used to the scar. My shoulders tapered out of sight at the bottom of the glass.

"I'd love to." Her reply brought me back to the moment, and I wondered why I'd felt compelled to look at myself at all. It wasn't something I did often.

"Do you want something to drink?" I lifted two plates from the cupboard. Hands outstretched, I reached them over the small counter which separated the dining area from the kitchen. She'd likely saw me looking at myself in the microwave but said nothing.

"I have my coffee," she said. "I would've gotten you something…"

"It's fine," I said. "I have had enough coffee today." I took a bottle of water from the fridge and joined her at my small dining table. She chose the chair I normally sat in and for a moment I felt a compulsion to ask her to move, but I swallowed it. It was only a chair. I looked at the food and my plate and for a confused moment was unsure how to proceed.

Pia laughed and went into my kitchen as though she lived in my house and began opening drawers. "Ah," she said, "I have found your silverware," returning with the utensils. She made our plates, taking little for herself, and said, as she watched me, "Have we met before?"

I shook my head. "No. Why?"

"I'm sure I know you."

I shrugged.

She studied me intensely. "I'm sure of it."

"Don't you think I'd know?" I asked.

"Maybe not. I mean, I feel like I do."

I must have looked alarmed because she held up her hands. "I swear to God I'm not a creep. I'm not crazy."

I made a face, pulling my lip up.

"Okay, I see how it might seem creepy. Me coming here. Me bringing you food. But I feel like I want to take care of you. Like I must."

"That's not creepy?" I asked.

"I'll give that to you. I really will. But help me figure out how I know you."

I shrugged, the spices in the dahl burning my lips. "I'm not sure what you expect."

"What do you do for a living?" she asked, her chin resting in her hands. She had a thumb ring on her right hand. Once again, she wore long sleeve thermals under scrubs, which were a pale blue. The light above the table showed me the small lines around her eyes and mouth, telling me she was older than I presumed. Her lips were full, eyelashes thick, and the ring in her nose was silver. I'd forgotten what she asked and met her eyes. We looked at each other for longer than is normal. She broke away first, and said again, "What do you do? Maybe that's how I know you." Her fork clanked as she pushed it around her plate.

"I'm a musician," I said. "I play the piano, guitar, and violin. Though the violin not as well as the first two."

"Maybe I've seen you?" she wondered out loud. Once again, I shrugged, eating bite after bite. I was starved, having forgotten to eat breakfast. "Did you play with orchestras?"

"Smaller orchestras in my twenties and early thirties. I teach lessons now." I said this with a feeling of shame, as if I should do more. I'd always felt like I was capable of so much more than I did. I wrote pages and pages of music and tucked them away in my closet.

"You're not from here?" she asked, and I answered this question and every other one after with "no." Finally, she held her hands in the air, exasperated. "You are not helpful," she said.

I flinched, until I understood she was playing, and then I smiled.

"I can't grill you any longer about your shady past, how you fit so nicely into my consciousness, or why I feel compelled to take care of you because I have to go be Nurse Nowak. But I will be back, and I hope you'll let me in again." I stood with her. "Oh, my plate," she said, turning to the table. I grabbed her arm to stop her.

"I'll take care of it," I said, and my fingers touching her arm felt feverish, but I could not pull away. It was as if a static spark had charged the air around us and I looked at my fingers on her skin, shocked and unable to move. Heat rushed up from my core, spreading across my chest and neck, and I gasped. I met her eyes, and saw she felt it too. She reached and touched my fingers on her arm with her own and lifted my hand. She intertwined her fingers with mine and stepped toward me.

Holding my gaze, she said, "I know you. We're going to figure out how." Then she was gone, and my hand felt cold and adrift, as it swung down to my side. From the window, I watched her get in a yellow Volkswagen. As if she sensed me, she waved, blew me a kiss, and slipped inside to drive away.

When Pia left, confusion draped over me like a dark heavy cloak worn for winter walks in open fields. It seems very dramatic. I'm trying to capture and frame the feel of the moment I touched her, the foreboding, the smell of damp corners, rain, and wet soil. I don't know why all that came up for me, or why I felt so alive, thrilled, and simultaneously forlorn, but I did. I was too shocked to ask her to stay with me. I watched her from the window, like a ghost who haunts an abandoned home. At the thought of her skin under my fingers, the air felt humid and my breath more constrained than it was the first hour I was at the hospital. As I watched her leave, I panicked I'd never see her again.

I sat on the corner of my couch and examined my sparsely decorated apartment. I travelled lightly, from place to place, never knowing how long I'd want to stay. My trust fund afforded me a great deal of freedom, which meant more to me than things. In the past ten years, I'd lived in fifteen different places. I was drawn to some locations by work in orchestras, but in the two years before I arrived in Sedona, I'd worked very little.

My mother accused me of drifting and my father was too preoccupied by work to care at all. I believed myself to be their obligatory only child, heir to the maternal fortune. My mother's brothers were all married, as were their children, so I felt no pressure to reproduce.

I'd been a stormy and moody child, a piano prodigy they said, before I broke the fingers of my right hand in the same accident on the skateboard that gave me the scar below my eye. I never played the same way again, though the doctor said my bones all healed as they should. My deepest secret was that something had shifted inside me, to the side of where my desire to play had been. I still enjoyed it, but the burning sensation I felt when I thought about notes on a sheet dissipated, and I only found it after in spurts during long stretches of solitude.

These thoughts led me to my mother, and I pressed her name in my contacts, putting her on speaker. She answered after three rings, her Texas accent thick. "Hello, Rikke. Are you well?" I told of her about the accident, my heroics, and sent, via text to her, a copy of the local news article that mentioned me. "Oh, my dear," she said, "you could have killed yourself! Why did you do that?" I explained my momentary lapse of self, the rush of the fire, the dog, and the elderly person. Then I told her about Pia, who dug in the rubble to find my phone, leaving out the parts about visions at her touch. Rightly, I assumed it was already too much for my mother. "Please tell me you remembered to pay your health insurance bill."

"I'd already checked. It's set up on my credit card to bill automatically." Each time I moved, my father's assistant found an insurance plan for me, and sent me the details to enroll. I felt like a kept child, but it was because in many ways, I was. I'd earn enough teaching or playing random music gigs to pay my utilities and eat, but my generous trust fund kept me in apartments and health insurance.

"Well, keep to yourself now. And do something useful, Rikke. Please." The conversation ended quickly after that, and I felt the absence of her love more solidly than I did when I called. When I was a child, I heard her tell a group of women friends, over for lunch, that I was a "strange, distant, queer" child, and she was uncertain where any of it came from, including my proficiency with music. Perhaps this is why the music stopped after I broke my hand, though a distant anxiety haunted me long before this moment, when I forced myself to remember it truly.

I looked out the window again, and then checked the time on the cable box under my television. Pia had left forty-five minutes earlier, but I felt her absence in the vacant space around me. Nothing hung on the walls, and what I owned was so minimal, I only needed a studio apartment instead of a one-bedroom. I grabbed my wallet, keys, and tucked my phone in the back pocket of my jeans. I slipped on my shoes and walked cautiously down the stairs. I didn't want to be alone, but I had nowhere to go. I'd park near the city center, and walk through the tourist shops, perhaps find a place to eat again. Since the fire, my appetite had increased, and I'd put on a few needed pounds.

I returned home, tired, a few hours later. My stroll through the city center was uneventful, and my leg ached where I'd been burned. It might have been an over extension of myself, but it felt good to be physically tired. I showered quickly, changing into loose shorts and a T-shirt. I sat on the edge of the bed and felt the burning sensation of notes behind my eyes. I closed them, watched the notes dance inside my eyelids, and opened them, to find myself in the closet. I picked up the keyboard I kept for such occasions and lifted it to my bed. I turned the volume to its lowest setting and played until the notes danced from behind my eyes into the air around me. I recognized the music as Chopin's Nocturne in E Flat Major Op. 9 No. 2.

As the music rose to a crescendo in my head, the pain in my leg retreated, the cough I'd fought since the fire dissipated, and the ache for a mother's love left. My life was what it was, and in that moment, I was at peace. There was nothing but me and my fingers on the piano keys. I looked at the small synthesizer on my bed and longed for a grand piano, closing my eyes to try and wish it so.

I finished, a moment of rare contentment, and sat the small keyboard on the floor. I looked at the blank wall as I fell into fitful sleep, thinking of notes, Pia, and my broken hand. I dreamed horrible dreams, of leeches on my neck, heavy lungs full of fluid, like swallowed pond water, and sickness deep in my bones, never leaving me be.

Chapter 3

Pia

After I visited Rikke and had the weirdest sensation of *déjà vu* as she touched my hand, I made a commitment to myself not to look for her anymore. I disliked feeling I was an intruder, a freak, when all I wanted to do was help. That and figure out why I felt such familiarity, such a pull toward her—I wanted to know the reason for it too. Obviously, it was a one-sided phenomenon. What a strange suspicious creature she was, all distance and reticence, looking at me with something akin to disdain. Who was she to disdain me? I had better things to do.

Things such as running my book club, a welcome change of pace and dynamics from the life of work and relative quiet I had created for myself. One part of me longed for the peace and solitude of my cottage, and the welcome company of my brother James, dear pup Orlando, and a few friends. But another part of me also existed, one that craved social entanglements, novelty, and conversation, and the role of the book club, among other things, was to provide community. For our get-togethers, the other members of the club and I baked elaborate desserts, wore period clothes and, in general, immersed ourselves in the universe of the story we were reading. Yes, that would be a much better project than taking care of a stranger who did not want to be taken care of.

On my next day off from work, I sat in my living room preparing the invitations for the upcoming meeting. The month of June was passing by quickly and causing the temperatures to rise. By the time we got together in July, we would be faced with the full majesty of summer in Sedona. Joanne, a thirty-something hygienist, had suggested we read George Eliot's *Middlemarch* next. After all, the work had been described by some writers as the greatest novel of the English language. We couldn't possibly go without having read that!

With my special golden marker, I wrote the details in every invitation, making sure to use my best calligraphy and a slanted cursive with exaggerated loops to mirror the sensibilities of that time. I then closed each envelope with real red wax and a seal with my PN initials. I was very pleased with the results.

In the back of my mind, drumming incessantly, was my annoyance over a woman feeling she needed a man's pseudonym to be successful and the sad reality that she was probably right. It is true that many good writers who were women existed and were up-and-coming in the 1800s, in George Eliot's time, but often they had to hide the social problems they wrote about under the guise of domesticity, and when they became well known, they had to face such affront as Nathaniel Hawthorne on the other side of the Atlantic, calling people like them "that damned mob of scribbling women." If only he, and others like him, could see all writers, of all genders, as equals. Suddenly, I felt grateful to be alive at a time when things, despite not being completely fair, made it possible for me to have my blue highlights and big tattoos with a bit more freedom. Had George Eliot wanted a man's name— fine—she should have had the right to have it. And who's to say that George had to be a masculine name? But she should not have felt it was the only way.

I've always liked my own name. My Latina mom had wanted to call me Maria Pia, a name full of the symbolism of old money in Latin America. But we didn't have any—old money that is. My Polish father proposed a compromise. "Pia," a short and sweet name, would sound good with the family last name "Nowak," which means "new." Thus, I got my moniker.

I prepared to go to the post office to mail the invitations, stuffing them all in my gigantic bag and wearing my summer hat. I was looking for my keys when the telephone rang. It was the house line, which I kept, out of a certain nostalgia.

"Nurse Nowak, it's Nurse Warren. I'm sorry to disrupt your day off, but would it be possible for you to come in?" She sounded more apologetic than I could ever remember, and I realized we were like TV characters calling each other Nurse This and Nurse That. "We have two nurses out sick and a third going home with a stomach bug, and I could use your help. It would be a short, six-hour shift, and you could have the whole of tomorrow off."

I sighed, covering the receiver. "Can you give me half an hour?" That would be enough time to mail the invites.

"I sure can." She sounded almost chirpy, which I registered as weird.

"All right then. I'll be there."

"Thank you, Nurse Nowak. I knew I could count

on you." Definitely a TV character.

Short lines at the post-office made it possible for me to be there with plenty of time to spare. I found an infirmary full of cold, flu, and respiratory complaints. Everyone coughed, everyone sneezed, and I anticipated a weekend of fighting whichever bug was going around, although over the years, I had developed quite the immune resistance.

A couple of kids needed asthma treatments, so I worked on that. A man had burned himself cooking at the stove, and I focused on his bandages, a task which reminded me of Rikke, so I cursed under my breath. Later, I was called to help with a man who had been off his medication and had developed delusions, and that is when it all happened.

The man, in his seventies, squalid with an unhealthy pallor, was agitated and sitting on his bed, making it hard for the attending doctor and his assisting nurse to take his vitals and perform any examination. They also needed a blood sample, which under the circumstances looked quite impossible.

Dr. Guedes, one of our favorite physicians for her combination of great expertise and calm reassurance, tried her best to talk to the patient, but he was not listening because he was beyond her words. As we all tried to calm him down, she signaled for me to ease him onto the bed by reaching for his shoulder and his arm. That was when things turned sour.

His eyes that had been blank, empty orbs suddenly were alive with fire, and they focused on me intently and with concern. At first, he could not speak, and it was almost like witnessing a person who is experiencing an awaken dream, one of those where we try to scream but no voice comes out. When he finally found his words, they were directed at me.

"You, y-you think you know who you are, and you think the here is where you live, but you are wrong. You are her and she is you, and time does not mean anything."

Dr. Guedes looked at me and I looked back at her, we both strategizing what to do next without uttering a word. Clearly, he didn't know what he was saying.

The old man then continued. "It is only by revisiting the past that we understand the future, and yet the past and the future are the same, so how do we draw the line between them? How do we tell the good from the bad? You! I know you!" He pointed at Dr. Guedes.

"Yes, you know me. I am your doctor. Remember?"

"Sir," I started, trying to be reasonable, "why don't you lie down and rest a bit?"

"No!" he screamed, and his voice was piercing and pained. With one swing of his arm, fist tightly held, he hit my forehead and I felt myself, in slow motion, fall back. My last memory was seeing the light on the ceiling and flailing my arms, trying to hold on to something, anything. Then all went dark.

I woke up on a hospital bed, this time a patient rather than a nurse. Not sure if it was night or day, I eventually discovered there was still light outside. I reached for the back of my head to find a large sore bump covered with a bandage. My temples throbbed, and I was slightly nauseated. A memory of the patient, his ominous words, and the hard fall surfaced together with a complicated feeling of anxiety and anticipation.

Dr. Guedes soon came into the room. Her short

bangs were parted a little off center and the rest of her brunette hair was styled in her usual bob.

"I'm glad to see you're awake." She took some notes.

"My head feels hollow and sore." I reached for it instinctively.

"It was quite a scare." She flashed light into my eyes, then made them follow her finger. "Any nausea?"

"Yes, but it's subtle."

"You'll be under observation overnight. It's a precaution." She took more notes.

"Are you sure I can't go home?" I would rather be in my bed. "And how's the patient?"

"No, you have to stay. He is sleeping now. We gave him some medication, poor man."

"He didn't mean to hurt me." I felt really sorry for him. He looked so scared.

"I know, but that does not make it less heartbreaking that nurses go through so much."

I smiled at her. It was true.

She continued. "Now relax. It's the only thing you need to do. I am sending you good food soon." And then she reached into her pocket, and I flinched, thinking it was medicine. "Here you go. I know how much you like her." It was an Agatha Christie book.

When she left, I started to flip through the pages of the book, appreciating the fact that they were yellowed and well read, and that they exuded that wonderful and lovely moldy-library smell. All of a sudden, a flash crossed my mind. I was transported to a blue room, with lots of pictures on the walls. It wasn't that I thought of a blue room. I *was* in a blue room, sitting at a table looking at the gold-framed portrait of a woman.

To my left, there was a piano, and above me a chandelier with tall, white candles. Beyond the table, a fire burned bright in the fireplace, and a dinner of green vegetables and potatoes gave out a delicious aroma of rosemary.

And then the room was gone, and I was back at the hospital.

Chapter 4

Rikke

Calling them "fitful sleep" and "restless anxiety" were understatements, and I was disappointed at my lack of adjectives to describe how awful I felt. After Pia left me that day, I called my mother, which of course made everything worse. Everything felt wrong. Before Pia, I was captivated by Sedona's beauty. The red rocks, mesas, and wide-open spaces called to me. I spent my days exploring my new surroundings, and I didn't feel lonely, out of place, or so anxious. Suddenly, it felt as though the space I'd built around myself was closing in. The alone time I'd cherished became an enemy. My empty apartment suffocated me, and the walls pressed me down into the couch.

I doodled in my sketch pad. I began a few pieces of music I would never play, unable to finish them. I turned on the television and stopped on a science documentary. In it, astronauts prepared for zero gravity. One said after the first moment in the anti-gravity chamber, "I lived my whole life not knowing gravity held me to the ground. In that moment when there was no gravity, I had no idea what to do." That was how I felt. I was not aware of something, though I could not name it then, until Pia touched my arm. Now I was flailing around, spinning upside down. For two days, rest, concentration, and sleep eluded me. I texted Pia, as a last resort, but she didn't respond.

She had texted back so quickly before and now ignored me. I wondered if she'd sensed my judgement and grown weary of it. I don't know why I reacted to kindness the way I did. Of course, it's possible she liked me. It's also possible she wanted to be nice when she learned I was alone and new in town and sought to help me heal. She was a nurse, after all. Instead of appreciating it, I probably gave her side-eyes and projected my desire to retreat. Perhaps I responded this way to interest out of some subconscious feeling of unworthiness. I threw myself down on the couch and looked at the blank wall behind my television.

A nice woman wanted to help me, found my phone in a burned building, brought me food and my response was to act like she was robbing me at gunpoint or stalking me. "Here! Take my wallet and phone. Do you want my watch? Are you reading my mail?"

I looked at my phone. Nothing. She still hadn't responded. The only thing I knew about Pia was that she worked at the hospital. I wondered how odd it would be if I showed up there. On the one hand, it would not be any stranger than what she'd done to me. She did dig through rubble to find my phone. She sat by my bedside all night and brought me Indian food. How much stranger would it be for me to show up at her work? I jumped up, put on my shoes, the pain from the burns a distant thought, and made it out the door, halfway down the stairs before I ran back into my apartment and slammed the door.

Breathing hard, I slid down the back of the door, legs out in front of me. Though I've never done it before, and not again, I think I was hyperventilating. I also remembered I'd not showered or brushed my teeth in two days and that seemed a prudent thing to resolve before showing up to talk to Pia again. While I attended to these necessities, I considered my reasons for seeking her out. So she'd not responded to my text message. I'd been ghosted by plenty of people after first dates over the years, though I wouldn't openly admit that to anyone. I really wanted her to respond. I also wanted to resolve my guilt and tell her I was sorry for my cold indifference to her outreach. I wanted her touch again, as well, though I was not quite ready to admit that to her. But being close enough for that was a necessary option.

I parked in an open visitor spot in front of the Emergency Room entrance at the hospital. I didn't remember how it looked, as I was brought in by paramedics, and I was too preoccupied by my injuries to notice any details. I looked around the parking lot to see if Pia's car was there. I saw the yellow hood in the space between two large trucks, and moved closer, to be sure. My heart hammered in my chest.

A thought clamored for my inspection. Was I being codependent? I'd gone to therapy and read a ton of books about it. I could unravel the pieces of every failed relationship from my mother's abandonment to my codependence. It seemed to me that humans were desperately flawed creatures. We needed each other to survive, but too much need left us dysfunctional. Our entire happiness depended on finding balance between self-sufficiency and mutual dependency. If we became too solitary, we were loners and if we engaged too much, we were codependent. I sometimes wondered if it wasn't the onslaught of modernity, industrialization, and destruction of the tribe of hunter-gatherers that caused all this.

I'd spent a lifetime exhausted by human relationships. I was always uncertain. Had I texted too much? Should I have called sooner? Was I too standoffish or did I act too eager? No wonder my default response was to judge and keep others at a distance. It was amazing anyone managed to connect to anyone in the modern era. Suddenly, I longed for the simplicity of knowing where home was. I never knew. I leaned against the front of a truck, worn down by my mind's reckless onslaught, and set off the alarm. I stumbled into another car nearby, nearly falling. I managed to right myself and ran across the parking lot, fleeing the scene. The mammalian brain I pondered defaulted lower, to the reptilian brain and my flight or fight was in full response and functioning quite well, I'm happy to share.

I skidded into the Emergency Room lobby and stopped inside the sliding doors. I attempted to right my t-shirt and pressed my glasses up on the bridge of my nose. I wished for my contacts, but my eyes were tired. At the receptionist behind the welcome desk, I smiled, wanly, vaguely guilty about the car alarm. "I'm looking for Nurse Pia Nowak," I said.

"Oh," she said. "She is in room six. Go through these doors.

I nodded, thinking Pia was working in room six. I stepped through the doors the receptionist opened for me. The hall began with room thirteen, which seemed counterintuitive, but I followed the numbers, turning twice before I saw "6" above the door. My pace slowed and my hands sweat. I wiped them on my jeans. I stopped shy of the room and tried to breath. "Hi, Pia," I would say. "I didn't hear from you and I was worried," or "Hi Pia, I have intimacy issues because of my mother's abandonment and my own codependent recovery, and also because our mammalian brains don't know how to live in modernity…"

I leaned against the wall, breathing hard again, head spinning. I put my hands on my forehead, willed myself to stop, and then stood tall, finding some sort of resolution. I walked into the doorway. Pia was on the bed, in her light blue scrubs, reading an Agatha Christie novel. I watched her for a while before she became aware of my presence. Her arms were exposed, and I looked at her tattoos with new appreciation. The blue in her hair was not as bright, as though washing had faded it. In the harsh light of the hospital fluorescents, I saw freckles on her nose and arms. I imagined her skin was soft to the touch. She met my eyes and put the book on her lap, upside down to keep her page. I stopped ogling her.

She tipped her head, a question in her eyes. Her body stiffened, but then I raised my hand to her, a tiny wave, and said, "I didn't hear back from you. I was worried." There, I thought, I'd done it. I was honest without exposing the inner details of every therapeutic conversation I'd ever had. Her body softened and she smiled at me. "What happened?" I asked, still in the doorway.

She waved me to the chair next to the bed, and I stepped gingerly into the room. I sat by her, crossed my legs, and rested my hands on them. Pia reclined against the bed. "A patient punched me, and I had an out of body experience." I sat forward, my instinct to touch her, but tempered by my conservatism, I sat back. She saw though it and smiled slowly at me.

"I felt so despondent watching you pull away from my apartment the other day. I almost chased after you," I said, the words tumbling from me before I could stop them.

Pia laughed heartily at this, and I joined her. A woman appeared in front of the door. "Obviously you're feeling better, Pia."

Pia held up her thumb, the one with the ring, and nodded. "I didn't mean to be so loud, Dr. Guedes. This is Rikke. Local hero of the apartment-complex fire. She came to say hi." Dr. Guedes offered her hand to me. I shook it, disliking her immediately.

"Quite the contrary, Pia. It was nice to hear you laugh, as it always is," she said, with a wink at Pia. I acted as if I didn't see it, but I met her eyes, and felt fury race from my head to my feet. She stared at me, and the air stilled and grew cold.

My senses sharpened, and I saw everything in the room with excruciating clarity. I heard the low, white noise of the air conditioning unit, the beeping of machines beyond the room where we sat. I was aware of the wrinkles in the white blanket on Pia's legs and saw the goosebumps on her arm. The beige tile under the bed curled in the middle and needed to be replaced. The blood pressure cuff was hanging slightly askew, and the dial faced away from all of us. She was tall and elegant, but I felt disgust when I looked at her. Pia rubbed her arms and put them under the blanket, watching me.

"Thanks for checking on her, Doctor. I'm going to sit here with her now. We'd like to talk privately if there is nothing else," I said. I couldn't explain my reaction, but I was too consumed with emotion to question it. Dr. Guedes smiled at me, eyes blazing, and turned with a wave.

Pia asked me, "What was that?"

I watched Dr. Guedes leave, not able to turn away until I was sure she was gone. I turned to Pia, leaned forward, hands on her hands under the blanket. "I don't like her," I said.

"Obviously." Pia lifted her hands from beneath the blanket and laced her fingers in mine. I felt the same jolt I'd felt in my apartment, but I wasn't swept away. Instead, I became even more present, and I met her eyes.

"You're so beautiful," I blurted. "I'm sorry if I was a jerk."

She nodded and touched my cheek with her right hand. I leaned into her touch, and we stared at each other until shouts disturbed us.

"Inbound. Multiple cars in accident on the state road. Two on-scene fatalities, six critical," someone yelled.

Pia jumped up, a little unsteady, and I stabilized her by the shoulders. She rested against me momentarily. "We're so short staffed. The flu. I need to help." I understood and watched her walk away into the mix, as stretchers came through the doors. I crept back down the hallway, my back pressed against wall, trying to stay out of the way. I turned as I readied to leave and made eye contact with Dr. Guedes. She smiled, but I didn't return it.

Chapter 5

Pia

I didn't tell Dr. Guedes about the strange episode that took me from the bed in the hospital to a fancy room somewhere else. I feared she would keep me from going home and instead run a million tests to see what was wrong with my head. If Nurse Warren found out, it would be twenty times worse. I couldn't help but worry that something was indeed amiss and that scrutinizing it would take us down a path of no return. After all, it was soon after the head injury that the strangeness started, so I couldn't help but connect the two. Yet, I shied away from discovering more, hoping that if I ignored the problem, it would simply go away. How many times had I done that before in my life, I wondered.

Instead of making a fuss, I stayed silent, as still as I could, but not enough that it would be perceived as some medically significant form of apathy. When Dr. Guedes came to see me in the morning, I let her do a final checkup and then readied myself to leave.

"Your friend doesn't like me," she said while she made my eyes follow her index finger from left to right.

"Oh, that's not true. I think she was upset to find me in a hospital bed." I tried to keep my head as steady as possible, and my eyes responsive to not incite further tests.

"Perhaps. Or perhaps she dislikes the fact that we are…friends?"

"Why would she dislike that?" I had never really thought of Dr. Guedes as a friend—more like a mentor, perhaps, or a strong woman in medicine whom I could look up to. I was not going to say that, though. If she thought we were friends, that was fine with me. "Rikke is a little reserved at first. Nothing personal."

Dr. Guedes smiled but her eyes stayed somber. She didn't press further. I was given three sick days to rest at home and had to promise not to come back to the hospital until my allotted shift, unless I felt unwell, at which point I should come to see her immediately. I was to take things slowly, not necessarily stay in bed but avoid overtaxing myself.

When I got home, I called James, who promptly appeared with a bag of fruit and a box of chocolates in his hands, and a frown wrinkling his forehead.

"I'm not happy." He walked past me toward the kitchen counter without saying hello. Orlando trailed him. "You could have told me you were literally in the hospital."

"It was not a big deal." I kneeled down for Orlando to come to me. "If it had happened anywhere else, I would have simply stood up and gone home. But over there, as you can imagine, they made a big scene."

"You're a nurse when it's about other people, but when it's with you? No selfcare."

I kissed him on the cheek. "Don't be dramatic, James. I can do selfcare as well as anyone else."

"Prove it and go rest. Orlando and I will cook lunch."

"Fine." I was half-annoyed and half-pleased with

his concern. It was good to be taken care of for once, but I was not used to it lasting very long. I always took back the reins of my own life. "But I know how to take care of things. Wasn't that what I did when mom passed away? And then dad?"

He knew it was true and did not retort. I had been a nurse to both our parents, to our mom at a very young age, and the experience had left a perpetual mark in my soul. I was a caretaker before anything else, and my heart ached for the chance to be useful.

Resting on the couch, I thought of my injury first and Rikke immediately after—specifically, her hands on my shoulders in a reflexive and protective gesture to prevent me from falling and from being that nurse when I was supposed to be a patient. She tried. She had looked out for me. Then I went to the hall, and Dr. Guedes sent me right back into my room. I couldn't say no to her. She was my doctor after all.

The feeling of Rikke's touch still burned my skin, as if the pressure of her fingers was still there, holding me together. It was impossible to deny that I wanted her embrace again, that being with her made everything better. I realized then that she hadn't prevented me from leaving the room. She had advised me with her arms. I liked that. I didn't feel constrained. Simply supported.

I must have fallen asleep soon after. I woke up with James by my side, presenting me with a bowl of noodles and vegetables. It smelled heavenly, and I identified the scent at once as a mixture of basil, parsley and lemon. "Eat up." He draped a kitchen towel over his shoulder and went back to the kitchen.

I was famished, and I ate with gusto. When I was finished, we swapped the empty bowl for a dish of ice-cream. James came to sit on the couch with me. I raised my legs and then lowered them again so that my calves rested on his lap. He passed me a bottle of chocolate syrup.

"James," I said, tagging at my sleeve. "I think I'm falling in love."

He looked at me and offered a placid smile. "I know."

"You do?"

This time he laughed. "I know you, which means yes, I know you are falling in love."

I sighed. "I'm all over the place. I can't sleep well, yet I sleep all the time. I'm distracted. Weird things keep happening. Yet, I'm so happy." I fell short of telling him about the visions because I was sure he would jump in the car and take me to the hospital.

"All the classic symptoms." He nodded. "And do you think the other party reciprocates?"

I thought about it for a second. "I believe so, yes." I'm sure I blushed. "I hope. I'm not sure. Yes."

He laughed at my second guessing. "Then why are you walking around like you're carrying a giant rock rather than skipping and singing sugary songs?"

I sighed. "Because it feels a bit overwhelming. It feels like nothing I've felt before."

"Wow, it's serious then."

"It's pretty serious."

He came to collect the ice-cream dish. "You'll figure it out. You always do."

Listening to the water run in the kitchen as he cleaned up after our meal, I fluffed a pillow and let the quiet of the afternoon—Orlando lying on the rug in front of me, birds chirping in the background—carry me away. I didn't go to sleep. I studied the feelings that were lodged in my chest. I touched my chest with my hand, as if doing so would help me understand them better. I don't know why I felt I had to decode them.

That's when it happened again. The same electricity through me. The same sense of unreality and the sudden realization that my cottage had disappeared and that I stood near a pond, with a battered leather-bound book at my feet, and wind blowing against my hair as letters flew up all around me. A second later, my feet were in the cold water, exactly like in my dream, and the familiarity of it all struck me and sucked all the air from my lungs.

I screamed.

In a second James was by my side, looking at me in fear. "What happened? Are you in pain? Is it your head?"

"I think I dozed off and had a nightmare." I lied.

"Shall we go back to the hospital? You really scared me!"

"For a bad dream?" I sat up. You want me back at the hospital because of a bad dream?" I felt horrible being so deceptive about it, but what choice did I have? I had no idea what was happening to me. There was no guidebook for what I was experiencing. It was not something nurses were taught either.

"How about you come home with Orlando and me? We can watch movies, eat popcorn, and I'll work while you rest."

I agreed without thinking. Maybe I'd feel better being away a bit, even if I hated leaving my house. I packed an overnight bag.

On the way to James's house, I let the wind blow

my hair back, much like in my recent episode. In my head, I called it an episode because I didn't have the exact words to describe it. In the back seat, Orlando seemed to be enjoying the ride. I thought of Rikke and how much I wanted to be with her, take care of her. Could I wish her into being? Into reaching out to me and telling me she felt the same? If I thought enough about her, would I cause her to think about me too?

"You're not here, are you?" James asked without any condemnation in his voice. "You are far away, flying high in the sky."

I smiled.

"Tell me how I can help."

"Jimmy," I said, resorting to his childhood nickname, "you already have."

We rode in silence to his house, a lovely if austere two-bedroom, north of the town center. It had a front lawn with canopied trees and a fireplace where we roasted marshmallows on cold nights.

He set me up in the spare bedroom, brought me a teddy bear and a glass of water, and turned on the TV to a silly sitcom.

"I'll be working. Call me if you need anything."

"You're great, little brother."

"I know," he said, his eyes glistening.

I was afraid to sleep. Between dreams and episodes, I had had more excitement than if I had been at an amusement park. It was like riding a rollercoaster all the time.

I picked up my phone and stared at the screen, as if I could make it light up with a text or call from Rikke. I looked at it blankly until it half hypnotized me. Then it went dark. For a few weeks, being awake and being asleep had blurred, further brought together by those visions which could belong to either camp. I wanted to separate those states again. Rest when asleep; live when awake.

Confused, I decided to deal with data the only way I knew how: analyze, synthesize, summarize. I picked up my little notebook. I started listing the elements of my visions. Water, a rose, a piano, a blue room, portraits, a book, shops, yellowed letters.

Nothing. They didn't turn into a coherent account of anything. I threw the notepad against the wall. Then I looked at the phone once again and felt like doing the same, but it was new and expensive, so I controlled myself.

I picked up the remote and drowned my frustration in the silly comedy in front of me.

Chapter 6

Rikke

After I left Pia at the hospital, my random wandering continued for a couple of days. I saw myself spinning like that astronaut in zero-g, and so, despite every shadow instinct telling me all the reasons I should not, I called her. I didn't text. I actually founder her phone number in "contacts" and pressed to call and talk live. Deep panic washed over me, and I leaned against the wall, suddenly fearful she wouldn't answer. I didn't know what I'd do if she didn't pick up.

She answered after one ring, her voice heavy with sleep. "Oh my god," I exclaimed, "I woke you up." Then, "But it's eleven in the morning?"

I heard her throaty laughter, a rasp in her voice. "I work nights. Time is irrelevant."

"That's fair," I said. I suddenly didn't know what else to say.

"Did you need something? Are you okay?" she asked when I said nothing.

"Oh," I said. Then in a rush of honesty and emotion, I completed. "I wanted to talk to you. I'd really not thought past that." I heard a little gasp on the other side of the phone and then rustling, as though she were sitting up. "But I don't need to keep you. You should go back to sleep. I am sorry I woke you. Maybe call me when you have time?" I felt embarrassed and nervous, as though perhaps I had revealed too much.

"No," she whispered. "I'm up. I'm spending time at my brother's. I'm bored, actually, even though he is wonderful and has been taking great care of me."

I looked at my legs stretched in front of me where I now sat on the couch, and the shadow of the tree on the wall where the sun broke through the branches. Maybe I should be caring for her.

She continued. "There is a craft fair today. I've had enough rest. Would you like to go?"

"Yes," I said quickly.

"Give me about thirty minutes, and I'll come to you. It's closer to you than to me."

"I'll see you soon," I said and hung up the phone. Sudden worry about the way I looked overtook me. I changed my shirt three times, and slipped in and out of cargo pants, jeans, and corduroys. I looked at myself in the mirror in the corduroys and grimaced. It was the poorest choice of clothing I'd ever made. I yanked them down and my boy shorts came with me. Half-naked, scrambling to find the first pair of jeans I had on, I caught a glimpse of yellow from the corner of my eye and looked out the window to see Pia park her car in front the fire hydrant, where red glaring paint marked a do-not-park zone. I rushed into the bathroom, grabbed the jeans and pulled them on quickly. I walked casually toward the window, where she saw me and waved.

I took the stairs a few at a time and practically leaped into the front seat of her car. There were four books on the back seat, but it was otherwise clean. A fresh daisy was in the flower holder, and I touched it with my finger. Hands on the wheel, she looked at me with a smile. I grinned back, as if in some sort of silent affirmation, and we zipped from the parking lot. I held onto the handle above the door as she turned corners. "This is not the Indy 500," I said when things got really scary.

Pia laughed and tucked a stray piece of dark hair behind her ear. "It's the Indy 500 every time I drive."

"Note to self," I said. "I will drive next time."

"Whatever." She glanced at me from the corner of her eyes, "Dare you to try and get the keys from me."

"I will and you'll beg to get them back," I said, with a smile and watched her drive, entirely too fast, through Sedona's back roads, taking us to a dirt parking lot around the corner from the art fair.

Pia whipped the car into an open parking spot at the back of the lot. I made the sign of the cross and she laughed and yanked her massive purse from the backseat. I stopped at the end of the car to wait for her, watching as she hoisted the purse onto her shoulder. She wore a light sweater over a turquoise-infused blouse and dark pair of jeans, with dark feminine shoes I was at a loss to describe. I imagined she had a lot of shoes. Her hands were strong, and they showed years of hard work, care, healing, and love. I watched her hands as she locked the car door, her long, tapered fingers moving with grace and ease. Movement seemed effortless for Pia, and when she turned to catch me looking, I smiled and turned away. I wanted her to know I was looking.

Oddly quiet, she came to my side, and we stood. "Well," I said, lifting my arm to her so she might take it. "Shall we, madam?" I grinned and she tucked her hand inside my elbow, leaning against me as she did, and we fell in step together toward the fair. Pia waved at a few people as we moved through the tables, stopping to look at artisan creations. We talked little about anything but what we saw, gasping our surprise and admiration of blown glass, and stained glass, carved woodwork and jewelry so beautiful it took our breath away.

Pia bought a ring with a rough turquoise stone that matched her outfit, and I nodded in approval. A folk band began to play as the sun rose high in the sky. Soft guitar and lute music filled the square, and I was drawn closer to it, as always. Pia walked with me, and we stopped to get apple cider before we sat on the benches to listen. The sun was warm on my face, but a gentle breeze created the perfect balance. I was powerfully aware of Pia's presence next to me and shifted so I could feel her shoulder pressed against mine. She leaned into me, welcoming the contact casually, and I looked at her profile, the soft angles of her nose and chin. She turned to smile at me, meeting my gaze, and I wondered how I'd tried to push away a woman with such warm brown eyes. A solo guitarist played the first notes of Chopin: Etude, Op. 10 No. 6, and I closed my eyes to listen, overwhelmed by the bright blue sky, red dirt of the mesas, and Pia herself.

With my eyes closed, each chord the guitarist strummed vibrated under my ribs, and as the piece continued into its second movement, Pia's beautiful fingers pulled my hand from my lap into hers, where she held it with both hands, her skin warm against mine. She traced the backside of my hand with her finger, while she held it tightly with her other hand. I opened my eyes and turned to her. She sat quietly, looking at our hands in her lap, and then lifted her eyes to mine. She pulled her right hand from mine, lifted her finger, and lightly touched the scar under my right eye, a question in her eyes. I mouthed, "Skateboard when I was nine," and she nodded, returning her hand to her lap, finding my fingers again. The song ended, and I said, with a grin, "I could do that better."

"You'll have to prove it to me," she said, and when she shifted forward slightly, I caught a glimpse of a sign which interested me. "Psychic: Tarot and Past Life Readings," I read out loud. "Let's go." I stood and pulled her with me. She followed but shook her head.

"Rikke, are you kidding? I am not paying a psychic for a reading."

I stopped in front of her, more alive and playful than I'd felt in my whole life, though it didn't occur to me as such then. I motioned wildly, "Pia, come on! I'll pay. Don't you want to know who you were in a past life? Maybe you were Catherine the Great, Cleopatra, or the inspiration for the Mona Lisa." She eyed me seriously, with deep incredulity, but I continued. "Or maybe you were a sad, peasant woman whose chickens got all killed by a terrible blight which is why you don't want to go." I held very still, my head tipped, fake compassion. "Are you still upset about the chickens?"

"I am not upset about the chickens, I watch people die from horrible diseases and accidents all the time," she said to me, hands on her hips. "When they don't die, they're not saved through any ridiculous superstition, religious or spiritual belief. They're saved by science. Which has never proved continuation of the soul or reincarnation, and really, I'm surprised at you."

Pia was adamant about her scientific rationalism, which only emboldened me to continue. Given the tattoos, thumb ring, blue hair, Indian food, and the purse, I had wrongly assumed Pia fit into the new-age spirit of Sedona. I was wrong, and I loved discovering so.

Feeling antagonistic and playful, I said, "Pia, you are so arrogant," She gasped, and her expression was horrified. "Do you really think you know enough about existence, and why we're alive, that you can discount spiritual belief so readily? I mean, I love pharmaceuticals, don't get me wrong, but come on. Maybe science doesn't understand any of this yet." And with that, I lunged forward, grabbed her purse from her hand and ran forward. "If you want this back, you're coming with me."

Pia chased after me, our laughter filling the wide-open space of the fair. I noticed a few people stop to look, with smiles on their faces. A woman selling jewelry said to her patrons, "I love happy people in love," and I felt a flush rush up my cheeks. Was I that obvious? I slowed and turned, and Pia crashed into me. I wrapped my arms around her, and her arms slid around my neck, and she said, "Give my purse, or you're gonna *git* it," in what was a surprisingly accurate John Wayne impersonation.

I laughed, hysterically, and handed the purse over, my hands in the air, and Pia smiled triumphantly, hoisting the bag onto her shoulder. I tugged her hand, the naturalness of her fingers sliding between mine comforting, even as I struggled to understand it. She let me pull her forward, and once again pliantly leaned into me as I moved her toward me. I felt a flash of desire rush through me, and I took a deep breath, averting my eyes from her, as we ducked into the tent. A woman wearing jeans and a t-shirt sat behind a card table. I was disappointed. I'd expected someone wearing a headscarf and flowing robes with ruby rings. She waved us forward and we sat in front of her.

"I'm Betty," she said. Again, the distance between my expectations and reality felt befuddled. That was not the name I was expecting and checked my own biases. Pia seemed to sense my thoughts because I felt the pressure of her fingers squeezing mine. When I turned to look at her, she raised an eyebrow as if to say, "You wanted to do this. It's your show."

I let go of Pia's hand and reached out to Betty. "I'm Rikke. This is Pia." When she let go of my hand, I promptly found Pia's again.

Betty pulled a stack of cards from the right of the table. "Let's see what the cards say about the two of you." She flipped the cards over, one by one, forming a cross of five cards. She turned over the first card from the middle. "This is your present. The Wheel of Fortune. It's fate. What's happening is inevitable, and it will produce tremendous change." Pia sighed a little but continued to hold my hand. I nodded for Betty to carry on. She turned over the next card, to left middle. "This is the past. Death."

I said, in spooky voice, "Ominous."

Betty looked at me with exasperation on her face. "Do you want me to continue?" I nodded, sheepish, and she turned over another card, on the other side of the same row. "Future. It's the Fool."

"I've been called worse," I offered with a smile and Pia laughed.

Betty ignored me because her gaze fixed on the table. Her posture had changed, and I was at a loss to explain when it happened. Something else changed in the room and instinctively I shifted on my chair toward Pia, pressing against her shoulder and turning my legs toward her. I extracted my hand from hers and put my arm around the back of her chair. I could see in her face she felt it too, and she leaned into me, and we both turned to watch Betty.

She took the card from the bottom. "This is the reason. Justice." Then she turned the top card over, not waiting for us, "Potential. Lovers." She seemed to be talking to herself and then she abruptly looked up at the two of us. Her eyes glazed and she stared at a space above our shoulders.

"You can't escape what's about to happen, and it has to be resolved, here, now because you won't get another chance. You think you never run out of chances, but you do. I think you do. How many lives have there been since this happened? At least two for you," she jerked her head to Pia and then turned to me. "You're not living, half-life, even when you're here alive, so it doesn't matter how many you've had." Then she slammed her hands down on the table. "You're always lovers," and I blushed, but Pia watched her with rapt fascination. "Always. No one competes but they want to, for you." Again, she snapped at Pia. "It's always the one who doesn't believe who gets to see. Makes it more interesting, maybe?"

"Um," I said, as alarm poured over my body, "Thanks Betty. I think we'll go now. How much do I owe you?"

Still looking at Pia, Betty said, "Something is happening to you, and someone wants you, but you're the fool. You can't see it. You never do. Why can't you see it?"

Pia gasped, and sat back, with fright and a certain degree of indignation. I stood, reaching for Pia's hand. "This is nuts," I said. "Come on." I pulled a twenty-dollar bill from my pocket and put it on the table.

Pia stood without hesitation and then stopped, tugging me back, to turn and look at Betty. "What do you see?" Pia asked, her voice trembling and quiet.

Betty's head snapped backwards, and her eyes rolled into her skull. I'd heard such a thing could happen, but I'd never seen it before. Abruptly her head snapped back down and she locked eyes with Pia. "You think you know who you are, and you think the here is where you live, but you are wrong. You are her and she is you, and time does not mean anything." Then Betty closed her eyes and opened them again. Confusion crawled across her face, and with her hand, she covered her eyes, and rubbed down her face with her palm. She picked up a glass, took a sip, and said, "That happens. Sorry if I scared you."

"Sure. No problem," I said and just wanted to leave. But then I looked at Pia, and her face was peaked, eyes wide, and her mouth slightly open. She looked terrified. I looped my arm around her waist and leaned in so she could see my eyes. She met them and steadied, and I motioned to the door of the tent with a nod of my head. Together we moved back into the sunlight. We didn't stop until we were well up the street from the crowd, standing in front of an open Sedona new-age church.

"Pia," I asked, as we stopped, both obviously convinced we were far enough from Betty. "What happened?"

"That's what the patient said," Pia said as she stopped to look at me.

"Whoa, what patient?"

"The one who hit me. Right before he hit me, he said the exact same thing."

"How is that possible? Are you sure? It could literally be the ravings of mad people." Pia shook her head, convinced, and I felt scared. "Or maybe Jung is right, and they all draw from the same archetypes."

"No. I mean, Jung is fine. But they said the exact same thing." Pia turned around, in circles, as if to find her bearings and be certain she knew where she was. "I like this church. Let's sit down for a minute." I followed her into the church and smiled as she held her hand behind her as she walked, inviting me to take it.

I followed her to a pew in the front of the open room. We were alone. I paused to look up at the vaulted ceilings and stained-glass windows. The afternoon light filtered through them, creating a cascade of color in the open hall. The stone floors held the cold, so the air was chilled, but so still peace immediately surrounded me. I felt like I'd been in the space before, but I knew I hadn't. Something about the moment struck a place deep inside me I was wordless to explain, like Pia herself.

Pia sat but I stood, looking at the blank walls, the strong stone support pillars, and that was when I saw the baby grand piano behind the slender podium. I fixated on it, an overwhelming urge to play consuming all my senses. I'd not felt such fixation since I was a child, and I wondered about it, as I'd wondered about so much since meeting Pia.

My thoughts and gaze returned to her. She watched

me, a small smile on her face, her eyes warm with both affection and attention. I walked toward her, and sat, questions in my eyes enough for her to understand. She shook her head, "I keep seeing things. Things like that keep happening. I don't know. I find it very upsetting."

"Do you want to talk about it?" I asked, concerned.

She shook her head and pulled my arm so I moved closer. "Sit with me for a minute."

I agreed silently, satisfied to do so. She rested her head on my shoulder, and I fixated once again on the keyboard. Pia must have followed my gaze because a few minutes later she said, "Go play."

"Can I? I mean, it's not mine."

"They won't care. Go. Play me something."

I ran to the piano. But once I sat, I was overcome with panic. What if it was terrible? The acoustics of the space would offer every mistake for scrutiny. Or what if I played something Pia hated? I didn't know what kind of music she liked. If I played something antiquated and classical, she might think me pretentious. If I played something modern, she'd think I wasn't serious. If I played one of my own compositions, it is possible she'd think it was terrible and then feel too bad to tell me about it. I touched the keys lightly, pretending to get a feel for the piano.

The sound rose from the piano and into the air, filling every pocket of space in the church. I picked up the pace, tentatively feeling my way into something and into my memory of playing on an actual piano. I pressed the keys, holding down B minor a bit longer than necessary. It was then I decided to play *Total Eclipse of the Heart*. I chose the song because if it sounded terrible, or if Pia didn't like it, I could shrug it off as a joke. I imagined myself saying, "Nothing like wooing someone with an '80s power ballad." I began to play and lost myself in the melody and the movement of my hands across the keys. It felt so good, and I felt so alive. Betty and all my anxieties disappeared. I closed my eyes, reveling in the feel of the music.

At the end of the chorus, I opened my eyes. Pia had moved toward me, and I'd been so absorbed in the music I'd not seen her. She stood by the side of the piano, and she was looking at me with such evident love. No one had ever looked at me like that before, so I didn't recognize the expression from experience. Rather, I felt it and I met her eyes while I continued to play. Obviously, I wouldn't need an escape plan if Pia didn't like what I chose.

From the look on her face, she was enraptured. I leaned into the music, tearing my gaze from her, playing my heart into each note. Pia sat next to me on the bench, and I finished the song with her there, a dramatic reprise for her benefit. Then I put my hands in my lap and looked at the piano keys, momentarily shy.

Then, her hand was on my back, and I turned. She grabbed my chin with her right hand and leaned toward me. I froze, not moving, anticipating her kiss, when abruptly she stopped and her head snapped back and she screamed, grasping at me as she fell backwards. I lurched forward and grabbed her, but not before we both lost our balance and fell from the piano bench. I rolled and scrambled to her, grabbing her in my arms. I thought she was having a seizure and panicked. I yelled for help, as I pulled her against me. "Call 911!"

Someone rushed through the doors of the church. The man wore a baseball hat and jeans, but I don't remember anything else, only that he pulled his cell phone from his back pocket and spoke rapidly into it, walking outside to see what street we were on.

Chapter 7

Pia

I was told I arrived at the hospital in a state of incoherence. I remember Nurse Warren looking at me like a concerned mother, her eyebrows so tightly held together they formed a V and her lips drained of all color. It is weird to realize what a person recalls from when they were in a state of panic. I also remember Rikke holding my hand and whispering to me that everything was going to be all right. I wanted to tell her to please not let go, that if she did, I might fall apart and never be put together again. It was the grip of her fingers interlaced in mine that I couldn't do without, as she said to me, "I'm here. I'll always be here." No words came out of my mouth, but still I thought she understood.

I was afraid the doctors would take me to the psych ward, and given my state, who could have blamed them? The visions had intensified, and I am sure I spoke of them to anyone who was there to hear. A crackling fire in the fireplace, tall trees penetrated by the rays of the sun, the water lapping at my feet, a rose, the piano, a blue room, a box of letters. They all came rushing to me in flashes that lasted only a few seconds each but had been repeating in an interminable loop since the episode in the church.

Yet, the psychiatrist was not my destination. Given

the recent head trauma, the MRI machine was where I ended up, covered in a light blanket and surrounded by close quarters all around, while the contraption scanned every dark corner of my brain.

The doctors found nothing, but still they wanted to keep me overnight. I refused. I had rested and been in the hospital more in the last two weeks than in all my other weeks combined. I longed for my house, for simple everyday things, for normalcy.

"I will take care of her at home." Rikke said. She stood next to my bed, arms crossed, legs slightly apart in complete certainty, so much so that the doctor on call, a young internist that had been with the hospital for only six months, looked afraid to protest.

When he left, I spoke to her in as kind a tone as I could muster. "I don't expect you to take care of me. I don't want to be a burden. I don't know what this is or how long it will last. You cannot commit to it. Got your own life to take care of."

"I'm committing to it right now. As long as it takes." She took my hand and kissed it gently.

My eyes were ready to overflow with joy, and a runaway tear escaped when I smiled back at her. Except for James, who as an adult had been always present, trying to thank me with his actions for taking care of him when he was a boy, I had no one else willing to rescue me when I needed it. I had grown so used to being the nurse that it was difficult to imagine the opposite. "As long as it takes." She repeated with more emphasis, looking me in the eyes.

I wiped my face and chuckled a bit. "You're going to have to fight James and Orlando. They both think they are my heroes."

She did not flinch. "I am pretty sure there's room in your life for one more. Hero, that is."

We decided that my house would be the best place for me to rest. It was cozy and comfortable, and James would not feel awkward about stopping by any time he pleased. I waited in the car while Rikke prepared a backpack at her place. When I saw her locking the door and smiling at me, my heart sang. She took the wheel, of my car and of my life, and drove us to the cottage without delay.

The week that followed was one of the best of my life. I slept when I was tired, woke up when I was rested. I ate when Rikke brought me food. We walked the rustic pathways near the cottage and gardened away the sunny mornings that filled us with energy and coated our skin with dew-like perspiration. Rikke asked for nothing and provided me with everything. When James and Orlando came to dinner, she prepared the most beautiful table to showcase the vegetables we had harvested and the pot pies she made from scratch. After that, she would play the guitar, my old learning instrument she had cleaned and tuned, and we would all sing love ballads, sitting by the fire while Orlando tried to nap nearby. I was never happier, more nurtured, and more valued. I could finally fully appreciate the meaning of home.

Rikke and James became fast friends, their banter much like that of loving siblings. They played hoops, cleaned the house, chopped vegetables and, in unison, sent me back to rest when I tried to help with anything. Sometimes James would sit in the dining room and code, while Rikke baked a cake or wrote music. Orlando had taken a liking to her as well, and I would often find him lying at her feet or sharing an armchair with her. My refrigerator was stocked, my house tidy, and my heart overflowing.

I did not have any visions or episodes during the whole week, and that contributed greatly to my happiness and good mood. By the end of the period, James announced he had to take a three-day trip to Phoenix to work with a client. He left Orlando with us and gave me a thousand recommendations about what I should and should not do.

That first Saturday, when it was only Rikke, me, and the pup, and we had hiked the mountains and stopped at streams, collected blooming flowers, and sunk our sneakers into the red mud of Sedona, Rikke set a table outside for two. She had installed cafe lights over the back porch, and the area sparkled with a soft yellow glow. By then, she already knew some of my favorite foods, and she had prepared a feast using them as main ingredients. There were roasted potatoes, an egg-and-artichoke pie, a selection of cheeses, fruit, and red wine. Small candles flickered in light-blue candle holders.

"I think I got it right, didn't I?" She was wearing a button-down black shirt I had bought her, and what I knew to be her favorite jeans. I also knew she had paid special attention to her hair, which looked soft and groomed, because I heard the hair dryer going for a long time. She smiled broadly at me, looking pleased with the outcome of everything. She brought me a rose and placed it by my plate. I shivered instinctively remembering my visions, but awareness of the sentiment behind the gesture made me recover almost instantly.

"More than right." I said, touched by her dedication. We had come a long way from our first interactions, and I had discovered her initial reactions to be ruled by a need to be guarded and in no way by actual coldness of heart. In fact, it was Rikke's great sensitivity and caring nature that caused her to put up those walls. I figured that now that she felt secure and protected from heartache, she was free to be herself. "This is one of the most beautiful things I have ever seen," I said.

She smiled broadly at me.

We ate in silence for a while, the flavors and the company unmatched. Between dinner and dessert, we told each other stories—from childhood, from college, from trying to find our place in the world and always thinking a piece was missing.

A little later, she brought out a strawberry tart and coffee. I found myself clapping and laughing because I like few things more than strawberry sweets. I realized immediately that she and my brother had been conspiring all along, and she had been fed all the necessary information to make my culinary dreams come true.

"I have another surprise for you." She looked as excited as I was.

"More? I couldn't eat another morsel."

"It's not food." She laughed. Her cell phone was on the table, and she pressed on an app icon while I looked on. The sound of the piano introduction to *Total Eclipse of the Heart* filled the air. "I never got to finish that serenade properly. That's not right, so I am fixing it now. That's me playing. Had to borrow the piano at the civic center." She extended a hand. "Would you dance with me?"

I felt my heart thumping in my chest as I took her hand. It was the corniest and most marvelous thing all at once. We danced under the yellow light while the song lulled us into a well-coordinated choreography. Close to the end of the ballad, Rikke took her hand to my face and combed away the strands of hair that covered my eye. "I would like to kiss you now." She said in a whisper. "Would that be all right?"

With a nod, I accepted her kiss, finding the last bit of joy that seemed to have been missing from an otherwise fairytale week. Kissing Rikke was like returning home. It evoked emotions that were as familiar as they were exciting.

I don't know how long we stayed locked in that kiss, neither one of us wanting to let go. The song had long ended, and we had continued to sway back and forth in a rhythm created by ourselves and the sound of the cicadas. "Violins with wings," they had been called. And what a perfect soundtrack for our love they were. At some point, we both realized the absence of music, and we laughed until my side hurt. I could tell we were both nervous, unaccustomed to being that unguarded and free.

"I don't care for the bed in the spare room." Rikke suddenly blurted out.

"Would you like to see if mine is any better?" I'm sure I felt my cheeks burn, but I held her gaze.

"Yes, I would."

I took her hand, and we ran inside, feeling as giddy as if we were dipping into a lake in the summer.

Outside my loft bed, the world disappeared, even the soft yellow light of the glass bulbs and the sound of the cicadas. There were only Rikke and me, and the feel of her kisses, and her hands that unbuttoned my blouse and held me tight. Her body found mine like the musician who finds in her instrument a well-known and beloved sequence of notes and rhythms, alternatingly powerful and sweet, fast and slow, loud and whispered. "Piano" in Italian means many things. Among them is "soft," as a musical term. Rikke's touch was the touch of a pianist, enticing and secure, the touch of someone who adores her art. I felt beautiful and revered, like music in her hands. I felt like her piano certainly did many times. In the end, I was overcome by a longing to wake up in her arms. But how could it be a longing if I had never done it before?

I fell asleep under her kisses, content and full, and I woke up still in her embrace, as I had wished. I couldn't think of any greater happiness.

In the daze of that early morning, as she ran her fingers lightly on my shoulder like she was composing, it took me a couple of minutes to realize someone was knocking on the door.

By the time I managed to find a long T-shirt to wear, Orlando was sitting by the entrance, alert and ready.

I opened the door slightly and peeked out, the sun temporarily blinding me. On the other side, stood a man, his dark hair shiny and his smile recognizable wherever I might be.

"Martín?"

"Hello, beautiful." He flashed his straight teeth at me and leaned against the frame of the door.

My blood cooled in my veins, and little icicles traveled faster and faster inside every artery.

There he was, in flesh and blood, and a tan that announced travel to faraway lands—the inspiration for tattoo number one.

Chapter 8

Rikke

Pia fell to sleep in my arms, but sleep eluded me. I watched her eyelashes flutter in a dream and her body twitched against me as she descended into slumber. Holding her in my arms felt unreal, and I think I kept my eyes open to prove to myself she was truly there. I'd long given up any expectation that I'd find someone to share my life. Relationships didn't add value to me; instead, they depleted me, and once I was empty, I typically found myself alone. I was beyond the point of blaming anyone else for it. I'd chosen each one of my lovers, whether consciously or subconsciously didn't matter. It had been a few years since I'd even tried.

I'd moved to Sedona because of its thriving arts community. I knew I could find work teaching, not that I worried about money. I'd not expected to meet Pia, and I didn't think it was possible I could fall in love. To fall in love is to let go. Living as I do—outside the boundaries of gender, adrift from family—makes protecting myself not a character defect but a requirement for survival. Letting go stopped being an option a long time before. The previous few days with Pia allowed me a glimpse into how life might be, in one place, settled, safe, secure, and loved. How it might feel to belong. I didn't know what was wrong with her, or why she was having visions and episodes. I didn't know if it was psychiatric or physical. I only knew I wouldn't leave her, regardless. For the first time in my life, I wanted to be where I was. I wanted to be with her. I wasn't sure I had a lot to offer, and didn't know why she'd want someone like me, but I loved her so much, I wanted to learn how to be still and loved.

I adjusted my arm, as tingling alerted me to a loss of blood flow. When I did, she stirred in her sleep and turned toward me, shifting on her side to face me. Her eyelids fluttered open and upon seeing me, she smiled, wrapped her arm around my waist and pulled me closer. I shifted to grant her wish, and she moved her leg between mine, falling quickly back to sleep. I moved stray hair off her forehead and kissed her there. Tears sprang from behind my eyes, and I willed myself to accept what she was offering and to trust her. I wanted her more than anything else in the world.

Pia was smart, beautiful, and kind. I loved watching her talk, walk, and hold her fork to eat. She filled the space with feminine warmth I didn't even know I craved until I met her. Her lips parted slightly in sleep, and I remembered how they felt against mine. I ran my hand down her back, the touch of her skin under my fingers the best sensation I'd ever known. I closed my eyes and recalled the tastes and sounds of her pleasure and finally drifted to sleep in her arms.

When I woke, Pia was gone. The bed felt empty and cold, and I sat up to the sounds of voices in the cottage. I heard Pia and a deeper male voice, and I felt confused. Had James returned so soon from Phoenix? I slipped on my jeans, tossed on the floor the night before, and the dark shirt Pia bought me. I dropped down the stairs of the loft and I saw Pia standing in the middle of the room, talking to a tall, dark, muscular and exceptionally masculine stranger. Something about their energy immediately made me feel nauseous, and I leaned against the railing to keep from falling over as a wave of jealousy and inadequacy swept over me. He saw me and stopped talking. Pia turned, abruptly, a confused look on her face.

"Uh—" Pia said, looking from me to him. I felt sick, and my face burned hot. I couldn't speak, so I turned the corner from the loft and walked down the hall into the bathroom. I leaned against the sink, turned on the faucet, and washed my face with cold water. Then I stuck my head under the stream. I knew with certainty he was a former lover.

Despite all claims to the contrary, I do not believe it is possible to be friends with someone once you've believed yourself in love with them. Once that energetic boundary is trespassed, a fissure remains. The size may be reduced, but there is always the possibility for it to reopen. This is what I felt when I saw Pia standing there with him. Should Pia choose, she could fall back into a relationship with him. He was unexpected, I knew this because I also felt her alarm at seeing him, but that made the whole situation even more dangerous for me.

Perhaps my extreme oversensitivity led me to this conclusion. My mother and father blamed the majority of my issues on my "lack of emotional regulation." The therapist they'd hired to help me after my accident gave them that term to describe me. Descriptors like "sentimental" and "overly sensitive" had plagued me since childhood. Countless people, family, friends, and lovers had all told me I needed to let things go. I ruminated and allowed thoughts to consume me.

What I couldn't articulate to anyone was that I really couldn't do any of those things because my emotions happened to me. I could manage my thoughts, as much as anyone, but not my feelings. When I felt something, it started somewhere in my thighs and rolled up my body, crashing in my chest, where it stayed, for as long as it decided, regardless of what I did. The only thing that ever made it better was music, and standing there, in front of the mirror, all I wanted was to retreat into the silence with an instrument and disappear into myself until I resolved whatever had overtaken me. It was so painful I doubled over, my breath catching in my throat.

I brushed my teeth, dread-awful fear spreading through my body. I thought I was different, and she loved me. I should have known it was all too good to be true. I breathed through the feeling, but my hands began to shake. I couldn't compete with him. When a woman like Pia was given an opportunity to be with someone like me, or someone like him, they always chose him. It was inevitable. Alarm filled my senses, and I sat on the side of the tub to decide what to do. I was going to the guest room to gather my things, and I would leave them alone. It was probably time I went home anyway, and Pia seemed to feel better.

I finished up in the bathroom and walked into the guest room. I put my things in my bag, not caring about organization or order. I heard their voices and then there was quiet. I sensed Pia's presence at the door. "Rikke," she said. I looked at her. She was wearing a long T-shirt, and she looked confused and shaken. I didn't want to add to her distress, but I couldn't seem to stop myself.

"I'll get out of here so you can talk," I said.

"No," Pia said, stepping forward. She put her hand on my arm, and I looked at it like it might burn me. She saw my reaction and withdrew. "What are you doing? I didn't invite him. He showed up. I'm letting him use the internet for a minute, and then he's leaving."

I zipped my bag. "Sure," I said, turning to her. "I saw you with him. I saw how you looked at him."

"It was unexpected, Rikke. Please. We can talk about this. He'll be gone in a minute."

"There is no need to rush," I said, retreating behind my expertly constructed walls. I'd let them down. I could get them back up. "From the way you looked at him, I'd say you have plenty to talk about." I picked up my bag and walked by her, without touching her or making eye contact, and out the front door. I'd not noticed I'd left my iPad on the nightstand.

"Rikke," she called again, as she followed me from the house, but I wouldn't be stopped. I held up a hand as I left, unable to look directly at the man who sat on her couch. I'd caught enough of a glimpse of him to see his legs were crossed, body relaxed, and he was settled into the seat as if he were entitled to Pia as matter of course. Men often acted that way with their wives and girlfriends, the energy evident only to someone like me, who always stood on the outside looking in.

My steps carried me down the hill from Pia's home where I finally stopped to order a ride. It came minutes later, and I asked the driver to take me to my apartment. As we turned into the parking lot, I impulsively asked, "If I give you $1000 cash, will you drive me to the airport in Phoenix?" The driver looked up, shocked, and nodded urgently. "Give me fifteen minutes," I said.

I wanted to be as far away from Pia as I could. I rushed into my house, packed clothes, laptop, and a few bathroom items. The air inside the apartment was stale and musty, but I didn't care. At that point, I didn't think I'd ever be back. I took my passport from the shelf in the bedroom, and left, locking the door behind me.

I ran down the stairs from the apartment and slid into the backseat of the car. "If you stop at the bank before we leave town, I'll get you the cash now."

****

I was in Phoenix within two and a half hours and standing at the gate of an airplane bound for London within three and a half. Pia had begun to call and text me non-stop almost forty-five minutes after I left. I turned my phone off and put it in my bag. Her visitor stayed for at least as long as it took her to begin calling me, and I viewed that as all the evidence I needed to justify what I was doing.

As I settled into a middle seat, tucked in the very back of the crowded plane, I finally breathed normally again. I don't know why I picked London and not somewhere else. The flight I'd chosen connected through Newark, but it could have connected anywhere or nowhere and I would not have cared. I heard the gears of the plane move and engines roar to life. The man next to me shifted in his seat, and coughed, before putting his elbow down on the armrest, pressing into my space, and against me.

I pushed my arm against his and made eye contact, angrier than I'd ever been. "Ever heard of male space privilege, asshole?" I asked. "Get your fucking arm off my armrest and don't touch me." Shocked, he pulled his arm into his own lap, and I leaned heavily back against my seat. I knew I was taking out my anger on him, but I didn't care. I put my headphones on and stared at the back of the seat in front of me. The in-flight magazine cover was ripped, like someone had torn it off to wrap their chewing gum. The barf bag stuck up from the pocket, and I felt so ill I thought I might need it.

I wiped tears off my face with the back of my hand. I thought about walking with Pia in the afternoons, harvesting vegetables, and dancing on the patio the night before. I thought about how warm and soft her hands were when she touched me, and the smell of her hair when it was still wet from the shower.

The dread in my chest broke into pieces, replaced with dark despair. The space around me, now dimmed in light as the plane lifted off the ground, felt like all there was in the world. The possibility of the future I'd briefly glimpsed with Pia dissipated as the plane jerked up from the runway. Heavy, suffocating darkness settled around my inner vision, and my chest tightened. The earth below receded as the aircraft climbed into the air, leaving behind my hopes for life with Pia.

Chapter 9

Pia

I wonder if the mountain is trying to break my resolve. Dry bush branches scratch my arms. I'm thirsty and sweaty. Toes have gone a little numb. I should have thought this through. To be in total disarray when I get to the top of the mountain won't do. Yet, if I consider it carefully, it is not such a big deal. Not in the context of the last few months. This is a placid walk, but my mind moves fast in many directions at once when my body remembers how I felt when she left.

Rikke's sudden and emotional departure shredded my heart into a million tiny pieces. My very soul ached. In so little time, I had opened up to her to such a degree that I hadn't taken any precautions to shield myself from pain. I was walking around with every nerve exposed, like naked wires in the rain, and it became very clear, very quickly, that she hadn't even noticed.

When she was gone, I stood in the same spot for a couple of minutes, frozen in place, looking at Martín like the stranger he had become. Time and separation had only confirmed what I knew when we parted ways before: that we should never have been together. Probably noticing my distress, he asked me to sit down. "Can I get you some water or something?"

I don't think I even responded.

"Would you like me to leave?" he said, already

picking up his things.

"Martín, I have to go. I have to find Rikke."

"Sure. If you need anything, I'll be at the Saguaro Hotel. It's good to see you, Pia. And I'm sorry. I should have called."

I didn't even wait for him to leave. I grabbed my keys and made for my car. Rikke was everywhere, impregnating the leather seats with her scent. She was in the daisy that, desiccated, had fallen to the floor. In the specter of our laugher while I drove, now only a ghostly memory of what had been.

At her place, I sat on the steps, waiting for her to come back, since I had knocked, and no one had answered. I must have sat there for forty minutes, crying and scolding myself for not having been able to keep her, for my failure to make her understand that together we were different from anything that had happened to me before.

I wished she could see that thoughts of Martín hadn't even crossed my mind, except for confirming he wasn't the one. He was a leaf from the past, one that had taught me much about who I was and what I could give, but still a page from a chapter now finished and archived.

Knowing in my gut all of a sudden that she was not coming back, I started to call and text compulsively. It was all I could do to prevent myself from going mad. Why did happiness have to be so fleeting? I had done nothing wrong, and still I was being punished.

I fell asleep on her doorsteps. I was homeless without her.

I woke up as the sun moved in the sky and found my face. The intense light made me frown. I hurried to look at my phone, but she had not replied. My chest was hollow. I walked back to my car, dragging feet that felt made of cement. I made it home and collapsed on my couch, no courage to even look at my bed, a place where so shortly before I had been so happy.

Orlando licked my face, and I'm sure he tried to tell me everything was going to be fine. A day later, James found me on the same couch, from which I had only moved for the bare necessities.

"Are you ill again?" He rushed to my side, loving concern evident in his eyes.

I told him everything that had happened, and he listened to me attentively, with the kind of compassion I had come to expect from him. "All in a split second," was what he said.

"I don't know where she is or how to find her. What if I have lost her forever?" I wrapped my arms around his neck and sobbed.

"Give it some time. Maybe she needs to cool off. She rushed into judgement about the situation, and she might realize that now, having stepped away."

"I don't know. The hurt in her eyes might haunt me forever." My chest was splitting in two.

"Let's not talk about it this way. I am going to insist you take a hot shower and stay there until you feel human again. Then we are going out for a bite to eat. We will figure out the rest later." He extended his hand to me.

I didn't have the will to protest, but I didn't have the strength to stand in the shower either, so I sat on the tiled floor, letting the water drape around me like a shawl. I wished away all the tension from my muscles, and all the heaviness in my chest, but water can only do so much.

When my fingers wrinkled prune-like, I found my bathrobe and a towel for my hair. Orlando dutifully waited for me outside the door, and I went back to the couch, knowing James would come to complain about my malaise any minute. When I heard thumping on the stairs, I turned around expecting a reprimand. Instead, I saw him brandish a tablet in front of me and say, "Get up, I know exactly how to find Rikke!"

****

"London?!"

"Yep. She's in London." James said between forkfuls of spaghetti. We were sitting in a little Italian bistro where he had dragged me with mysterious promises about locating Rikke.

It had taken me quite a bit of time to realize what his very simple ploy was. I should have remembered that Rikke was really bad about password-protecting her devices, and her tablet was no different: one swipe and everything, including the location of her phone through the "find my devices" app, was available to us. Because I care about people's privacy, I did have qualms about going through her things. Eventually deciding to do so weighed heavy on me, but I was desperate.

"I'm gonna follow her there." I said while moving my ravioli around the plate. The thought of eating made me queasy.

"You're going to London? Just like that."

"I see no other possible course of action, do you?"

James looked up, like he was searching for an answer on the ceiling. "It is kind of romantic, though."

"Will you take me to Phoenix tomorrow if I find a

ticket on the Internet tonight? I have a million accumulated vacation days, and with my having had the accident, I'm sure no one at the hospital will say anything."

He patted my hand. "I'll do anything to help."

I mouthed a silent "thank you" a little overcome by the emotions of the day.

London, I thought. Always my favorite place. I really wish it were under different circumstances, but it is always up to us to make the circumstances better anyway, and I knew I was invested, life and soul, in turning that one around.

Part II
Chapter 10

Rory

In October of 1840, I returned to Moorsgrange to find the place much altered from the image I had retained in my mind and in my heart for comfort. You see, I grew up in Moorsgrange—not in the main house, to be sure, but on its grounds, in a cottage set aside for the gamekeeper, who happened to be my father. It is a breathtaking property, with magical gardens and open fields, extending all the way to where one's vision becomes blurry, and the mountains and the sky merge into one. Moorsgrange spoils one to the point that no other place compares. It demands lifetime commitment in return, and it incites passions and emotions that one has to learn to keep as permanent companions, even if they venture away.

When I went back to Moorsgrange, I was twenty years old and had received an education that few of my station in life could aspire to. Not only had I completed the traditional schooling that wealthy girls received, but I had also received training as a nurse and was fully capable of caring for the young, the elderly, or the ill. Although becoming a nurse put me in the realm of people who worked for a living, it also gave me a taste of freedom of the kind that those girls, with their wealth and advantage, sadly never experienced. Their spouses were chosen for them, they would be told what to think and what to wear, and, in time, they would forget what their own tastes and opinions were. Their wants would give way to whatever was accepted or in fashion. They could not discern if they liked yellow or quite preferred blue. They abided by social rules and expectations and come to forget the joys of bare feet in the water and late nights by a fire listening to music.

Of course education did to me what it is designed to do. It taught me a vocation with which I could find a job. However, it also planted the seed of independent thinking, the love of books and ideas, and that discomfort that comes from acquiring knowledge that one can never really put aside or always see reflected in the world. I was a woman of science, and I planned to behave like one.

When the hackney deposited me in front of the main house on that foggy winter day, close to noon, I abandoned my belongings right there on the steps of the mansion and ran, in the most unladylike manner, toward the gardens that, although gelid, held all the mystery and all the beauty I had been dreaming of.

The air smelled like I remembered—a combination of the scents blown from the woods and wet soil—and I took it in as if my life depended on it. The scarcity of birds at that time of the year made the chirping of the very few all the more precious, and I attended to their melodies all the more carefully. That's how it happened in Moorsgrange. You were drawn in by the birds, or by the roses, and soon you noticed the pond or the forest beyond it. Next, there was this longing in the pit of your stomach, this caress of the wind against your neck, and you were lost to the world outside its boundaries. You were allowed incursions out, but Moorsgrange never left you. It was a state of heart.

I saw Jules for the first time in years in the rose garden, where naked skeletons of rose stems glistened with the remnants of frost that the weak sun had not be able to evaporate. He was sitting at the edge of the fountain, now waterless but still humid enough for moss to form. He had a small book in his hands and must have been so enthralled by its pages that he didn't hear me approach.

I stood there, opposite him, so close that I could observe his long eyelashes, his well-trimmed nails and the pin on his cravat, which I remember had belonged to his late father. His brown hair was longish, and a strand flopped to cover one of his eyes, encouraging Jules to run his fingers through his locks. His fingertips were exposed through fingerless gloves, and he used them to turn the crinkly pages of the book.

It was only when I feigned coughing that he realized I was there. He stood up all at once, like someone who is caught in mischief and has to concoct an explanation in a fraction of a second. Then his eyes recognized mine.

"Rory. It is you!" His voice was deeper but still his own.

We hadn't seen each other in six years, since we were both fourteen and still the tomboys that caused his mother to fret and worry over possible fractures, especially given our predilection for climbing trees, crossing creeks, and running over the moors like wild deer. We had been inseparable since the day I arrived in Moorsgrange at age eight, after my mother passed away. "Rory and Jules" became a unit, and staff and parents alike rarely enquired about one without referring to the other.

"Of course it's me! What are you reading?"

He was much changed from the boy who laughed easily and was happy to come home muddied, with a torn shirt and a scratch on the cheek. He looked like a gentleman now, polished and polite, tall but still quite thin, which only made him more handsome according to the fashion of the time. At first look, he seemed like a bit of a dandy, but there was something in his manner, an under-the-surface authenticity that did not fit with the required affectation. His clothes, elegant at first glance, were threadbare enough to disqualify him from the title as well.

"Oh, this. Nothing important." He hid the book behind his back.

"And you're just going to stand there and not give me a proper hug?"

He looked uncertain. We were not children anymore, and we could not, in the five minutes of our renewed acquaintance, have established what the new rules of conduct would be, but it was clear they would be quite different from before.

Tentatively, he walked toward me and stood close. "I like the way you wear your hair."

I had decided not to be subject to the whims of fashion, so I simply styled my hair the way I thought it would suit me better. At that point, it was a few soft curls of red hair framing my face and a long braid with a ribbon intertwined, over my shoulder. Breaking all etiquette, he touched a loose curl and the side of his hand brushed against my face, sending a pleasurable shiver through me.

"You are beautiful. Like you, but different."

"Different?" I repeated his word to give myself time to absorb the compliment and guess his meaning.

"I suppose we're not children anymore." He looked grave all of a sudden, like he was trying to prove his point.

"If you think that will prevent me from climbing trees or running barefoot you are sorely mistaken, dear sir." With that, I grabbed the book that he had now left forgotten at the edge of the fountain and dashed through the garden. "What have we here?" I said flipping through the pages and discovering it was poetry.

He ran after me, laughing like old times, past garden benches and flower beds, until he was overcome by a coughing fit and had to stop. He put each of his hands above his knees so that his spine was parallel to the ground and his rib cage moved rapidly in an out, with an urgency that scared me.

"What's wrong?" I was suddenly taken aback by how pale he looked and how breathless he'd become.

"I get these now. When I run, go up the stairs, or ride a horse. But I'm fine in a minute." He stood straight again and puffed out his chest, offering his arm for me to loop mine around.

We started walking in silence, reestablishing our common ground, and I was afraid to break the spell of that perfect moment either with words or with more of his respiratory distress. While seeing my childhood friend had brought immense joy to my heart, the nurse in me had become quite alarmed. I wanted to say I would take care of him, that I had the proper training to make him better, but I knew making him feel vulnerable in front of me would have had a terrible effect. In my mind, I vowed to do it anyway. I would do it out of love.

Yes, love. From the moment I saw him sitting there near the fountain, the undeniable truth rushed through me like the electricity of a bolt of lightning. I loved Jules, in that desperate way that allows little space for doubt or fear. A love that simply is, like the hills beyond Moorsgrange. From that instant on, my life would not be mine anymore. It would belong to him, to his needs, and I was happy to give it up. Understanding of my purpose in coming back to the manor hit me like lightening.

****

In my absence, Moorsgrange had aged. Like a lonely lady, unloved and uncared for, it had lost its exuberance; its walls were humid and cold, and its furniture more battered than I remembered. Of course it still displayed its grandeur: an unloved duchess is still a duchess. Yet I could not help but mourn the loss of the years of splendor, when we were children, when Jules's father was alive, and when fancy balls and formal dinners were the rule in Moorsgrange. Those nights, I often asked my father to bring me around to the house so that I could peek at the ladies' gowns from behind the corner of a window and admire the grace of the waltzing couples. On those occasions, I would go back to the cottage and try to imitate their steps and the coy way with which the women received invitations to dance. "Who, me, sir? Oh." I would say with affectation to my invisible companion in the room. "I believe I could, thank you."

Jules, once he recovered from his coughing fit, insisted on showing me everything and indicated he planned on asking his mother to provide me with quarters in the main house.

"I know my place, Jules. I belong in the cottage with my father, whom I have not even seen yet." Over the years, my father had taken an annual trip to London to buy what was needed for the mansion and to see me for a couple of days. The latest of such visits had happened nine months before. "I miss him very much." I felt my eyes tear up a bit.

"I know you do, but at this hour I am sure he is out in the woods hunting. Do you still refuse to eat meat?"

"Yes. Vegetables, grains, and fruit are enough for me. Not that I reject the occasional cake or tart."

"Come, I will ask Cook for some fruit. Maybe she's made jam."

We descended into the kitchen through pathways I knew so well, I could close my eyes and still get to our destination. Of course everything looked smaller now that I was a grown woman, but the smells were the same, as was Jules's smile when he took me by the hand and into the lower floor. The familiarity of those everyday blessings filled me with happiness. Yet not everything was bliss in the manor.

With the estate's decline, the once-large staff had been reduced to a housekeeper, Cook, a scullery maid, a cleaning maid, and a butler who also served as valet. I knew most of them well and was looking forward to renewing their acquaintance. They were the closest thing to an extended family I had had while growing up. The fact that a couple of dear friends were among the ones dismissed frustrated me, but I chose to concentrate on the nice people in front of me while also making a decision to write to the others as soon as I could.

"Look who's here!" Jules announced to those members of the group who were in the kitchen. Cook looked like herself, only six years more tired. She moved her gaze, from the dough she had been kneading to my face, and a smile of recognition came to her lips.

"Rory! Oh, 'ow wonderful you look." She dusted off the flour from her hands and came to give me a hug. "I was always so grateful for your le'ers and your stories about the ci'y. But 'tis so much be'er now that you're back."

Mr. Arnold stood up and straightened his jacket that now appeared a little faded. "Miss Allen." He nodded, circumspect as always, as if he had not been a witness at my parents' wedding or a guest in my christening. He was responsible for bringing my little family to Moorsgrange when we needed it, being that he had known Father for so many years. "I am sure your father is delighted with your return to Moorsgrange."

"I imagine he will be. I have not found him yet."

"In the woods, to be sure." Mr. Arnold concluded, echoing Jules's supposition.

"What did I tell you?" Jules smiled at me again, and my heart confirmed what it had hinted while we were in the garden—that I was back for him and that only his happiness mattered to me. That it took me so little time to realize should have astounded me, and yet it simply felt natural, meant to be.

"Cook, we came searching for some fruit, maybe some bread and jam for Rory?"

"Nonsense. You shall 'ave a full meal. Sit down, the lo' of you, please. Oh, this is Grace Smith, our scullery maid. Pro'bly about your age, Rory?"

Miss Smith did a little curtsy, and I caught her in time to shake her hand instead. "I'm sure we're going to be friends. Pleased to make your acquaintance." She blushed and smiled, and I remembered how much it meant to be acknowledged and visible, even if only for a second, when you lived downstairs.

Cook placed bread, cheese, jam, pears, a tart, and apple cider in front of me on the big kitchen table. I looked to my left and found the spot where Jules carved his initials when he was very young. A crooked J was still quite distinguishable. I ran my fingers over it, unable to contain a smile.

After pouring some of the cider into a cup, Cook started reaching for the cold cuts. That was when she remembered. "Still no meat?"

"No meat." I confirmed.

"You were always a queer one."

"Cook!" Jules protested while Miss Smith coughed.

"Wha? I don't mean any 'arm. You are just as queer, Master Jules. With your music and your 'ead in the clouds. And your books of poetry. And don't forget that 'air of yours."

We both snickered. I had missed her sincerity.

"Wha?!" She repeated, looking from him to me and back again. Miss Smith stifled a chuckle.

Jules went to give Cook a hug. "Nothing, Cook. We love you, is all."

After the meal, I announced my intention to finally go to the cottage, and Jules declared his wish to accompany me.

"Please don't, Jules. I have already taken too much

of your time today. I'm sure you have things to do."

He looked disappointed but did not insist. "I reckon you want time with your father."

I bid goodbye to everyone and went to collect my belongings. I looked forward to the walk to the cottage.

Moorsgrange had its enchantment enhanced by each season: it was abuzz with activity in the summer, as if the whole place had awakened to the sounds of birds and to the pungent smells of the garden. It was poetic in the fall, with autumn leaves collecting along the pathways, a rusty patina over everything. In the spring, the beauty and elegance of the flowers, as well as their bright colors, were almost overwhelming, and in the winter, the sweet melancholy of bare branches and foggy lanes made for perfect reading afternoons and dreamy nights by the fire. The best thing about Nature was that, unlike the architectural part of Moorsgrange, it did not need constant attention and refreshing with paints, oils, and tiles. Nature renewed itself perfectly if we only let Her do her own job. We should have realized that it was the same with our emotions. Sometimes, we should sit with them, in contemplation rather than action, but we were too young to know.

I longed for conversation with my father. Like Nature's, his form of wisdom was simple and direct and had helped me make decisions all my life. He was also my connection to my mother and to the love I knew he still felt and forever would feel for her.

With my mind lost in these thoughts, I made my way home, hardly caring about the weight of my bags or the tiredness in my feet. As I approached the cottage, I noticed the smoke coming out of the chimney.

Realizing this meant he was home, I couldn't help but run a bit, anxious to get to him as soon as I could.

"Father! Father" I shouted as I approached the door, and he came to open it as well as his arms to hold me in a hug. At that, the safety of home overtook me and removed all my unstated fear that I didn't belong in Moorsgrange anymore.

Chapter 11

Jules

I didn't expect to see Rory again when she left for her training as a nurse. My mother was never fond of our relationship. Rory, she explained, was beneath my station. It was her expectation I marry a woman with title, as she had married my father. After he passed away when I was sixteen, her insistence on such became a nagging, pervasive cloud in my life. It was a result of her pragmatic view of the world, one according to which things and people were useful or they were not, and if they were found useful, she then filtered them through additional layers, categorizing everything into tightly formed compartments, based on her expectation of reality.

It was Elizabeth, my mother, who sponsored Rory's education away from Moorsgrange. It happened suddenly after she caught us playing dress up in my parents' wardrobe. Rory had painted my cheeks with rouge, and I wore one my father's vests over one of my mother's walking skirts. Rory wore my father's trousers under her dress, and I'd painted a moustache on her lip. We laughed hysterically as we dressed, but then upon completion, found that we stared at each other, unspoken understanding passing between us. Really, it never mattered what we did, so long as I did it with Rory.

The image of us dressed as such terrorized my mother so completely, Rory was gone within a few weeks. She hired a male tutor for me with the explicit understanding that he would teach me grammar, math, biology, and how to be a man. Alexander was ten years my senior when he arrived at Moorsgrange, shortly after Rory left.

I'd moped about the manor for weeks, despondent and gloomy, dragging myself through the long damp corridors we'd once filled with laughter. Nothing Alexander did affected the depressive pallor which permeated my being, from skin to bone. With Rory gone, I felt an inconsolable ache in my chest, a sadness which never receded no matter how many tears I shed. I moved through the days, from lesson to lesson, my limbs bending in all the right places, but my muscles growing weak with loss. The only solace I found was composing mournful piano nocturnes I trusted I would one day play for Rory. I imagined her standing by the piano, all her attention for me alone, clapping when I finished, rushing to throw her arms around my neck, celebrating my gift to her, as she kissed my forehead and lifted my pain away.

For Elizabeth, it was an accomplishment to have a son who could play the piano and citra as I could, but it wasn't becoming to have a son willing to play dress-up with the gamekeeper's daughter. Alexander was employed to be certain it never happened again, and it didn't. Under his strict, unrelenting tutelage, I learned to dress according to the rigorous standards of the day. With my father deceased, he escorted me to men's clubs and meetings all over the borough, when my health allowed. My mother's fear that my hands would be damaged in an accident prevented him from taking me hunting, to my relief.

They called me a prodigy when I sat at the piano in the parlor when I was six and played the hymn, I'd heard at church the day before. That fateful day set the course for all that unfolded after, from my travels to Elizabeth's obsessive protection of my talent, my station, and me, Rory's departure, my father's death, and my ongoing illness. My mother and father took me on a playing tour when I was fifteen, and when we returned home, my father and I both fell ill with what Cook called the graveyard cough.

I turned sixteen in my bed, the shades drawn, the room dark, the world outside beyond my reach. Some unknown evil had overtaken my body, killed my father, and in feverish rants, I saw it watching me from the far corner of my bedroom, waiting for my eyes to close so it could pounce. In my hallucinations, the fever took form, eyes red and glowing, arms long with talons instead of fingers. While I soaked my bed sheets in blood, sprayed from my mouth in coughing fits which made it impossible to even control my bowels, outside my window, they dug the plot where my father rested.

The days bore down on me, in endless torment and I begged my mother, Cook, and Rory's father to kill me. My limbs ached and grew cold then roared back to life with fire so hot I feared I'd dropped into hell. Doctor Milson came every second day, administered serums and leeches, then hot and cold compresses. Beyond that, only bedrest and fresh air. Nothing he did mattered. The thing that possessed me was waging a victorious war, and with Rory gone, I had no reason to fight. After months of torment, I begged him for enough laudanum to end my suffering, but instead, the dose he administered allowed me to sleep for two days. I cried for Rory, again and again, and saw her in my dreams when I did rest, chasing ahead me through the grounds, her hair blowing behind her as she ran, eyes alive with laughter.

Then, one day, many months into my sixteenth year, I woke as the sun broke through the small crevice in the heavy drapes. The room was stale with sickness, closed off to the world outside, and that tiny patch of sunlight was heavy with dust. I watched it from the bed, rolled on my side, and put my feet on the floor. My intention was to stand, throw open the drapes and open the windows, regardless of what waited outside.

I didn't know what season it was, whether sun or snow and sleet. Then I saw my legs, exposed where my dressing gown pulled up, touched the skin which hung directly on the long bone of my leg and despair welled inside me. I was able to wrap my hand around my own leg, and I screamed. My mother's housekeeper, Miss Smith, rushed in to find me in the throes of anguish, naked, as I viewed my emaciated body in the pale light of the single ray of sun to which I'd awakened.

My whole life then revolved around recovering more strength, eating, walking, and not overdoing it. I asked to play my piano soon after awakening, and my mother arranged for the servants to carry me downstairs. I still played as I had before, but my body would never be the same. I would never be healthy again. I'd escaped hell to dwell on the boundary between life and death, content to not suffer but not live either.

Until I saw Rory again.

****

After Rory left me in the kitchen, I walked slowly through the halls of the manor, pausing to study paintings I'd not looked at in all the years before. I was tired from the excitement of the day and my chest felt heavy. I coughed, holding a handkerchief over my mouth, and ignored the spittle of blood as I tucked it back into my pocket.

Rory had not seen her father in many months, since his last trip to London, and I wanted to respect her privacy and desire for solitude with him. But I'd not seen her in many years, and being with her made my heart beat faster, like the heart of someone who is alive. Strong wind raged outside, and the manor shrieked at its onslaught. I stood in front of a window and felt the pulse of the air as it leaked into the house. I trailed my hand on the damp walls.

I wandered down the stairs to the kitchen and then the servants' quarters where I stopped to talk to Mr. Arnold as he readied himself to rest for the evening. He stood immediately upon seeing me outside his door and I waved him off, as I always did, uncomfortable with such displays.

"The windows leak so, Mr. Arnold." The damp on the walls also worried me, though I did not know enough to fix it.

"That they do, sir. I will see to as many as I am able once we resolve the leak in the ceiling on the third floor and in the attic." I nodded, content to have passed on the information. As much as I wanted to resolve the issues, I was not able to do so. "You've been up and around a great deal today, sir. Please take care to rest and not strain."

I agreed, leaving him to wander into the kitchen, where Cook stood, wiping her hands on a well-used towel. She smiled when she saw me, her right-side missing tooth offering the only glimpse into the crippling poverty she'd lived with before coming to us at Moorsgrange.

"Cook," I said, "I was wondering…" but she held up her hand, stopping my line of inquiry.

"Master Jules wants to know if I will make Rory a chocolate sweet for 'im to take 'er." I blushed, flustered my affection was so obvious. "Good for Master Jules that I've already done so." She lifted a baking towel from a small chocolate cake in the center of the table to show me. Then she tucked it under the towel again, picking it up to hand it to me. "'old on!" She rushed from the kitchen, while I stood, humbled that I was known so well. When she returned, she carried my citra carefully in both hands, handing it to me so I could take it with my open hand. "Come, now," she said, pushing me toward the back door, which she opened. "Go see your lady."

I traipsed through the dark, bungling and stumbling, unaccustomed to being outside at night. I was further inconvenienced balancing the cake and citra, uncoordinated by my long infirmity. I stopped mid-way through my journey to Rory's cottage, set the cake down while I tucked the citra inside my waistband. They were loose enough to hold it, and I laughed at myself as I continued toward Rory, a cake in my hand a citra in my pants. I imagined telling her this, and her laughter as I described it all, acting it out for her. I realized I often imagined everything through the filter of how I would tell it to Rory. I wanted her to witness all my life, from nocturnes to chocolate cakes on stolen, windy nights, under the cover of darkness.

I arrived finally, tired, sweaty, and out of breath outside the cottage door. I took the citra from the waist of my pants and sat it against the door. I wasn't ready to knock, as I wanted my breath back before I saw Rory. I turned to look at the manor in the distance, at an angle I'd not often seen it, glowing with candlelight and fires. The door opened behind me, and I startled as my citra fell inside. It was Rory, wearing a simple dress, her hair pulled up high on her head, skin flushed as if she'd just washed. I tried to speak but nothing came, so I held out the cake for her.

"Jules, what are you doing out at night?" She took the cake and lifted my citra with the ease I associated with the way she moved through the world. "You look waxen. Come in. Hurry." I stepped inside, as she set the cake and citra down on the wooden table. With her hands free, she grabbed my arms, and pushed me down on a chair. "Jules, what has become of you? Are you ill?" She knelt in front of me, hands on my face, and I pulled her up and against me, arms around her waist. I knew it was inappropriate to do such a thing in her father's home, but my desire to hold her close was so strong I couldn't resist. She wrapped her arms around my neck, and we held onto each other as if we would never see the next day. Finally, I released her, and she pulled away from me reluctantly. I saw her wipe a tear from her cheek.

"I was very sick for a long time, but I feel better now," I said with a smile. "And I brought you a chocolate cake." She looked at the cake on the table and stood.

"My father has stepped out for more firewood, but he will be back. Should I make tea for us?" I watched her ready the kettle for the fire. On the citra, I played a silly tune we liked as children, and she paused as she lifted the kettle to laugh with me. Her father returned to find us together with surprise, but also a welcoming spirit, and I played her favorite songs into the night, while we shared tea and chocolate cake, until I was so tired I worried how I'd get home. I bowed to Rory when I left, overcome with vicious desire to hold her in my arms again. Instead, I tucked the desire in my stomach to power my walk home. Her father took my elbow and escorted me to the main house, into my bedroom, settling me into bed before he left.

He paused at the door as he left my room. "My daughter loves you, Master Jules. Be careful of that." Then he was gone, and I was alone, carried away by my exhaustion borne of overexertion for love.

Chapter 12

Rory

Returning to Moorsgrange had been rewarding and taxing in equal amounts. Seeing Jules again brought me great happiness but also great distress. He was very ill—there was no denying that obvious fact, and, for days at a time, he stayed in his room, too tired to walk with me. Likewise, living again in my father's house was wonderful, as it reminded me that we were a family. Yet, that also meant living by his rules and watching him work until exhausted, without much hope of progress or betterment. Finally, dwelling in Moorsgrange meant being able to stay among beloved people, from my father and Jules to the household staff, but it also meant having to face Mrs. Elizabeth Emsworth, the lady of the manor, who was both my sponsor and my ruler, my supporter and my enemy. I noticed that in life, every happiness had its counterpart.

It was because of Mrs. Emsworth that I had received an education, but her motives had never been pure. She could not stand the affection that always existed between Jules and me, a sentiment that transcended time, space, and class, as made abundantly clear by my absence and subsequent return. As children we had defied conventions out of the pure joy of being who we were: I was equally adept at wearing pants and climbing trees as Jules was of applying color to his cheeks and singing in a lovely falsetto. As adults, we were still what we had always been, if not more. Tea at the cottage—and everything that had transpired between us—meant Jules agreed with me.

In the days that followed my return, as much as I tried to confine myself to the cottage and to the gardens, it was to be expected that I should be summoned, and so I was, one mid-morning, half a week into my residency, as I walked near the pond and studied a detailed account of lung infirmities from a book I had brought with me from London. Jules's extended stay in his quarters had left me with plenty of time to study, which except for being with him, was my favorite activity.

It was Mr. Arnold who came to fetch me.

"Miss Allen. My employer has asked to see you. She will be in the morning room."

I had dreaded such encounter from the moment I'd arrived, and I considered myself lucky to have avoided it for a few days. As I walked toward the mansion, I decided to not rehearse what I was going to say. I concluded that any artificiality would only make me weaker.

The powder-blue morning room looked different from what I remembered, and the air inside smelled moldy. The wallpaper was faded, and a yellowed watermark stained a corner where the ceiling and the wall met. The furniture had been rearranged and was sparser. The piano was still there, but at least one chaise longue and a secretary desk were missing, and the curtains, once majestic and bright, looked faded. I could not help but decide that all that humidity was not good for Jules's health.

Mrs. Emsworth sat on a tall armchair, the many portraits of family members behind her, like escorting companions. She did not stand as I came in. Her face looked only slightly more aged, a feature most pronounced around her mouth, where thin vertical lines showed as she pursed her lips. She wore a green dress with ivory embroidery around the neck, and her hair, now peppered with grey, was arranged in braids that were then made into a bun. She would have been a handsome woman if her demeanor was not always so severe. That added the most years to her overall appearance.

"Oh, Rory. Come." I stood in front of her, and she examined me, as if I wore a dress she was considering buying, only that couldn't be true because my clothes were those of a person in service.

"Mrs. Emsworth." I said, between polite and curt.

"I see you are doing fine. Welcome back to Moorsgrange. I reckon you found your father well and the cottage in good condition."

"Yes, Mrs. Emsworth. I did. Thank you."

"And I've a letter that indicates you completed your education and have become a capable nurse. I am pleased."

"I wanted to make sure I made good on your investment."

She chose to understand my commentary as an expression of gratitude even if I had intended it much more as a statement of obligation. "Well, I am happy to have been in a position to help."

To help or to demand, I thought to myself and then bit my lower lip in an effort to prevent myself from saying as much.

Mrs. Emsworth had used a walking cane for as long as I could remember, and she had both hands on it now. Her posture became more erect every time she held on to the cane like that, and, even at a young age, I had realized that when she moved to hold on with both hands, she was about to say something she considered important.

"It seems of the essence to think of the future. Have you any plans?" She kept her chin high.

The question surprised me more than it should have, but indeed I had considered the answer many times before.

"I believe it would be prudent if I started looking in town. I could become a lady's maid, or I can be hired to take care of the sick while they heal. I have broad training and can even assist a surgeon."

At that last remark, Mrs. Emsworth made a face. Certainly, she was considering and discarding the idea of surgery and all its bloody ramifications.

"There's a new doctor in town. Perhaps he is looking for an assistant. There would be no harm in asking."

"I agree. If you have any information on where to find such a person, I would be happy to travel to town tomorrow and enquire."

"Good. It is set then." She stood up and walked to a side table, from where she retrieved a note, which she handed to me. Clearly, she had prepared it in advance.

"Thank you. I will make preparations right away."

As I was leaving, I gathered enough courage to speak to her about Jules. Something told me it would not be a welcome subject, but I had an obligation.

"Mrs. Emsworth, I could not help but notice that

Jules's health is a bit fragile at the moment. I could help if you'd let me."

"That will not be necessary, Rory. He has a doctor. In fact, the new doctor has been very helpful too, and I am considering a patronage. His methods are more advanced than Dr. Milson's, being that the old doctor is now almost eighty.

I was not about to stand down. Every time he coughed or heaved, I felt a dagger through my heart. "I do not presume to know as much as a doctor, but I have seen great improvement in respiratory ailments in a hospital in London. I have assisted in many cases."

"I'm sure you have. Should your help become necessary, I will be the first to let you know. Good day, Rory." And with that dismissal, she walked out of the morning room, making it impossible for me to argue any further. I fumed in silence, as I often did, being that I was not allowed the privilege to speak my mind given my station and being a woman.

On my way to the front door, I found Jules in the library. I rejoiced at the fact he had left his bedroom. Noticing him alone, and reassured that we would not be disturbed since his mother had gone up the stairs, I went in. I had decided to help him whether she liked it or not. "I've come to help you feel better." I remember saying, and I followed up with arguments about how his health did not make him a burden to me, that he could never be a burden, no matter what he said which was contrary to that—and try to contradict me, he did.

"What are you reading this time?" He had at least five books spread on the library desk.

"These are books on music. And where, pray tell, do you come from?" He put in a joyful voice, certainly to reassure me he was well.

"I came to say hello to your mother."

His whole body stiffened. "Why?" he asked as if my actions were quite absurd.

"Because she is the lady of the house. Because she sponsored my studies. Because she is my father's employer. Shall I go on?"

His shoulders relaxed a smidge. "I don't like it when she meddles."

"She wasn't meddling."

"Oh, no? What did the two of you talk about?"

"This and that. My future."

"There you have it. Meddling."

"She wants to make sure I am settled and employed. That's all."

For a second, it seemed he would retort, but in the end he did not. He did stand up and come close. He put a hand on my arm, and I realized I did not want him to remove it. "I'll watch out for you. She will not take you away again." He placed a kiss on my forehead.

"Do not worry, Jules. I belong in Moorsgrange."

The next morning, I left early to cover the few miles that separated us from town in a coach that was going in that direction anyway. I travelled with Mr. Arnold who had been tasked with bringing certain provisions back to the house: sacks of flour, fabrics, new brooms. We arrived in less than an hour, and I almost gasped at how much Rosemead had grown in my absence. What had started as a village now prospered, and displayed many new houses, stores, and the forementioned medical practice. I could not help but eye a lovely tea house at a corner. The church, which had been there forever, looked well-kept and tidy.

As I exited the coach, I noticed a tall man, who looked to be in his late twenties or early thirties entering the practice. He stopped, looked at me, removed his hat, and smiled. It was a nervous smile, made more so by his sallow cheeks and the fidgeting nature of his hands. When I got closer, he addressed me in a casual tone, as if we were acquainted with each other.

"Coming to see me?"

While his face was young and his smile tentative, his eyes were older and more pained than he would likely have wanted to give away.

"If you are Dr. Cain, then yes sir, I am here to see you."

"Nothing too serious I hope."

"No, sir. I am not ill. I'm a nurse. I am here to offer my services in case you are considering hiring an assistant."

"What a great prospect, Miss…?"

"Allen. Rory Allen."

"I am pleased to make your acquaintance, Miss Allen. Shall I escort you in?" And with that he used his arm and hand to show me the way.

It was a well-equipped practice he ran, in comfortable quarters that were sure to attract the well-to-do dwellers of Rosemead and properties nearby. "I also visit patients in the great residences surrounding this area." he told me. I thought to ask if he did charitable work and cared for those who could pay little or nothing at all but felt the question premature given our very limited acquaintance.

After a brief narrative of my history and my education, I went silent, patiently awaiting his thoughts on my blatant request for a job.

He stood up and with his hands together behind his back, walked toward the window in a pensive state. He stopped there, and, without looking at me, said. "Serendipity is a wonderful thing. It so happens that this very week, I'd been enquiring about an assistant and wondering if I would have to travel to York or Leeds to find someone with qualifications. Suddenly, you, Miss Allen, simply walk through my door."

"Coincidences are wonderful!"

"Oh, I think it is more than a coincidence. It is true that as a man of science I should not dwell on superstition, but what if it is fate? It is too perfect to be otherwise."

I sat there, unsure of what to say to his reflection. "Does that mean I can have the position?"

"Yes, Miss Allen. That is exactly what it means. You shall work here in the practice twice a week, and we will take an extra day to visit patients in their homes. Apart from any emergencies that might occur, you will have the rest of the week for yourself. Those will be long days, so it seems only fair that we should start with three. What say you?"

"Thank you, Dr. Cain. I accept."

We agreed that it might be a good idea for me to lease a small room in town. There were two widows who could use the extra income, and Dr. Cain indicated the practice would pay. This way I would not have to arrange for transportation other than to be delivered on Tuesday and retrieved on Thursday. My poor father would not have that additional task, which was enough reason for me to assent.

I shook the doctor's hand, and we agreed I'd start a

week Tuesday, which would be a short eight days
away. There was so much to be done. He offered to
take care of my housing. I would take care of
everything else.

As I rode back with Mr. Arnold, a strange anxiety
took hold of me. I didn't want to leave Jules, not for
three days at a time, not for one, really. He needed my
care, and even if I tried to reason that I would leave
instructions, I knew he followed the ones I gave him
because they came straight from me. This was not a
misplaced sense of importance. It was simply an
acknowledgement of the reality, of how he felt about
me. I was sure of it because I felt exactly the same way
about him. Yet, I needed a job. I needed a life in which
I could be self-reliant. Without wealth or name, that
was my existence, and I embraced it without complaint,
but with a certain angst.

Given my awareness of my forthcoming change in
situation, I spent every possible minute I could with
Jules until the day I was set to start work. We walked
the gardens and read to each other, sitting under the
sun, on iron chairs cushioned with throws. We played
cards, he played the citra, and I played the little I knew
of the flute. We wrote poems, laughed at impossible
rhymes, and collected flowers for my bedside table. I
fed him delicious foods, whetting his appetite with
stories of all the places we would go together and all
the things we would do.

And everything was good and wonderful for eight
days. For eight days, time stopped, and we were the
only creatures on this earth. We ignored his mother's
nasty looks from the second floor of the mansion while
we pretended I had no money concerns and Jules had

no health ones. For eight days, it was like I had never left. We were back to finishing each other's sentences, to laughing with abandonment, to knowing exactly what would make the other happy at what time. For eight days, Moorsgrange was again our paradise.

Chapter 13

Jules

I was overly tired when I left Rory the night of cake and citra, but I was happier than I'd been since she left. I woke and tried to climb from my bed, but my legs betrayed me and a coughing fit left me writhing on the floor where Mr. Arnold found me. He helped me back into bed, brought a basin for me to wash my face and hands, and then a breakfast of Cook's homemade bread, jam, and poached eggs. Despite my fatigue, I ate ravenously, and when he returned in late morning for my tray, I asked him to bring me lunch right away. He returned with soup made of potatoes, carrots, and rabbit. I ate it greedily, as well, demanding more of Cook's bread. My goal was to restore my strength with food. For years eating was a chore, and I put little effort into it. But with Rory returned, I felt new motivation.

At high noon, I rose to dress, shave, and wash but failed. I climbed back into bed, and Mr. Arnold brought me a stack of books from the library. I wanted Rory but did not want to let her see me as I was. So I hid away in my room, the servants bringing me food and books for the remainder of the day. My mother visited, though she didn't know about my visit to Rory, and Cook and Mr. Arnold seemed content to conspire with me and keep it so. Mother assumed my illness flared because of the change of seasons. In her mind, the falling leaves and temperatures caused the demon inside me to awaken, and I wouldn't change her mind.

I spent the day confined to bed, but forced myself from it the next, as I grew desperate, and my own heartache strangled me. I was weak, ill, and not worthy of someone like Rory. She was alive, vibrant, and thrilling. The air pulsed around her as she talked and moved. It was selfish of me to pursue her. My earlier hopes and joy about Rory's return diminished in the reality of my situation. With failing health, what kind of life could I possibly offer her? Strong enough to leave my room, I retired to the library to decide on what books I would read next. Then, I planned to play for a while, work on a few new piano pieces I'd neglected. I was resolved to let go of my childhood infatuation for Rory until I saw her in the doorway of the library. She'd left my mother's company, and her face was drawn and pallid. I understood the feeling all too well.

I wanted to protect her from my mother, provide her cover in any way I could to pursue the life she wanted, because I was not able to do so. Even if I knew how to extract myself from the obligations to which I was born, and my mother, I was not physically strong enough to live beyond the walls of the manor. I hoped Rory would find her path as a nurse and a way to a happy life beyond the walls which confined me as surely as my illness. Perhaps the best way to protect her was to let her go. But Rory wouldn't make any such resolution easy for me. She found me in the library again, the next day, after her visit to my mother. Rory looked more resolved and certain than she was the day before.

"Jules," she said, tearing my attention away from

the book. "We must make you well."

"Rory, I am not well." Seeing her in the doorway erased all my noble intentions. I didn't want her to ever leave me. I could not fathom Moorsgrange without her there again, but I knew I must be honest. My mother called me overly sentimental, but I felt the threat of tears behind my eyes, though I resisted them. I sat, back straight, remembering Alexander's lessons, and tried to recover my dignity. Worried I'd exposed too much, I looked away from her, and watched the rays of light filter through the stained-glass window at the apex of the room.

I shouldn't have worried because she rushed to me, her dress moving in a fluid wave with her long gait, a characteristic I'd noticed but then forgotten in her absence. Rory moved as if subjugating the earth, with such bold confidence, unlike other women whose little steps kept them in their places. I looked up into her eyes as soon as she sat next to me on the couch. I faced her and covered her hands with my own.

"No one has been able to make me well. Whatever lives inside me allows me occasional freedom, but it always comes back. My trip to visit you left me shaken." I held her hands but tore my gaze from her, looked at her long fingers intertwined with mine. "I want to be with you all the time. I've not stopped thinking of you since you returned, but I am not well. I don't wish to burden you with it, Rory. With my mother. With me," I emphasized. Shame burned from inside my belly and I'm sure my cheeks glowed with it, as well. I was afraid of how she would respond. Perhaps she would agree with me and leave me there, in the library. The thought was intolerable, even if I knew it was the most noble outcome.

"You fool," Rory said, and I gasped, shocked. "Like you would ever be a burden." I turned and met her eyes, lifting my hand from hers, and touched her cheek with the back of my hand. She leaned into my touch and kissed my hand. "We are going to make you well. Then we can take on your mother together." She smiled then, the glint of mischief and disobedience unchanged since we were children, still there in the depths of her eyes.

In the following days, Rory supervised my diet, sending me rich soups, hearty pies, steaming tea, herbs, and tinctures. She gave me a vial of ointment with peppermint to apply on my chest. I do not know if it was her healing efforts, or the love with which they were infused, but my strength renewed. We spent every waking moment together, but I consciously did not overexert myself. When she left to begin her new job, I rested for great lengths of times while she was away working. I was building my strength, saving it all for her. I engaged Mr. Arnold in my plot to spend time alone with her, though we did not address it directly, and he helped me clean our secret space on the easternmost side of the manor.

Rory and I found it as children, quite by accident. On a game of chase through the house, I tripped over my gangly, awkward legs and the wall panel shifted when I crashed into it headfirst. After Rory made certain I was not maimed, she pushed it open with a swift kick of her foot and the panel swung wide, on hinges. A steep staircase of stone, chiseled by hand, led to an abandoned food cellar, unknown to even the servants. It was much larger than any other cellars in the house, but still smaller than the smallest bedroom, and the stairs and hidden nature of it engaged our imaginations and we turned it into our private fortress.

I took wood planks from the stables, smuggling them into the manor under the cover of night, to conceal the dirt floor. The block and mortar walls had mostly withstood the passage of time, and I smiled to see my childhood patchwork where I'd wedged blocks back in place. Rory and I hung blankets over the walls, trying to create an impression of the tapestries in my mother's receiving room. We lifted a cast-off table and chairs from the attic, so we had somewhere to drink tea and eat cookies. The last candle we burned was still on the table where we'd left it, standing on top of a thick layer of dirt.

Mr. Arnold helped me sweep the wood planks, and together we scrubbed the walls, making small progress each day, until the space felt refreshed, and the heavy smell of mildew evaporated. He brought a bucket with hot water and soap down before me one day and wiped the table and chairs. I thanked for him for his help, and he only nodded, leaving me by the hidden passage. I shut the door and the small space disappeared again, as if it were not even there. Rory was in town, and I decided on a small constitutional, following her advice, and walked to the garden, where I sat on the stone bench and watched the sun rise to its noon-time peak.

Now that the space was cleaned, I wondered how I might surprise Rory with it, and enhance it for us. Sitting there, the sun warm on my face, the air crisp and clear, it came to me in a rush. I hurried into the manor, to discuss my idea with Cook and Mr. Arnold, as I only had until the next day, before noon, when Rory returned with her father, to implement my plan.

I stood at the window on the third-floor landing, watching the path to the house, waiting for Rory's return. I'd bathed and combed my hair, rinsed my mouth with herbs and tea, and despite not having much facial hair at all, I'd shaved. My face felt soft under my fingers, which smelled of the peppermint from Rory's ointment. Finally, I saw her approach and hurried down the stairs, taking care to walk steadily and slowly so as not to wind myself. Her father would take her as far as he could toward their cottage, so she would not need to walk, and I wanted to be there to greet her and ask her to join me in the later afternoon.

Despite my best efforts, the trips up and down the stairs left me gasping for air, and I leaned against Cook's counter for support. I wiped my forehead with a clean linen, exasperated by my ill health and inability to do anything. For a moment, self-pity roared to life with my fatigue, but then I saw Rory's smiling eyes and I pushed it down. I would get healthy for her, because of her, and life would be good again. I pushed off the counter, refusing to acknowledge how tired the trip downstairs had left me, and I stepped into the back garden of the manor. I saw Rory walking toward the cottage, her bag in her hand and I yelled.

"Rory, you are home." She waved wildly. I rushed toward her, as quickly as I could, tripping over my steps as I left the garden. I found my balance and she moved toward me, meeting me halfway. She looked up at the manor, and hesitated making physical contact with me. "My mother is gone to the city for two days," I said and hugged her. She held me close. Her breath on my cheek and the smell of her chased away my ill health. Fire stirred inside me. I wanted her, and I would have her. Neither my mother nor my health would take her from me again.

"I've missed you so," she whispered into my ear and reluctantly, so we were not a spectacle for the servants, I let go.

"I've missed you, Rory," I said, heart blazing with love and devotion. "I've waited for your return. Counted every hour since you left. I have a surprise for you."

"A surprise?" She asked. She took my hands, holding them between hers, and I nodded, pleased with myself.

"Can you join me in the kitchen this afternoon? Later, after lunch, when you've rested and settled in."

"We can go now," Rory said.

"We cannot," I said, as I laughed. Even when we were children, Rory could not wait for surprises. "I have a plan. A whole evening if your father will allow it," I added, remembering my respect. I would ask his permission to marry Rory, but first, I needed to ask her, and it was too soon for either. A proper courtship was in order, whether my mother liked it or not.

****

The hours between Rory's return and our time together passed slowly. I prepared slowly, deliberately conserving my energy, and then retired to my room to rest. I slept soundly for three hours until Mr. Arnold woke me, as I asked. I washed again, wanting to be certain I smelled and looked my best. I dressed in a clean suit and vest, but I decided I would not wear my jacket. It felt restrictive against my chest, and I already labored to breathe. My mother told me my illness left my skin a lovely pale white, which accentuated my dark hair and eyes. I was also thin, something else my mother thought should be celebrated. I wished to be sturdy like Rory's father, strong and capable. I pushed self-pity and inadequacy away. Rory liked me as I was.

I took the stairs slowly and found Rory already waiting for me in the kitchen. She sat at the servants' table, talking with Cook and Mr. Arnold. I paused out of sight to listen to her lovely voice as she finished her story. "Then, we treated a patient with such terrible sores on their feet and legs, open wounds which will not heal. I saw many things in the hospitals in London, but I never saw anything like that."

Cook said, "I tell you 'tis a miracle there are people the likes of you. Lea'me to my pies."

"I imagine such experiences, over time, will help my sensitivity to it," Rory said.

I turned the corner and she smiled so genuinely I felt as though I were the most important person in the world. "I doubt it." I said. "It is your sensitivity which makes you as perfect as you are."

Rory flushed and looked at her feet. She wore a simple dress, one I'd seen before, but it was clean and well pressed. I realized she didn't have as many clothes as I did, because of our different stations, and I made a mental note to speak to my mother's maid about getting her more.

"Well, there's the gentleman of the 'ouse," Cook said. "Up to no good with his mother away, I reckon."

"Shush," Mr. Arnold said, and I think there was a twinkle in his eye. "Now, that's enough." He put his arm on Cook's arm and escorted her from the kitchen.

I walked toward Rory and held out my hand. She

joined me and tucked her hand in the bend of my elbow. We walked from the kitchen, into the hallway, and I stopped in front of the wood panel hiding our secret spot. I let go of her hand and she covered her mouth with it.

"Jules, what have you done?" I smiled pointed to the panel.

"Do it, Rory," I said. She laughed, bunched up her skirt and kicked. The hidden door opened. I led her down the stairs. I'd lit candles in our secret room before I met her in the kitchen, and it glowed with dim light. On the table, I'd left a poem I'd written during her absence, tucked inside an envelope for her to read later.

"It looks as it used to," she said, and I clapped at her excitement and surprise. "What is this?" She pointed at the envelope.

"It is for you. For later." Rory picked it up and held it in her hands, as if she would never cherish anything more. Now that Rory was there, I knew we'd outgrown spending too much time in the hidden room, but I wasn't finished yet. I lifted a candle from the table and walked to the far corner of the room. "Come here," I said, and Rory stepped toward me, trusting. "Look." I held the candle to the stone wall, and she leaned forward.

"Oh, Jules, it is still there!"

"It was buried under so many layers of dirt, but Mr. Arnold helped me scrub it off. Once it was clean, I worked on it some more, so it will always be visible." When we were children, Rory often drew a geometrical flower symbol everywhere she could—from school papers to the dirt while we played in the garden. She'd decorate it with different symbols and words each time, but she always added a J and an R. She told me it was us, always going around, perfectly balanced. I didn't really understand what she meant by it, but she loved it, and so for her thirteenth birthday, I'd carved it into the stone wall of our hidden nest, complete with our initials.

"I love it," she smiled and faced me. She placed both hands on my face and kissed me lightly on the lips. Shyly, she looked away, and I tried to still the fire once again burning inside me.

"I'm so glad. I have more for you." I waited for her to climb the stairs and blew out the candles. "I've planned dinner for us, in the parlor. Mr. Arnold and Cook are setting up now." I offered her my arm and we walked through the halls. I held open the door for Rory, and she touched my face as she walked by. The light in the room was settling into dusk, and I pulled the drapes against the setting sun. A fire burned, biting back the impending cold of night, and took the moist chill from the room. My piano was on the opposite side of the room from the fire, our table near it. The table was freestanding and we commandeered it for my dinner plans. Rather than moving dining hall chairs to it, I'd relocated cushioned chairs with arms to serve as our dining seats. I'd tested them earlier in the day to be sure they were comfortable.

I pulled out a chair for Rory. I took my seat, tired and shaky, though I didn't want Rory to see. Cook had made a vegetable pie and another chocolate cake, and Mr. Arnold left us a bottle of wine. I poured her a glass, and Rory served our food. We ate, talking about the adventures and time we'd spent in our hidden alcove. She confessed she still drew the flower symbol often.

"But do you still add a J and an R," I wanted to know, as I took a bite of the pie.

"Always," she said with sincerity. "I always will." I nodded, satisfied, and asked about her work and time in town with the Doctor. She spoke about it with hesitation and changed the subject, so I did not pry. Once we finished eating, I gathered my strength and walked to my piano.

"I have a new song for you," I said. I lit the candles on top of the piano from one I'd carried from the table. "I'd like to play it." Rory came to stand by the piano. "You can sit if you'd like," I said, motioning toward the bench.

"I want to see you." she said. I flushed, I'm certain, but I began to play a new nocturne I'd written since she returned to Moorsgrange. My body was tired, lungs heavy, and legs weak, but my fingers glided across the keys as if all were right inside me. I played effortlessly, closing my eyes to focus, hoping that each note transmitted my love for her, to her, in such a way my inadequate words and body could not. I played until my eyes watered and I opened them, finishing the last few notes, and sat my hands in my lap, suddenly shy. I looked down at my fingers, splayed open on my thighs, and Rory sat next to me.

She kissed me, less chastely than before, and I responded and pulled her to me, at least as much as our awkward angle could accommodate. Blood rushed to my head, and arousal raced across my body, so intense I was momentarily shocked. Given my ill health, I didn't realize I could feel so much physically.

"Rory," I said and pulled away. "I love you."

"And I love you, Jules. This was all so beautiful." I

smiled, pleased, and remembered the clock on the mantel above the fireplace. Time was always against me. It either exhausted me or moved too fast or slow.

"It is getting late, and you must get home to your father, I'm sure."

Reluctantly, we stood holding hands this time as we walked the long manor halls. I ached for her nearness and wanted to take her to my bed and sink into her arms and warmth. But I controlled my impulses, knowing that if I was successful in my courtship, we would be married after, and I would never have to spend a night without her. We stepped into the night from the warmth of the kitchen, where we'd stopped to put on cloaks.

"Please don't walk in this cold, Jules. You will become ill. I'll be fine getting home."

"No," I said. "I will not allow you to walk home alone."

"While your chivalry is noble, I am more concerned with your health, and it is an order from your nurse. You can be gallant when you are well."

Once again, shame burned my face, and I stumbled for words. "I feel so inadequate, Rory," I admitted. "I want to be strong for you. Able."

"You fool," she said again. "I only want you to be you."

Then, we heard her father's voice. "I've come to bring you home," he said as he opened the gate into the back garden. He'd seen us from the lantern light, streaming from the windows of the kitchen.

"Yes, father," Rory said, squeezing my hand. "I'm ready. Thank you." She winked at me and whispered. "This was the most beautiful night, Jules. I will see you tomorrow." With that, she walked toward her father and faded from my view. I retired to my bedroom, exhausted but exhilarated, and fell into a deep and dreamless sleep, Rory's face the last image I saw as I drifted from the world.

Chapter 14

Rory

One Wednesday afternoon, shortly after I began working for Dr. Cain, I found myself in a room in town, where blood had pooled on the ground and a grown man screamed on the table. On his arm, a deep wound gushed and Dr. Cain himself looked unsure of how to proceed, his hands moving from one instrument to the next, only to go back to the last one. Every time the man's voice pierced the air, the doctor seemed to cringe in return. I myself never came to understand why I was always able to display—and feel—such calm in those circumstances, but it was with tranquility and deliberation that I made my decisions.

In that case, I had to do something about the fast loss of blood the man was experiencing. His face was already drained of all color, and his limbs were limp on the table, making it evident that he had no more energy left to fight. I couldn't leave the poor man, who had fallen while carrying a large number of empty bottles, to bleed until expiration, nor the doctor to feel so utterly demoralized.

"With your permission, I would like to work on something that might help, Dr. Cain." I was hoping to try a technique I had learned in London.

"What is it?" he asked with some anxiety in his eyes, putting down the long needle he had been toying with.

"A quilled suture. I can pass a double thread through the lips of the wound in an uninterrupted manner, but we will do so at greater intervals, with a curved needle, and then we will anchor everything and avoid tearing with a piece of bougie on each side."

"That is not a bad idea. This is quite a deep wound, and he is losing a lot of blood."

"If you could hold the skin together, I can work quite quickly. And doctor?"

"Yes?"

"Would you wash your hands? With soap?"

He looked at me, raising his eyebrows, no comprehension showing in his face. "What for? We are covered in blood anyway."

"Trust me." I said simply.

He did as I suggested and fifteen minutes later, the laceration was closed and the patient resting, with the help of a sizable dose of whiskey. I then used a clean cloth and boiled water to rinse other, more superficial wounds. Dr. Cain looked quite pleased at the results.

"Your help is immensurable, Rory. I look forward to discovering what other techniques you learned in London." He wiped his hands in a piece of cloth and went to the next room, leaving me to attend to the sleeping patient, but not before stopping to observe me.

I had started to notice that Dr. Cain sometimes spent long minutes looking at me. It happened while I worked or when I sat at the end of the day to update our records or a patient's file. Every time I looked back at him, he would quickly avert his gaze and pretend to be otherwise engaged. Yet, I was sure I was the object of his observation more often than I would have preferred.

The occurrence was not invasive to the point of justifying the termination of my employment, which was, in all other terms, going very well. Yet, it drove me to distraction, this tendency to treat me as an item to be studied.

Word of our professional services had spread throughout the region, and the practice was full every day. Our Wednesdays of home visits were long, and I often arrived at my quarters in town quite exhausted, much past supper time. Mrs. Tilcott was kind enough to always leave some bread and cheese, or cake and butter, out for me. I would then wash and fall into a deep sleep, readying myself for one more day at the surgery before returning to Moorsgrange.

In town, I always made a point of visiting the bookstore and studying more about Jules's infirmity. The owner, Mr. Doyle, had become my friend, and he let me borrow what books I found without any qualms. "You help our town with your knowledge, Miss Allen," he said handing me an anatomy volume he thought would interest me.

I would then buy oils and herbs at the apothecary to take with me to treat Jules during my four days at the mansion. I had come to think that his mother knew about my methods, but seeing that he was improving visibly, she kept the illusion of ignorance, and that suited me well. Since Dr. Cain visited Jules often, Mrs. Emsworth chose to believe it was all his doing, and more than once, I saw her compliment him lavishly. I had the impression the doctor thought likewise, and I was fine with either overestimation.

Jules had put on some weight and his breathing had become much more stable. He only coughed occasionally, and one evening, we even found ourselves dancing. It all happened while we cooked and dined with the staff, being that Mrs. Emsworth had been invited to a banquet at an estate nearby and had left in the early afternoon. We set a table outside, now that the winter was giving way to early spring, and we feasted on such delicacies as the duck my father—not me, to be sure—had acquired while hunting and strawberries, potatoes, a vegetable stew and snow peas. Afterwards, the group brought out spirits, a violin and a concertina, and those musically inclined took turns playing local songs while we clapped our hands and danced. Candles were lit when sundown came upon us.

Jules took the violin first, and he was very proud to show off his skills. His eyes shone bright, and his fingers moved expertly, making the task look simple even though we knew it was not. He was so talented that for a while we forgot to sing along and sat, astounded and enjoying the harmony that came out of the instrument. When Cook started playing the concertina, Jules offered me his hand, and we twirled around, as if we had not a care in the world. This time, his energy held, and he laughed, grabbing my hands and then embracing me, while I put my head on his shoulder and heard his heart pounding, fast but strong.

When we tired of dancing, we left the group and walked to the rose garden, now in bloom, and sat by the fountain, where we had first seen each other upon my return. The fragrant air of the night left me pleasantly dizzy, as did Jules's kisses, urgent as they were, as if we hadn't a moment to lose. Lying on a blanket over soft grass, we promised to take care of each other while a full moon illuminated our smiles. I kissed his eyelids shut and we fell asleep like that, hands interlaced, my head lying on his chest, time standing still.

It was Cook who woke us. "Quick, your fader is comin' and I reckon 'e will not care to find you lo' like this." We straightened up as best as we could. Jules tied the sash of my dress in a bow, and we sat by the fountain again, laughing uncontrollably at our own mischief. Before I left with my father trailing at a short distance, Jules gave me a red rose, which he kissed lightly before handing out. I walked all the way home almost floating in midair, with my feet only lightly touching the ground. Love had made my heart full and my life quite complete, and love had also made Jules better.

****

One additional week of work with Jules constantly on my mind, and Dr. Cain invited me for tea, saying he had something important to discuss. At five, he escorted me to the tea house I had spotted on my first day and asked for a complete tea service. A lovely, tiered tray of scones, cucumber sandwiches, madeleines, and *petits fours* arrived, together with a beautiful teapot.

He served the tea himself, using a silver strainer and adding a splash of milk. We then ate the delicious sandwiches, talking about the practice, some of the recent cases, and improvements we wanted to make to the office.

"Speaking of improvements, Rory, I asked you here because I wanted to discuss the possibility of extending your hours. As the practice grows, we receive requests for more appointments, and if we were to add one more day—Friday, for example—we would serve more patients. What do you say?"

Caught by surprise, I thanked him for the offer. It was clear he was pleased with my work. Yet, there was an eagerness in him that bothered me, his fidgeting fingers against the table and an unsteadiness that made this cup and saucer clatter. He was the doctor and could see patients independently from me any time. Why should he be nervous about whether I accepted or not?

"Dr. Cain, most of the time I spend in Moorsgrange is dedicated to the care of Jules Emsworth. Three days away is already plenty. I would not like to be in town longer and compromise his health."

He nodded repeatedly, as if agreeing with me. Yet his lips were terse, and his face contracted. "Jules is under my care too, Rory. He gets plenty of attention. One day will not make a difference."

"I am sorry to disappoint you, but Jules is one of the most important people in my life, and I want to make sure he stays healthy. He has improved so much in recent weeks, as you very well know, and I shouldn't like to see him regress. I'm afraid my decision is final. If you prefer to look for a nurse that can work longer hours, I fully understand."

That final comment was met with further agitation from him, as if I had uttered blasphemy. "I would not think of it, Rory. The success of the practice is directly linked to your work, and I shall be very sad should you ever speak of leaving me…I mean, leaving the practice. We will continue as you suggest."

"Thank you, Dr. Cain. You can count, as always, on my full dedication on my assigned days."

We finished our tea in what would pass in polite circles as pleasant conversation, but, in reality, dialogue had been halted by our opposing positions. I was relieved, nonetheless, that the doctor did not insist any further.

His demeanor changed after that. He seemed more guarded, except that his staring at me intensified. Often, I found him looking out of the window, as if waiting for someone, while I made my way from my quarters to the practice. Whenever I met his eyes from the street, he would retreat from the window, and I would find him fully immersed in preparations for the first patient once I made my way in. At that point he would bid me good morning but limit our interactions otherwise. Our conversations became more transactional with each day.

Two weeks passed in that manner. More and more patients were coming to the surgery, and I worked as nurse as well as secretary. Eventually, Mrs. Tilcott started to come in the morning to help with the filing and handling of appointments. Some people would ask to see me directly, especially if their lungs were the source of their ailments of if they needed sutures. Words spreads very quickly in a small town like that. In gratitude for advice and care, patients would bring me breads and cakes, bouquets, or ribbons for my hair. I would often take the treats back to my father on Thursdays, when I made it back to Moorsgrange.

At home, Jules continued to improve, and we spent every possible moment together, while he practiced and wrote music, while I read and studied, or while we simply strolled the grounds, content to be arm in arm. Dr. Cain was always circumspect during his visits to Moorsgrange, and I suspected he did not approve of my friendship to Jules, nor our constant laughing and banter. I imagine the source of his discontent was mine and Jules's different stations and the fact that when together, we always behaved like equals.

One evening, after the doctor had left, Jules pulled me to him for a kiss and then, still holding me in his arms, commented on the doctor's demeanor. "Why is he always so uptight?"

"I don't know. I wonder if he thinks I am putting on airs," I speculated.

"What do you mean?"

"Well, I have to say I taught him a medical trick or two, by virtue of having been in London and having learned new techniques. I sometimes worry that he thinks I am stepping beyond the tasks that a nurse should be concerned with performing. I have patients coming to see me, asking for me directly."

Jules thought for a second. "I find it unlikely that he is intimidated by your skill. Didn't he ask you to work more, exactly because of your expertise?"

"That is true."

"I think it is more likely that he was upset precisely because you said no, and he relies on you so much. He must still be sad about not being able to extend your hours." Jules laced his arm around my waist and pulled me close to him. "But enough about the good doctor." And he kissed me until my lips felt aflame.

The following Tuesday, I arrived at the surgery quite early to find that Dr. Cain was not there. Instead, a note rested on the desk indicating that I should see what patients I could in my capacity until he returned in the afternoon. A separate letter invited me to lunch at the one more elegant inn of the town. It indicated a coach would come to pick me up, given that the establishment was several miles from the surgery. I was confused and preoccupied with this new development. Dr. Cain had behaved so differently, erratically, and stoically in the last several days, that I did not want to venture a guess as to this new unlikely development.

I checked the clock all morning, distracted by the anticipation of this mysterious meal. It was fortunate that no complicated cases appeared, and by the time the coach arrived, punctually at eleven thirty, I was ready to make my way to the inn. Mrs. Tilcott informed me that the next patient would only come at two-thirty, which afforded us plenty of time to resolve what might be on the doctor's mind.

Twenty minutes passed before I made it to the inn. High in the sky, rain clouds were forming, and the smell of the upcoming downpour was all around me. Upon my arrival, I was directed to a private room, which had been set up for a meal. Dr. Cain stood next to the table, wearing his dark hair greased and combed back and his mustache freshly trimmed. On the table, there was a large meal of chicken with potatoes, asparagus, peas and bread. I realized I never told him I did not eat any animals. As a centerpiece were flowers in shades of pink, yellow and red. A yellow flower was also in his lapel.

"Rory, please come in." At the table he moved the chair back so I could sit. He then took the seat across from me.

"Dr. Cain." I said without much ado. "I am confused by your request to join you here. Confused by this meal."

"It is a special day, and I wanted to celebrate it with a special meal."

"Oh? And what is special about it?" I had a knot in

the pit of my stomach that was making it difficult to relax or to avoid asking direct questions.

"How about we enjoy a bit of this delicious food first? Would you like some chicken?"

"Dr. Cain, I apologize for not saying this sooner, but I do not eat meat. I will have some of the potatoes, asparagus and peas, please."

He turned very pale with visible disappointment at this revelation but served the vegetables, nonetheless. He then put a minute amount of food on his plate.

We ate in silence, seemingly unable to find any comfortable subject matter to discuss beyond our shared interest in medicine. After the meal, a barmaid came to offer fruit and cheese which neither of us ate much of. I was readying myself to announce my departure when Dr. Cain touched my hand. His own hand was clammy against my skin.

"Rory, please." He had beads of sweat forming in his forehead. "I called you here for a very important reason."

I predicted that this was to be a good-bye meal. Clearly, he was dissatisfied with a nurse who could only work thrice a week. He had likely found another who could labor every day, and he was trying to let me go as kindly as he possibly could. I lowered my head and waited for the communication, which was certainly making him quite uncomfortable.

When he uttered the words, I thought I had misunderstood. For they were so different from what I had anticipated that I had no idea what to do with them. In one single breath and bracing himself for the answer, the doctor asked. "Rory, will you marry me?"

Chapter 15

Jules

I was delirious with love. Thoughts of Rory consumed me, and all my energy went to planning our time together and the life we would live once we escaped Moorsgrange. I wrote her songs, playing the piano more than I had since I became ill. While my mother discouraged my continued interaction with Rory, she was emboldened by my playing, and one day, in late fall, she threw a large party for all our neighbors, acquaintances, and friends. They came at high noon for a lunch Cook spent days preparing, and as the sun began to set, she pushed me to the piano, where I played a number of well-known pieces and three original compositions inspired by Rory. I looked up from the keys and saw amazed faces, teary eyes, and the glaring absence of Rory. She should have been by the piano while I played, but she was not invited. She was likely helping her father with the horses of our guests.

I feigned fatigue to my mother after the guests finished applauding and slipped from the room and then the manor from the kitchen door. My steps were heavy on the damp, cold earth as I wound my way to Rory's cottage. I was openly weeping when I got to the door and pounded on it, my desire for Rory so strong I felt as though I would break it down. She opened the door quickly, alarm on her face. "Good lord, Jules! Are you okay?" She pulled me into the cottage and rubbed my arms, trying to warm me. "You should not be out without a coat!" Then she wiped my face with her hands. "Why are you crying? Oh, Jules, what is wrong?"

"Rory," I said, my emotions so strong I felt overpowered. I fell to one knee. I reached into the pocket of my vest, where I had tucked away my grandmother's ring as I waited for the perfect moment to ask Rory to marry me. I pulled the ring out now, a gold, silver, nickel, and copper ring, with an exquisite purple and blue stone. In the previous weeks, I'd quietly guessed the size of her ring finger when we held hands, touching it with my fingertips, so I could be certain the ring would fit well enough for her to wear in secret, until we were married, and she could wear it all the time. I'd wound thread carefully around the diameter of the ring, to make it fit Rory's long, strong, and slender finger.

I held it up to her, and said, "Marry me, Rory. I want nothing but you. I have played for all these people and without you, nothing matters. We can live beyond these walls. You can be a nurse. I will play the piano, teach, and do whatever else I must. I will go anywhere with you. I will do anything so long as I am with you."

Rory looked at the ring and at me, and her tears joined my own. She pulled me up from my knee and slipped the ring on her finger, where it fit well, and hugged me. "Yes, Jules. I will marry you. We can go to London, Paris, Berlin, or even Manhattan. We can go everywhere, see the whole world or live in a room in London. I just want you, too. Moorsgrange is my home and I thought I was finally back to stay, but you're my forever home. I am to go where you are."

****

In the days that followed, Rory and I planned our secret wedding. We knew my mother and her father must never learn of our plans. They loved us and believed they knew our best interests, but their love rested in control, and Rory and I would have none of that. We knew our own hearts. My primary concern was financial, as I wanted to be sure I could provide for Rory.

She told me she could care for herself, and I teased at her sentiments as much as I admired them. When she was in London, she met women who believed it was time for them to have greater economic equality and that change was on the horizon. She narrated stories of women who lived in Paris and Berlin completely independent of men, who wrote books and had many lovers. Her eyes burned with conviction, and I reveled in her passion, her energy infusing me with strength. I longed to see the world as she did, and, quite unlike Alexander and other men in my station, my desire for her flared when I witnessed her goal of pursuing her own independence.

Perhaps she didn't want my financial support, but I knew she wanted my emotions, music, and friendship. Financial security was what I felt I needed to provide, and I had a deep abiding need to be able to produce and care for myself, separate from my mother and family fortune. I felt bound and controlled. I admired Rory's desire for independence so much because it rivaled my own. Being able to earn my own money meant freedom, which is why I agreed to the three-week playing trip my mother arranged for me in December, leading up to the holidays. It would be the first time I played for crowds since my father died and I became ill. I sensed my mother wanted me to go to keep me from Rory.

I agreed to the scheme, not to please her, but because I knew I would meet benefactors at the concert halls and churches throughout England. I could then generate an income to take care of myself, and perhaps, should she decide to let me, Rory. I could not believe I thought myself once incapable of living beyond Moorsgrange. With Rory by my side, everything felt possible.

Rory was deeply concerned about my health and asked me not to go. I assured her I was well enough to travel and play, and I saw it as an opportunity to emerge again in the world. I wanted to prove to myself I was worthy of her. She deserved at least that much in a future husband, and so despite her protests, I prepared to leave, reassuring her through stolen kisses.

"Rory, I will earn money on this trip. Meet people. It is three weeks. When I return, I will have arranged our marriage. I plan to ask a priest at a nearby church to marry us, in confidence, during confession. I've thought it all out. We will sneak away and by the time your father and my mother learn of our plans, it will be too late. And I will have savings, from my own efforts, for us to begin somewhere new."

Eventually, Rory surrendered to my desire to travel and play. Instead of arguing with me, she began to help me prepare, concocting medicines and cooking food which would travel with me. She gave me explicit instructions about sleep, when to take herbs and when to rub the ointments on my chest. She cried when she left me to go town for work the day before I was to leave, but I calmed her with kisses and said I would be fine. Dr. Cain had assured me, and my mother, that my illness was well under control, and when I conveyed this to Rory, she was unmoved by it.

"I am capable of deciding that on my own," she snapped, and stormed away. "I'm better at medicine than he is."

I chased after her, coughing as I extended myself. "I'm sorry," I said. "I know you are the most capable healer in the whole of the world." She playfully swatted at me.

"Now you are playing to my pride," she said with a smile, and I wiped her tears, holding her face in my hands. "I am upset because you're leaving so I am not being reasonable."

"I know," I said, and I kissed her. "But I will make some money and contacts, and we will begin our lives when I return. I am so excited."

Rory nodded but looked unconvinced. "I feel as if I will never see you again."

We held each other tightly. I didn't know what other assurances I could give her, so I said nothing. I watched light filter in through the library windows, arching toward its morning peak. A single beam of light flooded the space, and Rory stood in it as she rested in my arms. I was still in the shadows of the room, and I saw it with awe and a deep feeling of sadness, which began in my stomach and spread upward, exploding through my damaged chest.

Even as I marveled at Rory's beauty in the rays of the sun, the deep auburn curls of her hair lit bright, the warmth of her body pressed against mine, hands on my back, clinging as though she would never let go, I also could not escape swimming in the same feeling of doom. I believed it to be the weight of my sadness for leaving Rory, but it was a deeper fear neither one of us understood then. It warned us in the best way it could, but we had no words to understand it and no equivalent prior experience to reference.

I left as planned for my playing trip. Being trapped in a carriage with my mother was a Dante-like experience, and I am certain I moved through at least three layers of hell those three weeks. Mothers can inhabit such large portions of our minds and hearts that even as we push them away in our desire to create our own space and lives, we also cling to them forever in our childish impulses to be safe and protected. Mine fussed over me constantly, but unlike Rory's care and concern, her attention was suffocating, and I looked forward to my time at night when I closed the door to my own room. I then had space and solitude.

On that very first day of travel, when we arrived at a small church a few furlongs from Moorsgrange, I did exactly as I had told Rory I would. I spoke with the priest and requested his help. At first, he hesitated, for fear of my mother, but I appealed to him, with promises to play for every holiday event he held.

I think he saw increased tithe and donations, as surely as I saw someone with the authority to bind Rory and me together forever. I was unsure about my own belief in God and the church, but I knew Rory's acquiescence to a priest would begin and end with a marriage ceremony, and a part of me actually delighted thinking about her reaction to the "love, honor, and obey," part of the vows he would read for us.

I scheduled our quiet ceremony for a Wednesday night, three weeks later. I would return to Moorsgrange two days before, and Rory would be in town working with the Doctor, even closer to the church than I was. My plan was to leave Moorsgrange quietly, as soon as the sun began to set, so we would both arrive there as darkness descended. I thought constantly about the moment I would see Rory at the church.

In my mind, she always arrived first, and I would throw open the old wooden doors, a wake of cold air filtering into the stone church. I would see her standing to the front of the church and marvel at my good fortune. My vision was so complete as to include the sound of the doors clanging shut against the ancient iron which held them in place. I could feel the stone under my feet, see the moonlight filtering through the stained glass of the chapel window, poised directly above the podium, and feel the warmth of the stove to the right of the door. Candles would burn, and the space would bask in the glow of their warm yellow light, and a soft wind would howl, as it seeped through the windows, serenading us.

This vision carried me through the next few weeks, and I wrote Rory letters every night, sending them to her at the doctor's office. I provided all the details of our marriage and included my vision for her. I imagined her reading it, at night after she finished work, curled up on her bed, legs tucked under her to the side in the way she liked to sit. When I played at the concert hall in London, the crowd cheered, but when I looked up into the audience, my smile felt hollow. I wished I could look up and see Rory sitting in the balcony, clapping for me.

Newspapers wrote up reviews of my performance, raving about my skill, and I began receiving invitations to visit other concert venues, and while in London, I was shocked and thrilled by an invitation to play in Washington D.C. and Manhattan. I agreed, readily, asking that any correspondence be sent to Moorsgrange. I was overcome with joy. Rory and I would travel to America, as we always dreamed. By the end of the second week, though, I grew more and more exhausted, and my breathing became more labored each day. Women gathered around me in throngs, talking excitedly about my pale, gaunt, thinness as though my ailment enhanced my appeal for them. I thought about Rory's insistence that I eat more and gain weight, and their insipid admiration of me and longed even more for her.

When I was not playing, or entertaining crowds right after I played, I slept a deep sleep which left me groggy and uninspired to rise and begin again. As I approached the final two days of the trip, and we wound closer to home, I was so tired I neglected Rory's letter and instead collapsed, exhausted. I woke the next morning at the inn, the light breaking through the heavy curtains, but was unable to move on my own. My limbs felt as though they were full of stones from the bottom of the river. I was certain my fever would kill me, and I would never see Rory again. My mother found me a short while after, crying and shaking, and with the help of the house porter, got me on my feet and into clothing. We cancelled my last performance and left for home a day early.

Seeing Moorsgrange from the window of the

carriage infused me with new strength and hope. I would sleep in my own bed, rest, and with luck, see Rory before she left for town. But my hopes were dashed. Rory had been summoned early by the doctor. An outbreak of influenza had left almost a full third of the village ill and she was occupied in their care, I learned from her father and Mr. Arnold. Instead of her care, my mother summoned Dr. Cain, and I watched them talk in the hallway, their conspiratorial nature together worrisome to me beneath the layers of my physical distress. I fell into unconsciousness as I watched them in the hallway and woke with leeches on my neck and chest. Rory hated them and told me never to let anyone use them on me. She thought it cruel to people and the creatures. I ripped them off me, furious, frantic, and raging. I flung them to the far corners of my room and fell from the bed, banging my knees on the floor.

The door opened wide, and Dr. Cain walked in, briskly, firmly, and lifted me roughly from the floor. He threw me onto the bed, his face red with anger. "What have you done?"

"I do not wish to have those, those…creatures on me!" I yelled back at him, my voice catching in my throat, my chest tight.

"Well, that seems an overly sentimental reaction, Jules." He stood there, hands on his hips, and I stared at him. He took a deep breath through pursed lips and shook his head. "But it is your health. I only wanted to help you." I began to calm some and straightened my nightgown and felt suddenly inadequate and exposed. Dr. Cain was a tall man, with thin shoulders, long fingers on narrow hands, a slightly pinched face, as if a door closed on his face while he was a boy when his skull was still soft—or at least so I thought. Rory often admonished me when I said that out loud. He always had scraggly hair on his face, and while unattractive, he was healthy and stronger than me, which is what I resented most. I covered my thin legs with the blanket and sat back against the headboard. He stared at me and finally looked up to meet his eyes.

His gaze was on me, but his attention was elsewhere, as if he were making up his mind about something. We sat in silence for quite some time until he finally spoke. "I have a message from Rory. She asks that you meet her at the church tomorrow night, instead of Wednesday. She says she has arranged for everything with the priest."

I sat forward. "You know?"

He nodded, his jaw tight, teeth clenched. He jammed his hands in his pockets. "Yes. She confided in me. I do not think it is the best idea, given your health, but she seems intent upon it."

I smiled and tried to stand. I wished to shake his hand. He waved his hands at me, unable to meet my eyes. "No. Rest. You need your strength." He left the room. I waited a few minutes and then stood to rinse the blood from my neck and chest. I saw myself in the mirror and grimaced. I tried to stand up tall but could not keep my posture upright. I longed for Rory but knew she was busy in town. Her father and Mr. Arnold relayed the details of the illness outbreak, and my decision to not alert her to my failing health intended to give me time to recover.

I cleaned myself as well as I could and changed into fresh bed clothes. I called for my mother's maid and Mr. Arnold, and they changed my bedsheets as I sat in the chair by the fire, wrapped in a blanket. Mr. Arnold helped me into bed, and I rested there, thinking about seeing Rory the next night, and then returning here, to my room together, where she could help me heal for good, and we could begin our life. I forced myself to eat multiple times the remainder of the day and into the next, believing my strength would return enough for me to make it to Rory and the church.

As the sun set, I climbed from bed, rinsed as best I could and dressed, haphazardly, my illness making it difficult for me to tend to myself for Rory as I wanted. I slipped on a heavy winter coat and took my father's walking stick with me. I walked quietly through the upstairs hallway and opened the door to the back staircase. It was rarely ever used and the god-awful sound it made opening should have alerted the entire manor of my whereabouts. I froze, anticipating someone coming to investigate, but when no one did, I moved unsteadily down the stairs, and out across the back garden, where my footfalls found the main road to town. I moved with determination, my breath heavy in my chest, sweat running into my eyes. I wiped my brow furiously with my handkerchief, thinking of Rory.

Rory was my beacon, hope, and destination. It had always been Rory, and nothing mattered without her. We fit together, not two halves of a whole, but two wholes, whose queer entirety meshed with the other, as though all of heaven conspired to bring us together. I would find her in the chapel, as my vision said I would, and when we were married, in a short time, I would find the strength to play her a song on the old piano next to the preacher's podium. I didn't know what song

I would choose. Instead, I would surprise myself and her with whatever came to mind.

And so I walked, onward and forward, and then the rain began to fall. Heavy torrents of water fell from the sky, but I struggled against it, a singular determination I'd never felt before. Soon, I would be married to Rory, and we would begin our life together. The wind began then, as well, beating against me as I walked into it. I viewed it not as an obstacle but as a sign that our love would withstand anything. Later, I would tell Rory of my heroics, how I stared down nature and the demon in my chest to get to her, and how I would do it again and again. The ice turned to hail then, and I hugged the side of the road, trying to seek refuge under the leaves of the trees. Some hail hit me with such force, I stumbled. Only my father's walking stick kept me upright.

When I finally saw the church, and the soft glow of the yellow candles, relief and new energy flooded my body. I moved quickly toward the door and swung it open, as I did in my vision. But it was not Rory waiting for me inside. It was Dr. Cain, sitting in the podium, facing the door. I looked frantically around the small chapel for Rory, but she was not there. I stumbled forward, losing my footing on the stone floor. My clothes were soaked through. Dr. Cain rushed forward and grabbed my arm to help me to a seat.

"Where is she?"

"I am sorry to deliver this news, Jules." Dr. Cain looked away from me, a forlorn look on his face. "But Rory has decided not to accept your offer of marriage after all. She has agreed to marry me. I think you'll agree that this is best for you both, especially given your health. You are not able to provide for her. In fact,

I think we both know you are likely to be a burden to her tremendous healing talents."

I stared at Dr. Cain, unable to understand what he was telling me. "No. Rory would not do this. She would not." I was slipping through the earth. I looked down to be certain my feet still stood on solid stone. The foundation upon which I stood was rocked by this news. "Rory and I have been in love since we were children."

"And you are no longer children, Jules, and you are very ill." Dr. Cain put his hand on my shoulder and looked directly in my eyes. "Else, would she not be here as planned? Likely, she won't even return to Moorsgrange. I have been fond of her, it is true. After I relayed her request to meet you tonight, instead, and I told her you agreed, I offered my hand in marriage. I had to, you understand, because I love her too. I think she deserved to choose. She sent me to you, unable to tell you herself. You know how female sensibilities are." He let go of my shoulder and walked forlornly away. "I expect you to resent me, and I understand. You see, it is that she will be better with me, than you. I am healthy and can give her children and a good life."

I watched him walk away, and I couldn't breathe. It wasn't my illness but Rory's shocking decision. It had never occurred to me that she would not come to meet me. In my vision, she was always there, waiting for me. I assumed she thought of me as often as I thought of her. I thought she loved me like I loved her, but I'd learned that wasn't true. While I'd been planning our future, saving all my energy for her, she was spending time in town with Dr. Cain, falling in love with him. While I sat in hotel rooms writing her letters these past three weeks, she'd been treating patients by his side, listening to him talk, awed by his talents and profession. I thought I'd been singular to Rory, but I wasn't. I was expendable, and she didn't meet me at the church like she said she would.

I left the church before Dr. Cain turned back around and stumbled into the dark, my eyes wet with the pain of Rory's betrayal, and the relentless rain and hail which beat down on me as if I were being punished for my youthful innocence. You only fall in love once, with all of your being, and when that fails, you are thoroughly rewritten, and no other devastation is ever comparable. This was the cost of betraying my birthright, mother, and responsibilities. I would never be so naive again, would never trust someone again. All the years I'd spent loving Rory were a lie. Who we were was a lie, because when I'd been consumed by her, she'd been consumed by her own ambition, desires, and someone else.

In my distress, I turned too often and walked in haphazard steps, stumbling and falling to my knees, only to pull myself up and stumble forward again. I remember nothing else but the lantern outside the butcher's shop in town. I slumped to the ground, my back against the door, and my last thought, as my view of the world collapsed into darkness, was of Rory. She would be so upset to find me in front of the butcher's shop.

Chapter 16

Rory

Working with Dr. Cain after refusing his marriage proposal was no small feat. Both of us looked uncomfortable all of the time, and we focused on medical conversations, patient files, and diagnoses to maintain an atmosphere of peace in the surgery, the artificiality of it poking at me from time to time. If anything, our days were even busier than before, each of us searching for additional things to do that would keep us engaged throughout the day and away from the other. The fact that Mrs. Tilcott continued to help us in the mornings was a blessing. She was kind, and I could always count on her to deflect the tension. When I had nothing to say to Dr. Cain, I engaged her in tasks or talking. Still the place felt very different and working became a chore rather than the vocation it once was.

I considered quitting the job immediately after my refusal. There was no long-term future for our professional association given what had transpired and because of my impending elopement. Yet, as my wedding day neared, it was prudent to save as much money as possible to start my life with Jules, and three week's pay was nothing to disregard as superfluous. Besides, with Jules away, the wait alone at Moorsgrange would have been grueling.

My concerns notwithstanding, I had to tell Dr. Cain

the truth, and I did. On the day of the proposal, I had simply said we could not be. After Jules's own bid, I explained to the doctor that there was no possibility of a union between us because my heart had always belonged and would always belong to Jules. I added that Jules and I were to be married as soon as he returned from his musical engagements. I even told him the date, so he would know that would also be my last day of employment. "I do ask for your discretion." I said to him, reasoning that the plan was not widely known. "And I thank you for understanding the situation I am in."

He was silent for a while, but in the end acquiesced. "I will not tell anyone," he promised me, as we heard the next patient coming up the steps.

There was much to do. I put together an outfit for the wedding, with the help of Cook, who had new additions for me every time I went home. We used scraps of ribbons she had kept over the years, a veil she had asked a friend to lend, and a dress I had found in a chest in my lodgings. Mrs. Tilcott was kind enough to let me use the lacy gown and to not ask too many questions. The days rolled out in front of me, one too similar to the next to be memorable, and I ended up working more than usual to help pass the time.

A couple of days from the Wednesday that was set to be my wedding day, I put the dress out to air, hanging it from my wardrobe. I admired it as I fell asleep and went on to dream of us in London and on a boat crossing the Atlantic. In my dreams, Jules was not sick, and we danced and ran unconcerned for his lungs and his real-life constant cough, which, in my musings, completely disappeared.

The preparations for the wedding were not the only thing on my mind. A letter addressed to my father also needed to be written, and that was one of the hardest parts of the entire scheme. My father was a good man, and he had never opposed the love that flourished between Jules and me. Yet, to tell him our elopement plans in advance was to put him in the precarious situation of having to conceal the truth from his employer, or, depending on what transpired, outright lie. Therefore, I decided I would time the letter to reach him after the ceremony had been performed. I placed the missive in my suitcase, which I had readied in advance, and stored the luggage under my bed.

The days away from Jules were long and morose. I took comfort in the letters that arrived with regularity. Anticipating the missives was what kept me going. They burned in my pocket until I could excuse myself from the practice to have a spot of lunch and read them. I was in awe of Jules's strength. His body might have been weak, but his spirit was true and valiant, and I could hardly wait to merge my life with his. With every word, he won my love again, and the certainty that what we were about to do was right drummed in every beat of my heart.

It was one Monday afternoon, however, the same day I hung my dress, that the arrival of one of his letters was not marked by the usual excitement and joy but rather by suspicion. I had been in town, on a day I usually did not work, because of an outbreak of the flu. Dr. Cain delivered the letter, as was common for him to do when he found it among his own correspondence. Only this time, he looked distraught, or at least more tense than usual when he spoke to me. Since our difficult conversation about my turning down his proposal, he had been gloomy anyway, and I could hardly tell his good moods from the bad ones. Yet, on that occasion, there was rage, or a version of it, that I had not seen before.

"It must have torn on the way here." He said referring to the folded letter with a big tear near the adhesive that kept it sealed. Jules had not been using the new envelopes because they were expensive, and he had been writing very often. Instead, he folded the letter in three. Through the tear, it was possible to read most of the words. "The post can be so careless." Dr. Cain looked down and then excused himself.

Once more, Jules had written of our love, of his success at concert halls, of wanting to take me to America, of additional details of our wedding. He described how he imagined my arrival, what everything would look, sound and smell like. It was clear he had thought of it all often and in great nuance and depth. I loved him even more for it. I thought that by then, he must have reached Moorsgrange already, and that only two short days separated us.

The next day I was to have no correspondence from him. All I could do was wait and finish my work and think of how disappointed Jules would have been not to find me at home upon his arrival if he had indeed made the trip already.

That Monday afternoon, when Dr. Cain left to see patients in the estates nearby, I wondered if he was to include a trip to Moorsgrange. If Jules had already come back, he would need some attention. I worried that the trip and the engagements would have been too trying for him. In retrospect, it is clear that I could have asked the doctor to carry a note for Jules. I could have even gone with him, but I had stopped trusting him, and so I said nothing.

Tuesday started with an overcast dreary morning and a line of patients outside our door. I worked as efficiently as I could to attend to them. Again, the post did not deliver any news, and I could hardly stand the wait for Wednesday. In the afternoon, putting his coat on in haste, the doctor left without warning, and I had to fend for myself and the patients. Not that he had been any help until then. Most of the day, he had paced or looked out of the window, and he hadn't even responded when I commented that it had started to rain.

I stayed at the surgery very late, tending to a woman with strong abdominal pains and an old man with a fever until they each felt better. Outside, the angry rain castigated those who ventured out, and an angst that was a mixture of premonition and dread overtook every last cell of my body.

Part III
Chapter 17

Pia

"What do you mean you're going to London?"

Dr. Guedes's eyes were like two laser beams following me across the nurse's quarters as I tried to explain why I needed a vacation immediately. It is often the case that a sense of urgency makes other people actually slow down, as if to show you the unreasonableness of hurrying. In this case, the doctor did it with questions.

"Is something wrong? You look unlike yourself."

"It's a personal matter, and it's very important. I'm sorry I haven't given any notice, but it's an emergency." I'm sure I looked disheveled and nervous, which is probably what, together with my hurried speech, prompted the additional questions and further scrutiny.

"Emergency how?" At that point she looked more doubtful than surprised, a hand on her hip in that typical teapot position that suggests skepticism. "Pia, I am concerned that you might be experiencing some form of post-traumatic disorder, you know, because of your head?" She moved her own head so that her right ear was visible, like she needed some preparation to hear better what was coming.

"I know how it looks, Dr. Guedes, but this has

nothing to do with my head. I must meet a person in London right away. The love of my life if you need to know."

She blushed at that revelation, and I wondered if I had said too much, but she had been very insistent, and I did not want her thinking I had lost all good sense.

"All right if you must. But will you keep me updated? Stop at HR next. I'm sure they will work it out with you. But I still think you should stay in town, under observation."

Ignoring this last part, I texted James that it would be a little longer until we could go to Phoenix. I placed my cellphone on a table nearby, together with my bag, and left for the business office. When I returned, Dr Guedes was not there anymore. By my phone was a note from her that simply read "Good luck."

The trip to Phoenix was painfully long, with the two and a half hours that separated us from the airport feeling like a lifetime. James, in his usual manner, tried to make things better by playing soothing music and telling stories to distract me from myself. At times, he almost succeeded, and I laughed at his tales of the time Orlando was found napping on the couch of a neighbor and the one about our childhood attempt at baking a cake that was equal parts flour and dirt from the yard. At other times, I looked out of the car window, watching red rocks turn into hills full of cacti and then the typical gravel, dirt, and succulents of the valley. How I loved the vegetation of the desert, equal parts melancholy and resilience. I wanted to learn to be strong like the desert.

At the airport I gave my brother a quick hug goodbye so that he would not see the tears about to roll from my eyes. Then I remembered something and needed to come back to his car window. So much for avoiding drama.

"You will need to run the July book club in my absence?"

"What do you mean run it?" His voice went into falsetto mode.

"You know, lead the discussion, offer food and refreshments, wear period clothes."

"What?!"

"We, I mean, you are reading *Middlemarch*. I'll send you instructions by email." I couldn't give him much time to protest. Too much was on my mind already.

We parted ways at the departure-area passenger drop-off upon my request, and he drove off with the promise that I would provide continual updates and a cheat sheet for the meeting. I felt alone and scared, but I recovered at the thought of seeing Rikke again, and that desire powered my legs and my spirit so I could make it to the airline desk. I had learned to focus on a goal when all else seemed to be crumbling.

I paid a fortune for my ticket but filed away that concern for later. On the plane, I chatted with a mother traveling with her baby daughter. She was very anxious about the trip, the first with her ten-month old who toothlessly smiled at me. We spoke of London, of family, of my job as a nurse. I realized she was counting on me for comfort. Reassuring someone else gave me back some of my own certainty. I wasn't helpless. I had done nothing wrong, and I could talk to Rikke and make things better. Exhausted, I fell asleep somewhere over New Mexico and only woke up when breakfast was being served. The baby, I gathered, behaved equally well.

London, the eternal and magical city, was as beautiful as always, a thick layer of fog encasing everything when I arrived. I longed for its parks, its museums and churches. I craved its history. As I rode in a classic black cab, I undid my scarf and wore it like a pashmina, covering my shoulders and protecting me from my surroundings even if I didn't know what was there for me to be protected from. I was depleted by the trip and in need of nourishment, both for my body and my spirit. At a coffee shop, even before I found a place to stay, I connected to the wi-fi and refreshed Rikke's tablet's "Find my devices" app.

Two miles. That was all that separated us, at least as far as physical distance was concerned. She had found accommodation at an old hotel, the kind to be seen in one of those curved streets with townhouses and lovely antique black fences. Sipping my piping-hot coffee, I pondered on the best way to approach her, and, in the end, decided I should do that exactly the same way I did it the first time. I needed to show up at her door with food.

By the time I finished my coffee, it was past eleven o'clock and lunch seemed appropriate. No more than two doors down from the cafe was an Indian restaurant, whose fragrant spices sieved into the open air in front of me. Inside, a world of culinary delights awaited. I bought some white rice and oven-baked eggplant and some nan, which the gentle old lady behind the counter nestled in a large paper bag with a handle. I thanked her, paid for my order, and made it to the corner where I took the next bus to the general vicinity of the address in which Rikke's electronic blue blip shone last on the tablet's map.

The hotel looked like something out of a Victorian novel. Red carpeting led to the front desk, which was predictably made of dark-wood panels. Large old-gold vases stood near corners, and the rose-color wallpaper, although well preserved, belonged to a far-gone era. Despite its long existence, the place smelled fresh, and a lovely bouquet of white flowers stood by the reception. From behind the desk, a young man with dark hair and a well-pressed blue suit greeted me with a smile and a slight nod.

"I have a delivery for Rikke Taylor. I would like it to be a surprise if you don't mind. I know you don't have any reason to trust me, so I can leave my passport here if it helps."

He raised a hand to dissuade me from that notion. "That will not be necessary. Go ahead. She is in room 303, our top floor. Stairs are on your left."

I mouthed a silent 'thank you' and went toward the stairs before he changed his mind. At least in my warped perception, and probably only in it, there was a risk he would.

Room 303 was in the middle of the corridor. Red carpet, much like the one downstairs, showed me the way there. In front of Rikke's door, it felt like my knees would buckle, and I fought back the tears at the first twinge of emotion. I needed to hold it together a little while longer. After regaining control, I knocked and inhaled deeply.

Rikke opened the door after the eternity of a few seconds. She was wearing grey sweatpants and a cuff-off tee-shirt. She looked at me like someone who had found water after a couple of days in the desert—half hopeful, half considering if I was a mirage.

I raised my arm showing her the brown paper bag. "I thought you might be hungry," I said simply.

She rushed into my arms, one hand around the small of my back and another around my neck. The bag of food landed on the floor. Her kiss felt warm and imperative against my lips, and a current of electricity circulated through my limbs. If anyone happened to exit their room at that point, they could have seen our bodies fused together, as if we were one, and, whether or not they liked our public display of affection, I had no desire to let go.

Rikke spoke first, her forehead against mine. "I am sorry for being an idiot."

"You're not an idiot. A little hot-headed, maybe, but certainly not an idiot."

"I acted like one. I almost lost you to my jealousy and lack of self-control."

I smiled. "You were not in any danger of losing me."

At that, she hugged me again, and despite the tight embrace, I felt I could breathe for the first time in days.

"How are you here? I mean, how did you find me?"

"The gift of technology." I tapped the messenger bag I was carrying.

She raised an eyebrow.

"I'll explain later." This time I was the one who hugged her. "I'm so happy that I am, though."

She took me by the hand into the room, but not before reaching down for the bag of lunch treats, which, luckily had survived the fall. She kissed me against the door, and we disappeared inside the room, to only emerge from it the next morning.

****

"So what would you like to do today?"

Rikke sat in bed, raised her arms above her head, and stretched, lazily like a cat. "I have not planned beyond this moment."

Resting on pillows, I was eating strawberries and looking forward to a croissant and some coffee, all of which Rikke had ordered through room service. I expressed my contentment in a long, cleansing sigh.

"Perhaps some sightseeing?" she asked, stealing a strawberry from my plate and resting her head on my belly.

"Where do you intend to take me?" I asked while running my free hand through her hair.

"I'm not a good tourist. I prefer to do things that locals would. Eat at unexpected places, discover an alley that leads to a gallery."

"I'd like that. I'll go anywhere with you."

We walked hand in hand through Hyde Park— Rikke had fish and I had chips from a cone made of brown paper. We rode the underground to the British Library and played with hats and fascinators at Camden Town. Rikke tried on outrageously expensive handmade shoes in Regent Street and bought me a ring with a butterfly on it at a nearby store. No Tower of London. No Big Ben. No long lines, lost tickets, and bad snacks. I could not have asked for a more perfect day.

At night, as we sat in the bathtub and Rikke washed my hair, we made plans for a trip. It was her suggestion, not mine, yet it immediately felt right.

"Where would we go?" I said, getting some suds off my eyes.

"I don't know…maybe get a map of England, point, and let fate do its magic?"

"It's not like there isn't a lot to see.

"Let's rent a car." She started to rub my hair dry with a towel.

"Can you drive on the opposite side of the road?"

"I've done it before. And you, ma'am, are definitely not doing it. Not with the way you drive on the *familiar* side of the road." She touched my chin so I would turn, and she could give me a kiss. "But you can choose the music."

I scowled at her, and then smiled. "You can get away with that—this time. And I will always choose the music."

We spent the next day arranging for the journey— getting the car, buying snacks and drinks for the trip, and working on the general direction we wanted to go.

We chose North. For some reason, I always dreamed of Yorkshire moors and vast expanses of land where we could walk with the wind caressing our faces. I wanted to lie on a field and look at the sky with Rikke, read, talk, then find a fireplace to snuggle by. Yorkshire seemed like a place where we could do that. Once all was resolved, I went out while Rikke worked on the maps from her computer. In my haste, I had packed the first clothes I had seen, and now, since I was so happy, I wanted to look pretty. There were a few boutiques near the hotel that I hoped to explore.

In less than two hours I bought two flowery dresses, a blue jacket, and a pair of traveling boots. I was walking down the street carrying my purchases and thinking of how much fun we would have when it happened again. My surroundings started spinning, almost as if I were seasick. It was lucky there was a bench a few steps away. I collapsed onto it, and the bags scattered at my feet.

In my mind, I left London, and the smell of humid soil invaded my nostrils. I was again looking for someone, from shop to shop, trying every door. It was like an awake nightmare and the tightness in my stomach made it feel all the more real. I wanted to scream but no voice came out. I bent forward in pain. My feet felt wet as did my hair. I was cold all over, and I could not stop shivering. My setting changed, and I stood in front of a gate, whose sides were brick columns with finials on top. I put my hand on the bricks, feeling their rough texture. It was the entrance to a country house, with one of those circular iron plaques that announce the name of the estate. I had seen pictures on social media and loved how each house, even the non-palatial ones, had a name. The plaque came partially into focus. The name of the property was embossed and started with an M. A branch covered the rest. I tried to focus harder, and the wind started to blow to allow me to read the whole thing. The word on the plaque was Moorsgrange. Everything started spinning again.

"Are you all right, deary?"

An elderly man dressed in old-fashioned attire touched my arm, and given his suit, handkerchief in his breast pocket included, I had trouble realizing I was back in London and sitting on the bench. The man's eyes were kind and he looked at me with compassion. He repeated, "All right?"

"Yes," I managed to say with a forced smile. "A temporary indisposition. I'm staying at this hotel, thank you."

He helped steady me and raised his black hat to me while bowing. He walked away but not before turning around one more time to make sure I was able to stand on my own.

In the lobby, I leaned against the desk. The visions were not over yet. I saw roses again, always roses. My feet in puddles of water. My stomach in tight knots. Torn letters, like confetti suspended in air. My eyes marred with tears. My voice caught in my throat. My hands, helpless. And a whispering voice kept repeating the word I saw on the plaque. "Moorsgrange." "Moorsgrange." "Moorsgrange."

I looked at my palms unable to understand where those thoughts had come from. I was a nurse. My hands were capable, dexterous, steady. Yet, now they trembled, and I could not control them. My ears deceived me. My own mind proved unreliable.

The young man at the desk, Arnav, who had helped me that first day, came toward me.

"Miss Pia! You are so pale. Come sit here. This armchair is very comfortable. I'll fetch you some water."

In a second he was back with a glass, which I sipped from slowly.

"Would you like me to call Rikke?" She had declined any form of honorific he had tried to use, and so reluctantly he accepted to called her by her first name.

"Oh, please don't, Arnav. I have to ask you not to tell her I felt indisposed. She would only worry, and I am already feeling better. I'm a nurse. If it were something serious, I'd be the first to look for help."

He looked at me dubiously.

"It's true."

"Fine, but Rikke would be really upset with me if she found out. It is clear she loves you."

I drank those words in big gulps, unlike what I did with the water. To be loved was the best feeling in the world. Rikke was back in my life, and I was not about to spoil it with fainting spells and visions.

I pulled myself together, grabbed my bags and went up to our room, to kiss Rikke and to make myself ready for our adventure.

Chapter 18

Rikke

When I opened the door and saw Pia standing in the hotel hall, I thought the extreme emotional stress I'd felt since I came down the ladder from her loft, and fled the country, had triggered some sort of psychological event. I couldn't quite believe she was real, and that her response to my flight was to follow me. I'd not reached out because I was afraid I'd encounter anger and eventual rejection. I had to touch her to know she was truly there. Her response to my kiss was equally shocking and it wasn't until then that I realized how wrong my assumptions had been when I left with such haste. I'd not been loved before and didn't realize her reaction would be to find me.

She looked so tired when she arrived. Once I'd kissed her, again and again, reassuring myself she was real, I ran her a hot bubble bath, washed her back and hair, wrapped her in the hotel robe when she climbed from the tub, on tired, uneasy legs, and ushered her into bed. She refused to sleep until I promised I'd not leave again, and I curled up behind her as she drifted into a deep sleep, eyelids fluttering in dream. Pia slept like this for about five hours when I finally had to move to restore the blood flow to my right arm. As I extracted my arm and tried to stand, quietly, to make my way to the bathroom, she sat up with a gasp.

"Rikke?" she cried out, and I rushed back. The sun had begun its descent about twenty minutes earlier and the room was darkened by dusk.

"Here," I said, sitting back on the bed. "I'm going to the bathroom." Pia nodded, hand on my arm, her eyes adjusting to dusk as if her awareness returned after sleeping so soundly.

"I had the most horrible dream. Something was wrong with you. There was water and it was so cold," I brought her hand to my lips.

"It's fine. Lie down. I'll be right with you." Pia bunched the pillow under her head. I looked at her, saw her eyes close, and watched as her body relaxed into sleep. I took a shower, the hot water waking me up. She'd come to London for me. I'd completely dismissed her feelings. I was so overcome by my own emotions and fears, it had not even occurred to me how my behavior would make her feel. She'd opened herself up to me completely, pursued me even when I tried to dismiss her, and had never been anything but honest with me. I repaid her courage again and again with my disdain and neglect. Then, despite that, Pia followed me around the globe.

When I finished in the bathroom, I found Pia awake and sitting up in bed. She'd turned on the light on the nightstand and was sipping a bottle of water. She'd combed her hair and pulled it up in a tight bun. Her eyes were swollen from sadness, fatigue, and heavy sleep. When she saw me, she smiled and my love for her overwhelmed my fear, and I said, "I'm so sorry."

Pia came to me and held my face in her hands. "I know and you don't have to apologize." Then, she let go and walked by me into the bathroom. I sat heavily on the bed. I wanted her to be angry. Somehow, I think that would have been easier for me to process than her relief and reassurance. A few minutes later, the bathroom door opened. Her face looked freshly rinsed with water.

I held out my arms and she came to me without hesitation. I pulled her down on the bed and untied the waist of her robe, exposing every inch of her perfection to my gaze. What I couldn't convey with mere words, I offered with my touch. We'd left the curtains open; the sheer fabric underneath obscured the view into our room, but not the light from the full moon. We moved together in it as if we'd waited centuries for each other.

After, I nuzzled into her neck, arm draped across her stomach. Outside, a car honked, and someone yelled. We both looked toward the window.

"I really don't understand my reaction, Pia. I can't explain the despair, the certainty of your rejection." She clasped the back of my neck with one hand and pulled me closer, locking me in tight, her legs anchoring me to her body.

"It simply will never happen," she said, her tone even, full of emotion and conviction, and I believed her. I pulled away, and she reluctantly let me go. I raised myself up on my elbow by her head and leaned to kiss her again. "But maybe we can work on you not fleeing to England next time and talk about things." I laughed and agreed, and she smiled, and I understood what it meant to be in love.

The next few days were glorious and when Pia decided, upon my suggestion, we'd drive North, I was more than happy to go with her anywhere. We gathered up our belongings and made our way to the rental car without incident. Pia seemed quiet but reassured me she was fine. As we situated ourselves in the car, I turned to look at her. "You're beautiful," I said. "You look gorgeous." She blushed, pleased with the compliment, and kissed me.

We began our journey, whole and reconnected. My guilt for my behavior still nagged and confused me, but I was resolved not to project it onto Pia. She seemed relieved and content to have found me, and she deserved that peace. She was so conscientious, she settled into quiet as I began to navigate driving on the opposite side of the road. After a really busy intersection and roundabout, I took a deep breath and she leaned toward me, hand on my neck.

"You were amazing." I grinned at her, wondering again at my fortune in finding her.

"You're extraordinary, Pia. Your presence reminds me to practice gratitude. You barely seem real, your kindness, empathy, compassion. Capacity to forgive. I really, I —"

"Shush." She waved at me. "Watch what you're doing. Don't drive us off a cliff." She shifted in her seat. What I'd said was settling in and, for whatever reason, she was hiding her emotional reaction.

"Pia," I said. "I didn't mean to upset you. It's, well, I'm in love with you. I never want to spend another night without you. I don't want to ever do what I did again. I know it might take time for you to trust me, but I will earn it. I'm so sorry I hurt you. I can't imagine how you felt when I took off like that."

Her tears came then, and she pulled a handkerchief from her purse. I'd made it outside London and looked for a place to pull over. I found a large space off the side of the road, leading into a field, and I slowed the car, putting it in park. I undid my seat belt, leaning toward Pia. She came to me, and I held her in my arms, the center console of the seat digging into my abdomen. I was tempted to tear it from the car and throw it out the window.

"I'm sorry. I can't seem to stop crying," she sobbed into my shoulder.

"It's okay," I said. "It's been a lot lately. Us, your episodes, us, me, me fleeing to another country, abandoning you, me." I rubbed her back. "I'm a lot, generally." She laughed through her tears. "You're not arguing," I said.

"I was so relieved to find you. I keep expecting something to be wrong. To happen. I feel crazy. I was walking today, and—" She stopped, but I waited.

She wasn't offering me anything else, so I asked, "Does this have to do with your dream?"

"What dream?" she asked, her tears abating.

"The other day when you first got here. You woke up. Told me you had a bad dream that something was wrong. Water. Cold." Pia shook her head against my neck. "You don't remember?" She shrugged. "You were sleep talking to me, baby." Again, she laughed, her body relaxing. "Pia," I said, gently, "I feel you're not telling me something. You were quiet earlier too."

"I have to blow my nose and it doesn't feel delicate to do it in your neck." She opened the car door and stepped outside. I opened the console and found a small pack of tissues.

"Here," I said, holding them out to her. I turned up the radio, knowing she'd want privacy. I couldn't escape the sinking sensation that she was withholding something from me, but knew she'd already extended a great deal to get us where we were. She'd moved us forward together, and once again, I consciously embraced my gratitude for her. When she climbed back into the car and buckled her seat belt, her eyes were red and swollen but dry.

"Ready?" I asked.

"Rikke," she said, quietly, as she faced me. "I love you, too." I pulled back onto the wrong side of the road.

We arrived at our hotel in Yorkshire about six hours later. We stopped to eat and walk, take pictures and connect. I kept hugging Pia as if I needed to maintain contact with her or she'd slip away from me, into another dimension. About two hours into our journey, I grew accustomed to the road and relaxed enough to really enjoy the adventure. Pia returned to her normal state of emotional control after an hour or so of quiet and additional reassurances. I kept peeking at her from the corner of my eyes. I liked the way the northern sunlight danced on her dark hair as we drove, and I believed her profile was evidence of divine intervention in human life. I decided if someone wanted to argue with me about intelligent design, I would say, "Meet Pia." I told her this and she briefly unbuckled her seat belt to kiss my cheek.

We stopped at an inn on our way north. I told Pia I felt tired and would like to sit and watch television, order room service, and be with her for the evening. It was not the nicest hotel I'd ever stayed in, but exhaustion settled over me as I drove, and I wanted to be safe. When I pulled the car into the open space in front of our room, the harsh overhead lights of the urban street hurt my eyes. Night fell quickly and I was glad we stopped. I am not even sure now where we were, but it all unfolded with a sense of unreality. One moment, I drove on a windy road, open for whatever may come, and the next, I was parked in front of a two-story, modern hotel with hard angles and fluorescent overhead lighting near to a bus stop and a busy road.

The room was small and simple, with prefab furniture and worn industrial carpet. Pia pointed at a stain on the wall behind the ancient television and I embraced her and said, "Can we pretend we didn't see it?"

She grimaced and closed her eyes. "Fine, but I'm sleeping with my clothes on so don't get any funny ideas."

There was no room service, so we walked across the street to a small Indian restaurant, which picked up our spirits immensely. We ate heartily and then ventured back to the narrow, dingy hotel room and fell asleep, fully clothed in each other's arms.

During the night, Pia thrashed and moaned in her sleep, and I had to shake her to wake. She sat up, hand on her heart, a vacant look in her eyes, and then turned to me, feeling first my face, then working her way down my body.

"I thought you said no funny business."

"Rikke, are you well? Are you okay?" Her tone was panicked, confused, and I realized she was not yet awake.

I held her by the shoulders and shook her, slightly. Finally, she stopped inspecting me for injury and relaxed back onto the bed.

"Rikke, what is happening to me?"

"Were you having another dream?" I turned on the

bedside lamp. She nodded, hand over her eyes. "What are you not telling me?" I asked again, heart hammering. Between her episodes and dreams, I was concerned there was something psychiatric happening with her, which was fine, I thought. As long as she was with me, that's what mattered. We'd figure everything else out.

"It's okay," she said. "I think it's because I'm so emotional and out of my routines." She tugged my arm, urging me to rest next to her. I wanted to push but sleep beckoned and the same exhaustion which settled on me as I drove was still present. I needed to sleep, and I did so quickly, my head on her shoulder.

"I love you so much," she whispered as I drifted to sleep.

I woke refreshed but not entirely whole. I'd slept for twelve hours or better. Morning had come and faded away, and late afternoon was quickly approaching. She'd slept too. Both of us were silent and unsettled as we began to move around. I was concerned about Pia and a distant anxiety loomed beyond my grasp and understanding. I watched as she brushed teeth and hair, studying her for any hint of mental distress or illness. I found none. She rubbed cold water on her face and winked when she caught me staring at her. When she was finished, I did the same, wiping my face with the washcloth she refused to touch.

We gathered our things quickly and continued our drive north. We came upon a small village and wound our way through its small streets. I began to feel lightheaded. I told Pia this, and she insisted I stop at the small pub we'd just driven past. I found a parking spot on the street.

"We should have eaten earlier. Your blood sugar is probably low," she fussed, tugging me up the street. My legs didn't want to cooperate, even though I thought eating was a good idea. Instead, I stayed where I was, and bent over, hands on my knees. I felt the same vertigo I experienced in Pia's bathroom and my instinct was to flee. She saw it and came to me, strong and present, and took my shoulders in her hands. "What's going on?" I focused on her eyes and shook my head from side to side, forcing myself up.

"I don't know." I took a deep breath. "I feel out of sorts. Like I'm not in my body. I feel really afraid. I can't breathe. Like right after the fire."

"Are you asthmatic?" she asked. "I'd know that, right?" I shook my head and leaned into her, trying to regain my sense of balance.

"Let's get some food." We walked forward together. Pia pushed opened the door with her shoulder. Inviting warm light greeted us and a server waved for us to sit down in any empty seat. There were not many patrons. We settled into a small booth together.

The server brought us menus. I ordered a grilled cheese with chips and Pia ordered a piece of pizza. It seemed an out of character choice for her, one she acknowledged as soon as the server left.

"I'm eating my emotions," she said, and I laughed.

A few minutes later, we were sipping hot coffee and eating bread as we waited. Pia kept her hand on my forearm as if to be certain I was still with her. Some of my vertigo retreated and the world seemed almost right side up as I ate my food. We didn't really speak. A sort of silent understanding descended upon us.

Finally, as morning faded into mid-day, and the

food soothed my hunger, I turned to Pia. "I think I'm better." She kissed my nose. I insisted on paying for our food, and we walked quietly outside. Similar fear overcame me, but I felt more prepared for it. I breathed through it and slipped behind the wheel of the car as if I felt normal, like it was any other day.

"Where should I go?" Pia shrugged, oddly quiet, as she stared out the passenger window. I drove through the village, turning down random streets. We paused to look at buildings, and then we stopped at a park, where we bought coffee from a small cart vendor. We sat on a stone bench and watched children play and I skipped rocks on the pond. As we watched the approach of night, we climbed back in the car and left the village. Trees and bushes lined the path, but beyond them lay only vast, open fields, and endless horizon. Pia sat forward in her seat and looked through the windshield, as did I. She said nothing as we progressed, but her jaw was clenched. I reassured her with a smile and hoped she'd relax. I kept both hands on the wheel of the car.

I saw the manor in the distance, large and looming, its windows lit with electric candles, one in each, greeting its visitors. It was dark so all I saw of the grounds was what the light from the house offered, and all I could feel was the overwhelming sense of death, even if I couldn't articulate it then. I also had the feeling that I was home.

I slowed the car as we approached, with a sort of reverence.

"Pia," I said quietly. "What is that?" She said nothing but I wasn't waiting for any response. I turned the car up the long drive leading to a house I felt certain I'd seen before. I turned the car lights on bright to navigate better. I found an empty spot in front of the manor and pulled into it. Pia sat stonily silent in the seat, staring straight ahead. I caught a glimpse of a sign on the side of the house, next to the front door. It read "Moorsgrange," and to the right of it was a vacancy sign.

"Let's stay here," I said, opening the car door, not waiting for Pia to respond, my heart hammering. But she climbed out of the car and we both paused on the brick pavers, in silent agreement. I turned away from her to get our bags, and Pia walked ahead of me. I stopped outside the large wooden doors and looked upward, and from side to side. I was overcome with a sensation of being watched. I felt as though someone were standing over my shoulder, looking where I looked.

A harsh wind began to blow, and I held the bags closer to my body, turning one last time to look over my shoulder. Pia held the door open and finally called me forward. My legs felt fastened to the earth, but I met Pia's eyes, and her gaze tugged me forward. We stepped into the manor and the soft, warm light of candles. A single, low wattage desk lamp burned behind the desk, but otherwise, the entrance was period specific. Someone had gone to a lot of effort to restore the space to its Victorian era image.

The hall opened up to a grand entry and a center staircase like something built for a golden era Hollywood film about Victorian England. I knew it was not original the moment I looked at it. It was too perfect, curved, and polished. I felt as though it was too far to the left and had originally been situated at a more elegant angle. The stairs bothered me so much I leaned into Pia, as she spoke with the attendant, and whispered, "Those stairs are wrong."

I sat the bags by Pia, assuming I'd be back to carry them, and walked away from her, peering into the doorways along the perimeter of the room. A parlor, library, and music room. I turned back around, again and again, looking at the space. I heard Pia talking to the front desk attendant, getting us a room. I crept forward into the music room, compelled forward by a grand piano sitting in front of the fireplace, which burned with low light. I sat at the piano and began to play a few notes, as if it were the most natural thing I could do in such circumstances.

I began with a simple Chopin Nocturne and then moved into an original composition I'd written some years before. A few moments into it, I switched to a mournful piano melody without any conscious participation, and Pia arrived by the piano, with the attendant, an older woman with bright red hair, frizzy and unkempt. I'd left our bags in the middle of the room, and it wasn't until I saw Pia that I realized what I'd done. I stopped abruptly and made eye contact with the attendant. Her name tag said Emily.

"Emily, I apologize. I started playing." Only I didn't need to apologize.

"It was beautiful," she told me, with a distinctive Irish accent. "Keep playing. You'll bring all the guests down for coffee." She clapped her hands and rushed from the room. Pia smiled at me with affection moved our bags from the middle of the room.

I jumped up from the piano. "No, let me get those." She waved me back.

"You better play, maestro. Your adoring new fan is

readying coffee." Moonlight filtered through the stained-glass window in the upper middle section of the wall, and danced across Pia's hair. The room was soft with light but I felt lost in darkness.

I began to play again, pulse pounding, trying to outrun a creeping despair. Emily and others filled the room for my impromptu concert. After thirty minutes, I began to take requests. I jumped from Beethoven to Alice Cooper, improvising when I couldn't exactly recall the notes from a popular song. I forgot my initial hesitations about Moorsgrange, oddly at ease entertaining strangers. Finally, as the hour wore on, I held up my hands, accepting their applause. Pia leaned against me on the piano bench, watching me with adoration.

I felt more alive than I'd remembered being before, and as Pia and I made our way up the stairs to our room, my sense of familiarity grew, even as my ability to talk receded. Pia slipped the key into the lock, another period feature of Moorsgrange, and the door opened with a grating noise, scuffing against the worn wood floor. She walked in first, flipping a light switch. There was a large, four poster bed against the wall by the door. A gas fireplace burned to the left. A claw foot tub in the corner, next to a pedestal sink. In the far corner of the room, two walls obscured the toilet, and a door opened and closed to it. We sat the bags on the small table by the sofa and stood in silence, looking around the space.

Pia picked up a piece of paper from the nightstand, reading to herself. Then, pale and shaken, she read a passage out loud. "Moorsgrange was a glorious manor in its day, then it was abandoned, until the mid-twentieth century when an investor purchased it and made it into a hotel. It was owned by a landed family for five hundred years, until they lost their fortune in the late nineteenth century."

"Pia, are you okay?"

She looked up at me, held eye contact, "Then, the wars of the twentieth century changed the relationship of nobility and manors and such," she explained. As an afterthought she said, "I'm tired."

Pia turned on the water in the tub, looking at the assortment of soaps available for use. She opened her bag and pulled out the new nightgown she'd purchased in London. I sat on the edge of the couch and took off my shoes, watching as Pia undressed. She smiled when she saw my gaze on her, and lifted an eyebrow and a welcoming index finger, beckoning me forward. I slipped out of my clothes and sank behind her in the tub, the hot water blissful. We were both tired and simply soaked in the warmth—silent, but together. After, we dried off and dressed in our bed clothes, Pia turned off the light and the room disappeared into darkness, broken only by the low light of the gas fireplace.

Pia settled into sleep immediately, but my brain hummed, despite my fatigue. My arms were sore from playing, but I liked the sensation. The undercurrent of unease felt more present in the dark quiet of the room. I focused on the sensation of Pia next to me. I felt her leg over mine, her soft form pressed against my shoulder. When she snored softly, I turned to look at her with a grin, and kissed her nose. She murmured in her sleep.

I turned my gaze from Pia, back to the room, and that's when I first saw him, standing at the end of my bed. He leaned against the post, gasping for air, water dripping down his face and chin. I yelled, and scrambled from bed, searching for the light.

There was no one at the end of the bed, but Pia was sitting up, hand on her heart, looking at me, shocked. "Pia. Someone. There was someone at the end of the bed!"

Chapter 19

Pia

As the top of the mountain approaches, I feel lighter and lighter. The air here is rarefied and pure, and I inhale with all my might. What a difference a few months can make. I recall being in England and fearing my world crumbling around me and taking with it my sanity and my peace.

During that leg of the trip, my heart was heavy with the weight of a secret, and given Rikke's fear of trusting people, keeping things from her was always a danger. Yet, I had said nothing about the panic that overtook me when she drove us into Moorsgrange, a place by the same name I had heard and seen in my episodes. I walked toward it, trying to mask my shock, and I tricked her because I didn't know what else to do. Struggle to understand what was happening followed. Had it been the case that I'd heard the name in an ad and stored it somewhere in my brain? Was there a pamphlet in the hotel in London which could explain Moorsgrange's presence in my episode there?

I had no explanation for that phenomenon, but a force bigger than me told me that Moorsgrange had to be our destination in one way or another. And without knowing any of this, Rikke took us there. My biggest hope then became that if I went to the place, the episodes would cease, and she and I would be free to further our relationship and to explore the countryside. I didn't want to burden her any further in the meantime. It was wishful thinking, but it was also all I had.

When we arrived in Moorsgrange, I had my next episode, still in the car, as we approached the mansion. In my vision, Rikke was lying on the ground, wet and cold, and I screamed for help. The fear in me was so intense that I instinctively reached for her and was reassured by the warmth in her arm and the smile on her face. Once more, I didn't say anything. I was determined not to spoil our adventure, but I felt vulnerable, as if the house, from the start, had exposed places in me that I had safeguarded with so much care.

From the distance, Moorsgrange was imposing and ancient, and also in the distance, it appeared to be luring us in with its own mermaid song. Electric candles shone at each window, and despite the darkness, as we approached, I could see a rose garden to my right, made silver by the light of the moon. It was an enchanted spot, where shadows played tricks on our eyes, and this world and others came together in sounds, scents, and raw feelings.

As Rikke took us closer to the manor, its exterior became even more discernible, and a smell of wet dirt made it to the car when I rolled down the window to see better. Almost without realizing, as if the words were not mine, I issued a greeting, which came out of my mouth in a voice that hardly resembled my own. I whispered, "Welcome home."

Our first moments in the beautiful hotel were magical, if a little unreal too, with Rikke playing the piano with increasing passion and skill. Of course it was one of the first things she noticed in the house.

Being at the piano made her shine bright her fingers sliding over the keys with incredible dexterity. I was so in love with her that she could have played "The Itsy-bitsy Spider" and I would have thought her marvelous, but such was not the case. She played as if removed from time and space. She played like Chopin himself had descended upon her, and I knew that she also played for love of me. Moorsgrange was the ultimate catalyst for her amazing talent, and it was my privilege and joy to witness its unleashing.

At night, as we retired exhausted into our room, we sat in the bathtub trying to warm up. While lovely and inspiring to Rikke, the place seemed to be sucking up my energy, and all I could think of was a comfortable bed and sleep. I was halfway to realizing this dream when Rikke, lying next to me, screamed something about there being someone else in the room. I sat up, my heart beating a thousand times a minute, and looked at her.

"There was someone at the end of the bed!" she screamed once more, which was unusual since I had not taken her for a scaredy cat thus far. Quite the opposite. She had entered a burning building after all!

"I don't see anything." I said and reached for the lamp.

"You don't see it, but can you at least feel it?"

I did feel it. For the first time I took an interest in the room we were in. While it had been adapted to fit the expectations of its being a hotel room, much of what once made it a family-home room remained. There were antique bedroom curtains, and period lamps, and bucolic paintings, and wallpaper. Though I doubted much or any of it was original to the nineteenth century, great effort had been taken for the place to look like so. Besides our full bed, in a nook in front of us was a daybed or chaise, perfectly positioned to be a reading area. Even if I hadn't seen anything strange when Rikke called out, I was drawn to that corner by an intensely familiar feeling, one of great care and fear combined. I needed to find out more.

"Lie on this bed, Rikke. With your head close to the window." I guided her by the hand.

"What?"

"Lie on this bed, please. Help me out for a minute."

"What do you mean? How?" She had her arms open on the sides of her body, with her palms up.

"Trust me." I tried to smile in reassurance.

She did what she was told but looked at me with a sparkle of suspicion in her eyes.

"There." I said when she was positioned on the bed, as if sleeping or convalescing. I asked, "How does it feel?"

"I'm quite freaked out at the moment, thank you. Between the thing at the foot of the bed and this, I don't think I will sleep a wink."

But how does it *feel*? I insisted, using on her the expression she had used on me. I had taken a position near the head of the bed, having brought a chair to it. To me, it is always about feelings being one's guide.

"Like I said. Feels creepy somehow. Like the air is different here. Like it's not fresh but instead stifled and old. Stale, really. I'm also having a hard time drawing a breath.

"For me it feels quite natural, both the joy and the pain that this spot evokes. Had there been a bedside table, I'd say I feel as comfortable here as if I had sat by this bed many times. Look." I motioned to her, picking something up from an invisible small table to my right. "See?"

"No. What am I seeing?" She moved her head to the side but otherwise remained lying down on her back.

"How practiced this movement seems to me." I mimed the complete gesture again—picking something up from the table, talking to the direction of the Rikke's face, doing it again.

"You're a nurse. Many of your movements are practiced. Okay, enough of this. I need air, and we need to sleep." She cracked the window open and then went to our bed. It was clear to me that Rikke and I had developed different strategies to deal with feeling uncomfortable. To me, it was all about finding out more; to her, it was better to try and escape.

"But I want to figure this out. I want to understand how I know that there was once a bedside table over here. And another bed. And how those movements come so easily to me." I pleaded, but she was not having any of it.

"Come to bed. Perhaps if we close our eyes, it will all go away."

I lay down and nestled next to her, warming up from the contact with her limbs. A sense of security came over me, like I was meant to be exactly in that room with her, like we belonged together in that space. She extended her hand and interlaced her fingers in mine. I was asleep within a few minutes, but not before glimpsing a figure that stood for an instant at the foot of the bed—like Rikke had described—and falling asleep thinking of what he meant and what he had wanted from us.

* * * *

In the morning, scones and a full English breakfast waited for us on a sideboard in the dining room. Outside, the country greeted me with renewed generosity. Through the French doors, I could see the grass, the daisies and poppies that sprinkled the garden with color even in this unlikely time of the year. Following the delicious aroma of bread to the other side of the room, I made a large plate of eggs, cooked tomatoes and toast, as I was famished. Rikke had asked me to start breakfast without her, promising she would join me soon enough. "Why don't we ask for a tour of the house?" she had suggested as I was getting dressed, but not before saying, "You look especially lovely in that dress and those sandals," a compliment that made me smile and earned her a kiss.

Outside the breakfast-room, through the French doors, on a patio decorated with wrought-iron tables and chairs, I met a few of the other guests. A middle-aged couple with matching hats told me they were on a walking tour of the region. A young man wearing a wine-colored cardigan explained he was interested in the history of the estate and an adjacent village called Rosemead. Finally, an older woman with lush silver hair said she was in the area for the wedding of a niece. We made small talk for a few minutes and soon the couple announced they would be on their way out hiking most of the day. By the time Rikke arrived, with her hair wet and a dark-blue flannel shirt, the two remaining guests, and I were talking about the cottage that had once served as the gamekeeper's home.

"Go past the rose garden toward the woods if you

want to see it," said the young man in the cardigan, pointing in the right direction. "It was recently remodeled, but they restored it as closely as possible to the original. They even put furniture replicas of what was there in Victorian times. Same places and all. Those folks did not live a glamorous existence." He sipped his coffee and started on another subject with one of the guests.

I whispered to Rikke. "I'd like to see that. Maybe something for us to do after breakfast? It would be nice to take a walk."

She held my hand under the table and gave it a squeeze. "Whatever you say," she whispered back.

With our stomachs full of warm food and coffee, we went for a stroll on our way to the cottage. It wasn't a sunny day, and the mood of the sky matched that of the property: nostalgic, poetic, beautifully sad.

I inhaled the cold air of the morning. "If you lived here, would you prefer the mansion or would you be inclined to like the cottage?" I asked Rikke on a whim.

"As creepy as it is, I think I'd like the mansion," Rikke said with a pensive look, eyes toward the sky and a lopsided smile. "It is striking."

"I'd choose the cottage." I replied without her having asked me to.

"You haven't even seen it. How do you know?" She stood in front of me and walked backward to face me.

"I like cottages. I live in one! Big places are too much for me. I like cozy places. That house is not cozy. Its large halls and humid walls are fun for a visit, but I can't think of them as permanent accommodation."

She shrugged.

We walked by the rose garden and the fountain, and then past a small pond. The fountain was full of moss, which made it look like it had always been there, like a gift of Nature herself. The pond water looked dark in the half-light of an overcast day. I wanted to sit by the water and be, but I wanted to see the cottage more, so we continued on.

The cottage was a low building with a thatched roof that made it look several hundred years old, even if, in light of the fact that the mansion had been built in the late seventeen hundreds, the cottage must date back to about the same time. In the Americas, we have little notion that buildings can be as that and still serve as pubs and residences. We live with our minds in the future, on what to build next. We select a few structures for preservation, but, especially in my part of the country, we unfortunately believe a little too much in modernizing everything. In the process, we forget to learn from the past or honor the cultures that had been there before, for thousands of years. Although the cottage wasn't that ancient, it still possessed an aesthetic that belonged to another era, another world even, and approaching it was like traveling in time.

The heavy dark-wood door opened with a creak, and the floorboards whimpered as if in pain or effort under our feet. The room that welcomed us had a fireplace with chairs facing it, a dining table to the side and a large cupboard in the middle. This last item had been decorated with mismatched cups and saucers, likely remnants of sets that had once been used in the manor. An improvised cooking area stood to the left. A battered rug completed the decor. As I stood there, inhaling the old, moldy air of the building, I pointed my finger to the right and told Rikke, "There is a bedroom to that side. It has a small bed against the wall and a round, iron stool that serves as a bedside table. There's a wardrobe across from the bed. Don't ask me how I know. I simply do."

Rikke looked at me as if I had descended on Earth from Mars. "What are you saying? You have never been here, or have you?"

"This is my first visit. Shall we go check?"

We walked into the room, and, to our great astonishment, there were exactly the three items that I had described. Rikke sat on the bed and looked at me.

"Did you see this in the brochure? Did you search the Internet to play a clever trick on me?" She sounded a little frustrated, like she didn't know why I would do what she presumed I had. Her constant suspicion was hurtful and demoralizing.

"I swear I didn't." I made an extra effort to look serious because I needed her to believe me. I didn't know what was happening, but I wanted to keep my wits about me, and to do that I required her to choose to be on my side.

"Do you think this place is haunted?" she asked standing up. "Between visions at the foot of the bed and you having these premonitions, I am starting to think we should leave." She paused and sighed. "At least you are not having more episodes."

There was a pause. Very slowly, she turned her head to face me. "Pia, you are not having episodes, are you?"

She knew the answer before I offered it. "Very little ones." I said, looking down on the floor in shame and tracing invisible lines with the tip of my shoe.

"Pia, why didn't you say anything? It's not fair. I wouldn't like to think you were keeping things from me. You know how I feel about trust. It's everything." She put her hands on her hips and inhaled deeply. "I'm leaving." She started for the main room, but I stopped her.

"Don't go. You can't do this every time we disagree. Stay, be mad at me, but don't disappear every time you panic."

"I don't know how to do this. How to give you everything and not worry it will all be taken from me."

"So you simply go away and lose it all by your own design? Ever heard of self-fulfilling prophecy?"

That made her halt. When she did, I reached for her shoulder.

"Let's not do this again. You can trust me. I didn't want to worry you. That's all. I've grown accustomed to the episodes now. I power through them." I smiled at her when she turned around, hoping my expression would reassure her that I really meant it, even if I myself could not say I was that certain.

"This is not something you should power through!"

"What else can I do? I've accepted them, for as long as they might turn up. Fighting them won't help. That I'm sure of. And stop thinking I am always lying. I don't do it as a habit."

Her resignation came out as a loud sigh. "What else do you know about this cottage?"

I know there is another room, to the other side, with a larger bed and a chest of drawers, and a little round rug next to the bed.

Rikke grabbed my hand, and we hurried to the other side of the house, our shoes making hollow noises against the ground. She stopped at the threshold of the room when she realized I was right. The second bedroom was exactly as I had described. A little plaque by the door indicated that the room was a replica of what it had been in the eighteen forties, as was the rest of the house. The plaque also said that at the time the cottage was inhabited by the Allen Family.

Rikke walked to and fro. It was clear she was trying to make sense of these new revelations. "This is becoming stranger with each passing minute. I think we need to do some research. If this cottage is trying to tell us something, and clearly the manor was trying to tell us something too, we might as well find out what it is. We should start in the library. Tonight."

We spent the rest of the day walking the property, having lunch on the patio, napping in the afternoon. We agreed we would have more privacy in the library if we waited for the quiet of night to explore it. By dinnertime, Rikke looked impatient, and she fidgeted, with one of her legs moving rapidly under the pretty embroidered tablecloth.

"This risotto is delicious." I elbowed her lightly. Perhaps she would relax for a minute and enjoy a meal that was indeed very tasty if I called her attention to it.

"I'm not hungry."

"Would you eat it for my sake?" I made pleading eyes and reached for her hand. That strategy seemed to mollify her.

"Fine. I'll eat a bit."

Once she started, she ate the full plate. Then she had cake for dessert, and I had to hide a chuckle. I kissed her lightly on the cheek. "Thanks for making an effort."

"They are all for you. My efforts, that is." Her tone was more playful, and I took comfort in that.

Right after, we were invited for a cordial in the very library we wanted to investigate. Everyone sat comfortably on deep couches and large armchairs, drinking *crème de menthe*. We talked about the day, about the countryside and about the current state of the economy, while Rikke looked obsessively at her watch, as if she had an important appointment coming up.

"Was your walking expedition satisfactory?" I asked of the couple who had worn the matching hats. Now in the evening, they were not matching anymore.

"Quite," said the husband twirling a cigar between his fingers. "It is a most beautiful piece of country we have here, don't you think, my dear?"

His wife, Marylin, who was caught halfway to sipping her liquor again, took her time to answer. "Very much indeed."

The young historian who had been standing near the shelves of books decided to contribute to the conversation. "It's a part of the country full of nostalgia and magic, made more poignant yet by the history of this house."

Rikke and I looked at each other.

"Oh, do tell," said Marilyn, with even more interest.

He came and sat among us, taking a little ottoman from under an armchair. "In the eighteen hundreds, this was still home to one Emsworth family. While they had been numerous before, by midcentury, they had been reduced to only two people, Elizabeth Emsworth and her son, Jules Emsworth, and by then, the house was starting to lose its majesty. The upkeep was high. Jules was a musical genius, an especially gifted pianist, and enjoyed relative fame in his time, though his name did not survive the harshness of history." That last part he said in a very dignified manner, his angular nose up in the air and a hand across his chest, over his heart. Marilyn gasped a little. "But then, tragedy befell them. He was sick with consumption for quite a while and was one day found lying in a puddle of cold water in town during a storm. He did not recover." This time Marilyn's gasp was much more audible.

Rikke came close to me and whispered in my ear. "The specter at the foot of the bed. I bet that was young Jules, haunting the halls since that tragic day." I couldn't tell if she was serious or if she was mocking the historian and our strange days at the mansion. She was uncomfortable either way, and her expression was marked by lines in her forehead. I could tell her consternation by her fidgeting, and the fact that she was biting her nails, a habit I had not noticed she had before. I brought my index finger to my lips and gestured for her to be silent. I wanted to hear the rest of the story. Then I took her hand in mine to prevent her from hurting herself.

Marilyn reached for the bottle of cordial, the emerald-green liquid inside glistening in the lamplight of the room, and without taking her eyes off the historian asked, "What happened after that?"

"His mother closed the house in a few months, dismissed the staff, and moved to London. The manor was uninhabited for many years and fell into decay until it was bought in the early twentieth century to serve first as a school and then a hotel. At that point, the owners started to restore what they could to make it look like it had before."

"And a mighty job they did," Marilyn's husband concluded.

"Yes," the historian agreed. "The property has been in the hands of different generations of the same family ever since. It seems they are distant cousins of the Emsworths."

"Where were they when those two needed them?" Marilyn scoffed and her husband looked at her in reproach, tightening his lips, probably worried that one of the hotel employees might be there to hear. It was not like they had met the owners themselves. "What?" she said, noticing his silent consternation. "Family needs to help family."

The young man continued. "Young Jules was rumored to be on his way to eloping with the gamekeeper's daughter."

I mouthed to Rikke, "The Allens!"

"What happened to the young woman?" Marilyn was asking all the right questions, so we didn't have to.

"I do not know." The young man shrugged.

"How do you know what you *do* know?" Rikke was the one to ask that time.

"I have been studying this area for quite a while. I'm interested in the history of inheritance and the social practices of the time—who got to be lord or lady of the manor and such. There's actually a really good museum in town where I have done some of my research."

Looking at Rikke, I could tell where she was planning on going next.

We spent another half hour chatting with the guests of the manor. The lady who was in the area for a wedding came back from a rehearsal and sat with us for a bit. Then, one by one, the guests excused themselves to go to bed.

Rikke and I were alone in the library, free to discuss roaming the premises in search of clues of the Emsworths, and the Allens, chasing a story that I didn't yet know that we should care about.

"All right, we won't find any pictures, but that does not mean we won't find anything." Rikke was so categorical that I looked at her for an explanation. "The first daguerreotypes started being taken in the early 1840s, right at the time we are interested in, but they took about an hour of exposure, which means they were good for buildings and the like, but not people."

"Those are early photographs, the daguerreotypes?" I asked.

"Yep. If the Emsworths were really ahead of their time, there could be a picture of the mansion, though I doubt it. But maybe we can find portraits? Other paintings? And letters. Would we be lucky enough to find letters?"

"Yes, letters and portraits would be great," I said. "Do you think the hotel people are going to be upset if they see us rummaging around the place?"

"Let's be discreet so we don't have to find out. Let's go to our room and wait until the whole house is asleep." She gave me a kiss, and we moved upstairs to plot our silent scanning of the library.

Chapter 20

Rikke

I was grumpy from too much social interaction. Pia seemed at ease surrounded by the other guests, but then, she was a nurse and used to constant contact with other people. I felt drained and depleted, and by the time everyone ambled from the library after dinner, I was ready to hide away with Pia somewhere. I pulled a chair close to the door so I could listen. I pressed my ear against the wood.

"What are you doing?" Pia asked, an incredulous look on her face.

"Waiting for everyone to go to bed so we can sneak back downstairs."

"And you can't stand?"

"What? I'm tired."

Pia laughed and sat on the arm of my chair and put her own arms around me. "Are you going to be really ornery when we get old?"

When we get old, I thought. Pia was thinking about getting old with me. A flash of panic rolled up my middle, crashed into my heart, and Pia saw it. She kissed my forehead and leaned her head against mine. "I'm going to hang on here, so you don't run away to China."

"I think that was passive aggressive," I said, once I regained my composure.

"There was nothing passive about it," Pia said, with a light pinch on my shoulder. "Shh. Listen. It's quiet."

"See? My strategy of door-sitting worked."

"I'm not encouraging you," but she laughed, and I held her close.

"I get a little scared," I said quietly. She sat still listening. "That's all. What if I believe it? Believe you want to get old with me and then Martín comes ambling back, with his big arms and perfect teeth, and you leave me for him? Or someone else? Or you get tired of me?"

"I could say the same for you, couldn't I?"

I pulled a face which said that was ridiculous and impossible and she said, "That right there. That's how I feel too. Is that so hard to believe?"

Somewhere, down the hallway, a door closed. "Yes. Falling in love is letting go. People think all kinds of things are hard. Running a marathon. Ironman competitions. Getting a degree. Achievement at work. But the hardest thing of all is to trust. I'm being honest when I tell you it's hard for me to trust, but I really want to trust you because I think that is what love is," I said.

Then, I nudged her to stand. "Let's go sleuthing around the manor after dark, Miss." The mood lifted, the vulnerability of the moment before replaced with anticipation and excitement. I opened the door and we crept silently into the hallway. Pia held the hand I stretched behind me, and we kept to the wall, moving quietly past the rooms. I'd seen a back stairwell leading to the kitchen earlier and we moved quietly toward it, wanting to avoid contact with the front desk staff attendant who kept watch all night. Really, I doubt the staff would have cared that we spent late hours in the library, but what I didn't want was to talk with people.

We took the stairs quickly, giggling a little. As we stepped from the steep, hidden staircase, Pia paused unexpectedly, and I lurched forward, let go of her hand, and stumbled a little. I laughed as I righted myself, but she looked dazed, and my mirth evaporated.

"Pia, are you having an episode?" Strain was written on her face, and I could tell it took effort for her to reorient to the present. She turned toward where we'd come down the stairs, walked a few steps, and kicked the wall.

"Holy hell, Pia. What are you doing?" The sound of her foot hitting the wood paneling reverberated through the hallway. I grabbed hold of her this time and pulled her toward me. As I did, darkness descended. Where there was once at least moonlight and outdoor illumination coming in through the high windows of the hallway, there was nothing. I felt suffocated and leaned into Pia with the dual purpose of holding her close and steadying myself. I shivered and I felt Pia's skin turn to ice under my fingertips.

"What is happening?" Pia sounded confused. She was back with me, but we were drifting in empty space. It felt as though all matter had disappeared, and we were standing on the vacant expanse between stars and planets, somewhere on the other side of the galaxy. I looked down and saw nothing. I heard nothing either, which scared me the most. The silence was so full when Pia took a deep breath, it sounded as if a tornado touched down. I looked from the right to the left and saw nothing. I looked at Pia, who stared ahead, her eyes fixed on something, and I followed her gaze. As I did, matter re-substantiated around me. The temperature warmed and the sounds of the manor returned—the hum of electricity, whir of the central air unit, and the clerk's television, faint from the front of the house.

Pia pushed on the wall where she had kicked. "What are you doing," I asked again, not eager to repeat what we'd experienced a few moments before.

"I have no idea," she said, but then, the wall opened. A hidden passageway separated me from Pia, and I pushed forward against the door, following her. She'd turned on her cell phone flashlight and I pulled mine from my pocket, doing the same. The stairs were stone and steep, and we crept down them carefully. When we arrived at the bottom, we stood side by side and shone the light around the space. We stood on wooden planks. A small table sat in the middle of the room, covered in dust and cobwebs. Disintegrating fabrics hung on the walls but for one spot, in the far back corner. Pia walked carefully toward the table, holding her flashlight above it. I held my flashlight up to look at her and saw she was crying.

"Are you okay?" It was obvious Pia was distressed, but I didn't know how serious it was.

"Rikke, I am so sad. I can't breathe," Pia said. I was overwhelmed with my own despair. I put my hands on the table, unable to comfort Pia, and struggled to catch my breath. Once again, as had happened in the village, my chest tightened. Pia saw it and came to me immediately, pulled from her own sadness.

"What's happening to us?"

I shook my head and held the flashlight up to look around the room, feeling that something or someone was there with us. I saw him then, standing in the far corner of the room, staring at me as he had at the foot of the bed the night we arrived. Water dripped down his face, longish hair fell in his eyes, and his mouth moved, as though he were trying to talk to me.

"Look in the corner," I said and pointed.

Pia did but her question told me she didn't see what I did. "What am I looking at?" Surprised, I pointed, urgently.

"Him. The dude from the room. There's a ghost in here with us," I said. Then, he was gone. Pia walked to where I pointed and stood right where he was. "Pia, god, will you stop! Don't stand there. He was there." But she ignored me, as she liked to do, I was finding out. She kneeled where he had been, with her flashlight held out in front her.

"Rikke," she said, gesturing me over with her free hand. "Get over here.

I was hesitant as I moved toward her, flashing my light around the small space, when I noticed a wooden box on the table. It was covered in cobwebs and dust which is why I'd not noticed it right away. I wiped off the top and lifted it gently from the table. It was heavy, sturdy, and had a small lock on it. I felt entitled to it and held it close to my body with one arm.

"I found a box," I said.

"Rikke," Pia said, and even in the dark shadows of the small stone wall, I could see her fear. "This is my tattoo. Please come here."

I knelt next to her and studied the carving in the stone. I followed the lines of the design with the light from Pia's phone and then took a long, drawn breath. I'd spent enough time studying all Pia's tattoos to know it was the tattoo located on her right-side ribs, reaching around to her back.

"Hold your light up," I said, and she did. I snapped a picture of the wall with my phone. "How is this possible, Pia? Did you find this tattoo somewhere and like it?"

She shook her head. "I drew it myself one night when I was traveling home from one of my younger adventures. Out of nowhere. When I arrived home, I got it as a tattoo."

"You must have seen it somewhere." Pia shrugged and turned to me, away from the wall. She motioned to the box in my hand, and it was my turn to shrug. "It was on the table."

"Let's get out of here," Pia said, taking a final look around the room.

I agreed and followed her up the stairs. A movement from the corner of my eyes caught my attention. He was back, but he was closer to me, and now he pointed at the box in my hand. "Go, go," I said to Pia, wanting her to move faster up the stairs. "He's back." I leaped from the hidden passageway into the hallway and Pia shut the door behind us.

We were silent as we struggled to recover some sense of self. Pia was shaking. We held onto each other as though we were on a sinking boat, facing our last moments together.

"Pia, what's going on?"

"That was my tattoo. How is my tattoo on a stone wall in North Yorkshire?"

"Why did I flee to England, and you followed, only to end up in North Yorkshire, where your tattoo is on a wall, and I'm being haunted by a wet spirit?"

"I think that's in your head. I don't see anything,"

Pia said.

"It's not. I swear to god. He was there," I said.

"I'm sorry. It's not that I don't believe you, it's that…"

"You don't believe me?"

Pia laughed and then so did I. She took my hand and pulled me from the dark corridor, heading toward the library.

"Whoa. We're still going?"

"This all defies logical explanation. My familiarity with the place. That carving. Your hallucination," Pia said.

"It is not a hallucination," I said, insistent.

Pia ignored me, leading the way to the library when I was stuck by a thought. "Oh my god. Do you remember the psychic at the fair? What was her name? She said you are her and she is you and the past is present or something. What if that is what this is?"

Pia pulled me into the library as I struggled to remember what I'd heard that day. Before I played the piano for Pia at the church, and she had her episode, and I came to stay with her, leading us to where we were.

"She said it's always the one who doesn't believe. That's what your episodes are. They're glimpses of this. Of something here. Maybe these spirits are trying to talk to you, to us. You don't believe, so you can't see the wet dude following me. They jam images into your brain." I was certain of my new understanding, but Pia looked at me in the soft light of the library with a skeptical look on her face. "You're kidding. After everything that has happened, you still have doubts? Explain how you know that cottage so well. The room.

Remember the whole, 'help me out' thing when I woke and saw the guy?"

"Rikke," she said.

"Cognitive dissonance," I said. This made her laugh, and then I joined, fear and hysteria at the root of it. Pia laughed so hard tears came to her eyes. She sat on the small loveseat, bent over her knees, and grabbed the ends of her shoes. I sat next to her, and stuck my legs out in front of me, trying to unclench my stomach muscles. A few minutes passed, both of us in the throes of anxious laughter, and then Pia sat back, her shoulder touching mine.

"I have no idea what is going on," Pia said.

"Finally, you admit it. Why are we in the library?" I placed the box next to me on the couch.

"It seemed the best place to investigate the people jamming things into your brain and the specter haunting us," Pia said. We sat in silence for a while and calmed from the events of the night. "The box. Let's look in the box," Pia said.

I picked it up and wiped the dirt from it with my hand. It was a deep wood hue, ten inches by eight inches or so, and almost four inches high. It was heavy on my legs. Though I'd not noticed its weight when fleeing the secret room. I turned it from side to side while we looked at it and then I turned it over, carefully and we both gasped. Once again, we stared at Pia's tattoo. I took my hands from the box, suddenly fearful, and Pia reached forward. She ran her finger over the design. It was not carved deeply, but the dark room had preserved it well.

"What the hell," I said, and Pia nodded.

"Can we open this?" Pia asked, taking it from my

lap. She bent over, dark stray hairs falling from her ponytail. She blew out and tried to move the hair from her eyes, both hands on the box. I grabbed the stray strand and tucked it behind her ear for her. "Come closer. It's a lock," she said, squinting. It was difficult to see in the low light of library, but under the dust and dirt, I could see a metal lock.

"Let's go back to the room," I said. "Get more light." Pia agreed and we abandoned our quest to search the library, a decision we would later regret.

We crept quietly back upstairs, down the hallway, and into our room, avoiding contact with any other guests. Pia turned on the bright overhead light above us and sat at the small table with the box. She resolved her ponytail issues, and I watched her wrap the band around her hair, marveling at the beauty of her hands in movement. Once again, I berated myself for running away from her, but as the thought emerged, a different sensation surfaced. I was really convinced Pia would want Martín. That once he arrived, I'd be totally expendable. Why had I thought that? She'd done nothing to indicate anything but interest in me. The depth of my feeling could not be answered by the situation as it was, and for the first time, I sensed it was in some way connected to all that was happening.

I watched Pia's concentration as she worked at the lock on the box with a pair of pointy tweezers from her travel bag. They looked like little, tiny daggers and I wondered how she'd gotten them through customs. Small lines crinkled on her forehead as she focused and I loved her so much in that moment, was so relieved she was with me, not on the other side of the planet, that I moved toward, and standing by the side of the table, I reached for her hands. She looked up, met my eyes, understood my intent, put the tweezers down, and came toward me, without hesitation. Whatever I was feeling, she felt too, and we moved to the bed together, where we forgot the confusion of our day, the locked box, specters, and everything else, and remembered each other.

Later, as we rested tangled together in bed, the lights still on, I said, "I love you." I left the bed to retrieve the box and returned to her. I handed her the tweezers, and climbed into bed next to her and she opened the box on her first try. We smelled mildew and stale air but we what we saw made us both gasp— letters wrapped in cloth, bound with string, like a vintage prop bought at a Hollywood store. Pia gently lifted the letters from the box and set them in her lap.

We stared at them, paused in a sacred silence. Once again, I felt as if the whole world disappeared. The bed, manor, and earth was nothing but atoms bound together, moving at different speeds. Even our bodies were no more than that—a collection of organs, bound together by skin, for a moment, in the expanse of endless space and time. I scooted closer to Pia, and she glowed, formless, perfect, beautiful. I didn't see her momentary human body, the one that would grow old and one day die, but the eternal force which was her. I closed my eyes, willed myself to return to normal space, opened them and Pia returned with the world around me.

"I'm not sure I'm ready to read those," I whispered.

Pia agreed, put them back in the box, and closed the lid. She set it in front of us on the bed, and we stared at it, until our eyes grew heavy with sleep. I slipped down under the covers and Pia came with me, snugged into my arms. We were both so exhausted we fell asleep, the lights still on.

I woke with a pain in my leg. During the night, I'd shifted, and my previously burned calf was on the wooden box. I lifted it, my skin sticking to the wooden cover, and attempted to lift Pia from my arm without waking her. My attempt failed and she woke, sitting up. I rubbed my calf and she squinted, sleepy eyed, and reached out to touch my leg, reassuring us both it was fine.

"I slept on the box," I said, watching as she slipped from bed. I put my feet on the floor, lifted the box to my lap, touched it again, and then feeling an overwhelming urge to protect it, stood and slipped it into my bag, adjusting my clothes to make it fit. Pia arrived to watch me do it, nodding her approval. We bathed, dressed, and readied for the day in strange silence. Both of us were preoccupied with our own thoughts about what was happening. Finally, I looked at the time on my phone. We'd slept until 2:30 p.m.

Pia took my phone, and to make sure it wasn't broken, turned it upside down and backward. "Time zone jumping." I nodded, in silent agreement.

"We should look at the letters," Pia said, as she finished putting on eyeliner. She was sitting at the small table, her compact mirror open in one hand.

"We should," I said. "Or do they technically belong to the manor, and we should turn them over?"

"Yes, they do, and yes, we should but I want to look at them first." Pia was quiet. "Or we could look at them and put them back where they were."

"Now? Do you want to look at them now?" We made eye contact.

"No," Pia said, and dug around her bag for clothing. I watched her dress, perched on the side of the bed. Finished, she turned to me. "Let's go to town. Walk around. Get out of here a bit."

I agreed hastily, slipping on my shoes. On our way down the stairs, I took cash from my wallet, slipped it in my pocket, and handed Pia my wallet to put in her purse. "You like making fun of my purse, but you sure use it." I paused on the stair and kissed her. She stuck my wallet in the side panel of her purse, and I took her hand once it was free.

"Hello," I called to Emily behind the counter. She waved furiously at us, smiling broadly.

"Play for us again?" I held up my thumb in agreement and she clapped. "Holding you to it!" The last words followed us out the door.

"You couldn't have slowed to talk to her?"

"Nope," I said, unapologetic, opening the car door for Pia with a grand bow and gesture. Within moments, we were on the small road in front of Moorsgrange and the tightness in my chest released. "Phew. I feel like I can breathe again."

"I don't know what's happening."

"Have you had more episodes?" I slowed as we passed a wide-open expanse of land, strange recognition falling over me.

"Not since the last one I told you about." She shifted in the seat, put her arm on the door and looked out the window.

I told her about the sensation I experienced, of the world disappearing and seeing her soul, in a rush, as we turned the corner into the village. I parked the car as I finished describing how she glowed and put the car in park.

"You're having episodes, too." Pia concluded, and I nodded in agreement. She continued. "But yours are different from mine. I feel like I'm sucked back in time."

"That's the first time you've said that. I mean, you've not told me you felt like you were time travelling."

"I was thinking about what you said last night in the library," Pia admitted.

I waited, quietly, but Pia was finished. She opened her car door and I followed. I stood next to her, on the sidewalk. We both turned, looking around. Now that we were in town, neither one of us knew what was next. I realized then that Pia was finished talking about her episodes, so I intertwined my fingers with hers and gently tugged her forward.

"Let's see if we can find coffee and food." Pia hoisted her purse up on her shoulder and we walked silently down the street. The sun reached through heavy clouds and a ray of light struck the middle of the street, offering us a rainbow. Pia exclaimed and so did I, as we paused to marvel at the colors. On the other side of the rainbow, and the street, I spotted a cafe and pointed. Pia led the way, and we jumped over puddles in the road, the sobriety of our mood replaced with laughter and lightness as we simply enjoyed each other's company.

We chose a small table in the far corner of the cafe. Pia ordered an egg croissant, and I wanted fish and chips. I drank two cups of coffee, black, and Pia sipped her Earl Grey tea. I described the beauty of her soul to her in detail and she blushed, pulling my foot between her two under the table. Then I told her about how I think everything is really empty space, and we create inside it, somehow, and she listened.

"What about vaccines and the scientific method?" Pia asked.

I grinned. "We don't understand everything yet. But that doesn't mean we shouldn't vaccinate."

"I thought you were an anti-vaxxer, momentarily."

"The force animating the universe thinks the polio virus was a really bad idea. A miscreation. One of those ideas that seemed good at first, but then, once it was out there, well," I said and shrugged. We laughed together and ate our breakfast, ignoring our concerns about Moorsgrange and the letters inside my bag.

Patrons filtered in and out of the cafe and I watched the door open and close from my peripheral vision. Then a figure caught my eye, and I turned my full attention to the door. "You've got to be kidding me," I said, aghast.

"What?" Pia asked, and turned to follow my gaze.

"It's that f-ing doctor from your hospital!" Emotions boiled in me, and I hit my fist down on the table. "What is she doing here?"

"Calm down. You cannot act this way anytime someone from my life filters into your vision," Pia said.

Pia's comment was like tossing oil into a hot skillet on a stove. I looked at her incredulously. "You will not tell me how I can act. I have a mom who does that so much I don't talk to her." I stood and stomped toward the doctor. She grabbed her purse and followed.

"Did you follow us. Did you follow Pia?"

Dr. Guedes looked at me, tucked her dark hair

216

behind her ear. "Well, this is a surprise."

"No, it's not," I said. She remained silent. "Why are you here?"

Pia grabbed my arm. "Rikke, stop. Dr. Guedes. It's a surprise to see you here." I stared at her, overcome with raw fury.

"I grew up here. I'm here to see my mom," Dr. Guedes said.

"And it's a coincidence that Pia is here?" I asked.

"Very much so," she answered. "Listen, I don't know what I've done to upset you, but I'd like to think it could not have been that bad."

I shook my head and. "Whatever. Stay away from us." I dropped money on the counter and pointed at our table. Pia was unmoving, in the middle of the restaurant.

"Are you coming?" I asked.

"Give me a minute." I opened the door hard on my way out, and it bounced against the building's brick wall. I'm sure people stared. I walked to the car and leaned against it, arms crossed angrily across my chest. I waited fifteen minutes before Pia arrived.

"I was expecting you to have fled by now," Pia said to me. She was obviously angry.

"I don't like her," I said.

"Do you have to act like that?" Pia grabbed the keys from my hand and threw her purse into the backseat of the car.

"Yes. I do. Because you're all love and light with everyone, all the time. There is something off about her. I don't have that reaction to everyone I meet. When I have it, I am asking you to listen to me."

"Rikke, you don't even give me a chance. I work

with her. I can't be rude to her."

"She wants you. She is interested in you. Don't you see it?"

"This will not work if you are jealous anytime anyone looks at me. You don't own me," Pia said, hostility evident.

"I don't think I do. But she does. She's dangerous. I don't know how she knew you were here, but that's creepy. Let me see your phone," I said.

"No. I've given you no reason not to trust me," Pia said.

"It's not that. I want to see something. Give me your phone." Pia shook her head. "I want to see if you are on the tracking app together. I think she is. I think she can see your devices, like you can see mine. Like how you found me."

"She grew up here. That is all there is to it. Her mom lives in the village. She fell and broke her arm. That's it. This is like Martín. You need to stop. There is nothing wrong."

"Keep the keys. I'm going for a walk. I will see you later at Moorsgrange. And if you get too lonely, I'm sure Dr. Guedes can keep you company." I walked away.

"Dammit! Rikke," she yelled. I turned around. "You cannot walk away all the time and leave me."

"And you cannot control how I feel and disregard what I am telling you out of your desire for everything to be perfect. I need you to listen to me. I know I was rash with Martín, but that doesn't mean I'm always rash. It doesn't mean what I'm feeling isn't valid. You're not listening." Then, Pia started crying and all the anger I felt evaporated when I saw her tears.

I returned to her and tried to hug her. She pushed me away, but I persisted.

"You are such a hothead," she said, and I laughed. "Don't laugh."

"I'm sorry. The more time I'm with you, the more emotional I become," I said.

"So you're blaming me?" I laughed again and now so did she. I hugged her.

"I am a hothead. I know. But Dr. Guedes is dangerous, and I don't like her. It is weird she turned up here," I said.

"Okay, that's fine. That is how you feel. But do you need to act like that?"

"Maybe? I don't know." A strong wind blew against us, and I motioned for Pia to get in the car. I paused at the hood of the car and saw Dr. Guedes standing outside the cafe, looking at us. When she caught my gaze, she walked in the opposite direction. I held up my birdie finger. Pia honked the horn and pointed for me to get in the car. I slipped into the driver's seat.

"Really? Am I dating a sixteen-year-old?"

"Maybe you are," I said, turning on the car so the heat would blow. A damp chill came with the wind and my arms felt cold.

"Let me see your phone, please. I'm not being jealous."

"No," Pia said.

"We'll look together," I said.

"Either you trust me, or you don't." Pia crossed her arms and pulled away from me.

"It's not about trusting you. We are in the middle of some crazy ghost story with letters in boxes, flashes in time, mystical experiences, tattoos and now, all of a sudden, a person I hate with every fiber of my being shows up right where we are."

Pia stared out the window, and I could tell she was thinking. She wiped a tear from her eye. "You don't need to look at my phone." I waited patiently. She pulled her phone from her pocket, held it in her lap. "Last year, we responded to an emergency outside of town. A hiker got lost and then got hurt. All of us at the hospital decided to share our locations through the tracking feature on the phone."

"So she knew," I said.

"But that doesn't mean," Pia trailed off.

"It means exactly what I said it means," I said.

"Don't you dare gloat," Pia said.

"I'm too pissed and creeped out to gloat," I said.

"Rikke, maybe we should go home."

"I was thinking that," I said. But then, the car stopped running. I turned the ignition off and turned it back over again and nothing happened.

"Is the car really dead?" Pia asked and I leaned my head against the steering wheel as my answer.

****

The car rental company had a tow truck come pick up the car. After much deliberation, Pia and I decided to forego another car. We'd take the train, shuttle, or simply find a car service to drive us back to London. We'd both quietly agreed the car's operational issue, as soon as we mentioned leaving, was an omen, and given that I was haunted by a specter, and her tattoo was on a wall in a hidden room, we decided it was prudent to play along. Truthfully, I think we both felt moved forward by an unseen force. It moved inside me, deeper than conscious awareness, driving me toward a goal I couldn't fathom.

As we watched the tow truck drive away with our little car, I waved at it. Pia watched me with a smile and when I caught her watching me, I swept into elegant bow, pretending to move a hat from my head. She laughed and clapped and said, "Let's find you a top hat."

I agreed, readily, and we set off down the village street, pausing to investigate the windows of all the shops this time. Silently, by doing this, we both agreed not to return to either Moorsgrange or the letters upstairs. "Sorry about earlier," I whispered in Pia's ear when we paused to look in a window.

She leaned against me, said, "Me too," and it was gone as readily as it came. Such resolution was new to me, but I didn't resist it. The worst imaginable idea was for Pia to be upset with me. I bought her a few pieces of chocolate, and a large chocolate bar for myself, with two cups of coffee. We sipped our drinks and ate our chocolate as we walked and then stopped in front of the museum the historian mentioned the night before. Pia saw it before me, pausing at the entrance. A brick stoop led up to the front door, which was heavy wood, with iron rods, painted bright red. There was a candle in the window, unlit, and two authentic street lanterns by the stoop.

"We might as well," I said. Pia was chewing her last piece of chocolate. She didn't look at me. I nudged her. "I give up. Surrender. Let's figure out what all this is and then go home and never come back." I watched her swallow, turn, and break a piece of chocolate from my bar, and eat that too. "Hey," I said, meekly protesting.

"Old coping mechanisms," Pia said, mouth full of chocolate.

"You want to go in?" I asked, and Pia nodded. We stepped up the stairs together, side by side, and I pushed the door with my shoulder, holding it open for Pia. We stepped into the museum where the light was darkened with long shades. Velvet ropes formed a small waiting line to the front desk, but no one else was inside, so we moved directly, rather than winding through them. The clerk was young, with dark short hair, cropped close to his head, and clearly uninterested in his work. He took our entrance money without taking his eyes off the tablet on the desk and waved us in. The only thing he told us was that closing time was in twenty-five minutes.

We paused at a table replica of the village and found Moorsgrange on it, noticing for the first time it was one of seven large estates in the area. What the status of the others was, I am still uncertain, but it didn't seem important enough to pursue. Pia stopped in the middle of the first large room we walked into. The front portion of the museum was walled off, in part, with a door leading to the larger collection of items. I barely noticed we'd made a transition from space to space until I saw her stumble. I didn't catch her in time before she fell to her knees.

"Are you having an episode?" I asked, panicked.

She nodded, clasped my hand, and moved her legs so she was sitting on the floor. "Rikke," she said, and I remained by her side. "This place. I know this place."

I looked to see if the attendant saw us on the floor. He was still staring at his tablet. I sat next to her, held her hand, and waited for whatever it was to pass. That is when I noticed the wall directly in front of us. A painted image of the museum hung there but the plaque under it said, "Village of Rosemead General Hospital & Doctor's Surgery 1825-1968."

"Pia, this was the hospital and doctor's office. Look." She had returned enough to herself that she was able to follow where I pointed. I watched her already paled face pull back tight in a grimace, and she sobbed, covering her mouth with her hand.

"Oh my god, Rikke. I felt like you had died."

"What? You felt like I died?" I was confused, scared, and tired. I wanted to go home.

"Like how I'd imagine I'd feel if you did," she said. "I'm nauseous. I need to stand up." Pia bent over, elbows on her knees, trying to steady her breathing.

I didn't know how to help her, so I stood quietly by her, thinking I might lend her my strength. I turned around, to block any view of her from the front of the museum, and that is when I saw the paintings on the wall behind us. One was of a Doctor Cain, with a plaque which read, "Village Doctor—1840-1872." Another was my specter. "Jules Emsworth—1821-1840."

"Pia," I said, tapping her on the back. "That's the ghost." Pia stared at Jules Emsworth with a mixture of fear, grief, and love. Then I followed her gaze to the doctor next to him and watched as she shuddered. I took a picture of Jules Emsworth with my phone. I wanted his portrait readily available the next time he visited me.

We both stood in silence, next to each other, overcome by emotion and a deep understanding that whatever had brought us together, and to England, was readying to make itself known. Like the moment before a thunderstorm, when the clouds roll in from the distance, the air stills, animals retreat and hide, birds bunker down, and life retreats to protect itself from lightning.

Finally, it was Pia who spoke. "Let's get back to Moorsgrange before it gets too dark."

We left the museum two minutes before closing time. The moment I stepped from the museum, I knew exactly why I was there, and I slipped in time.

Chapter 21

Pia

I reach the top of the mountain, exhausted and elated. The climb means a lot to me. This mountain has taught me so much about permanence and impermanence, about standing tall with my convictions, about listening to the silence within more than to the chatter outside. Here, where the earth and the sky meet, I can fulfill my destiny and begin a life completely ruled by love, acceptance, and joy. I can't wait to finish what started when I entered what had once been the surgery where Rory worked and where the documents that told us that story were located.

Something stirred inside me at that museum that was unmatched by my previous experience, so I was unprepared to face it and to deal with it. Yet, somehow, I knew my whole life had been a rehearsal for that moment: taking care of my parents, developing such a friendship with my brother, becoming a nurse, watching over Rikke after the fire. I had previously thought they were my avoiding life, focusing on others to forget about myself. But in reality, they were all connected.

They had all been experiences designed to expand my capacity for love and acceptance. I also knew that whatever was to happen needed to be resolved before I could move on, and I knew that Rikke had come into my life as much more than a friend and a lover. She was there to help me become who I was meant to be and to reclaim what I had forsaken before. That realization brought a mixture of anxiety and hope; I stood at the verge of a change that would define me, perhaps forever. What if it were a change for the better? But then again, what if it weren't?

Rikke and I left the museum and former doctor's surgery with the intent of going back to the hotel. We were each shaken by the unexplained circumstances that had brought us to that place, and we were each dealing with those emotions the best way we could, which at times meant not very well. To me, that included trying to take control of the situation, boss my way out of what scared me, address the matter as quickly and efficiently as possible. If I were to become the real me, if there was something momentous in my path, I'd rather it happened sooner than later. To Rikke, it meant retreating into her own world, but not without kicking and screaming her way there. I could tell that every time an event or person shook her to the core, or got near her to a significant degree, she retrieved her trust and stored it away while lured by a seductive desire to run. She played it tough at those times, though she could not fool me anymore. She did not retreat because she was tough—she did it because she was scared, perhaps instinctively fearing the explosion of growth and self-knowledge that would come from allowing complete openness to the opportunities that life presented. Maybe that was the reason she became so distracted at times. Maybe that was the cause of the accident that left her unconscious on the ground of a village's main road.

We had crossed the street toward a taxi stop not far

from the museum. *Such a 1980s thing to see in the age of apps that bring you a car with a driver on demand*, I thought, but Rosemead was a pretty idiosyncratic place anyway.

It was a line of local shops with a small gallery in the middle that separated us from the vehicles, one of which could easily take us to Moorsgrange. We reached the sidewalk, and I heard a loud thud. Rikke gave a slight whimper. While she looked back and scanned the area—and I am sure Dr. Guedes was the object of her concern—she hit a metal pole and fell down, unresponsive.

It took me a second or two to realize what had happened. Then, panic overtook me. I was screaming for her to wake up, and yet she did not move. On the deserted street, my voice reverberated against the buildings, but no one was there to hear.

Even with all my training, I was unable to control my nerves—it is different when it's someone you love, which is the very reason why doctors don't operate on family and friends. I checked her eyes but got no reaction. I spoke to her softly and then in a shriek. Desperate, I started roaming the streets, frantically trying every store door to no avail. It was late afternoon, and everything was closed, no matter how much I shook and rattled doorknobs.

I had done that before, I was sure, the anxiety attached to the movement still vivid in my body. Suddenly, I was back to visions of me searching for someone I didn't know. Only they weren't visions anymore. Time melted away and the stores became more old-fashioned, their neon signs and storefronts disappeared and were replaced by hand-painted signs that read "apothecary" and "butcher shop." Inside each shop window were wooden panels and glass jars, women's hats and baked goods. I had started to cry, suspended in some time and space situation I could not tell apart from the one where Rikke lay unconscious and lost to me. When I looked her way, she was still in the same spot, immobile. I shouted for help yet again.

Where the taxis had been, I saw a hackney. Across the street, the museum had given way to the surgery, its sign announcing that it was the place where Dr. Cain saw patients three times a week. I remembered a tea house, right at the corner. Then I stood in the middle of the street, shouting, but I couldn't tell anymore if my voice was coming out or echoing in my head. With no person in sight, I returned to the shops and knocked on their windows. Maybe someone was doing accounts or tidying up after hours.

Nothing. I turned to Rikke once more. I was crying so hard that I hiccupped from time to time. "Jules, wake up!" I screamed at her, shaking her shoulder as if I was overtaken by a delirious fever. "Jules, it's me."

Rikke stirred a bit but did not wake up. I was cold and wet even though there was no rain and no water. "Jules, don't do this to me." I insisted. "Jules!" I cried once more. Feeling the adrenaline that pulsated inside every vein, I lay next to Rikke, not knowing what else to do, and closed my eyes. Maybe if I did, everything would return to normal. Magical thinking had kicked in.

A hand landed on my shoulder, and then it reached for my arm, lifting me. In my confusion, I was still able to tell that Dr. Guedes was on the scene, assessing the situation. She went from me to Rikke and to me again.

"Pia, did your friend faint or hurt herself? Pia?"

Once I was up, she held onto my shoulders and shook me. No words formed in my brain. I did not reply. "I'm going to make a quick assessment to see if it's advisable to move her." Dr. Guedes moved fast, like she did every day in our hospital back in Sedona.

While the doctor worked, I stood next to her, unable to power my muscles to move or help. Fat tears rolled down my face and clouded my vision. Loneliness and pain like I didn't know possible embraced me.

In the midst of it all, Rikke moved and started to blink.

"Rikke!" That gave me the strength to go to her. I held her hand and saw in her eyes that she was back.

"What happened?" she asked reaching for her forehead and flinching as she touched it.

"You hit your head and fell." I kissed her hand trying very hard not to disturb the rest of her body. I then made room for Dr. Guedes to do her job.

"Don't move yet," Dr. Guedes urged while holding her hand and lightly pushing her shoulder down.

"Take your hands off me!" Rikke jerked on the ground, and I went to her.

"Please don't move. Dr. Guedes is only trying to help." I pleaded with her to no avail.

"No!" Rikke screamed.

"All right, all right. I will never understand why you hate me so much." Dr. Guedes let her go and stood with her back toward us.

Rikke sat up.

"Listen to me." I touched her face lightly. "Dr. Guedes and I will put you in that taxi over there, and we will take you to Moorsgrange, where you are going to lie down and let her examine you like the doctor she is, understood?" I spoke firmly and left no room for protests. This was certainly not the first time I had to deal with a difficult patient. She nodded almost imperceptibly.

I whispered to Dr. Guedes. "I think we have a small window of opportunity here. Please help me." She came toward Rikke like someone forced to approach a lion. This time, Rikke did not reject help, but her eyebrows were drawn together, and her fingers crawled inside her palms forming fists.

We took her to the taxi where she laid her head on my lap, as we both rested in the back seat. Dr. Guedes took the front passenger seat. The driver, looking at us, did not say a word but drove us directly to Moorsgrange.

Hills and valleys, purple moor-grass meadows and flower-dense pastures rolled in front of us. I took them in with everything I had, while keeping a hand against Rikke's hair. I wished we were still driving the small rental, the two of us, enjoying the English countryside and each other's company. The colors and the light overwhelmed me, and I started to cry. How was it possible to feel so many things at the same time, from the deepest sadness to the greatest love? How was I to move forward with my heart so crowded with feelings? As if reading my thoughts, Rikke reached for my hand and held it tight. It was like crossing a threshold that we had tried to cross before but had not succeeded. "Everything will be all right. I promise you," she said.

In the front seat, Dr. Guedes looked ahead as if she was telepathically helping drive the car. Once or twice she turned back to check on Rikke, and confirming that she was conscious and coherent, quickly reclaimed her role as side-seat driver.

"You don't know that everything will be all right." I said sharply without looking at her. I was scared. There was too much outside my control, and I was really mad at Rikke this time.

"Pia, why did you call me Jules?" Rikke asked, her eyes glued to the back of the driver's seat.

"What?" Her question helped me to let go a little bit of the anger and replace it with surprise.

"You called me Jules. I was only starting to come to at the time, but I am sure you did."

"Why would I do that?" Something within me could not deny the feeling that it was indeed what I had done.

"I heard it too." Dr. Guedes intervened, reigniting Rikke's rage.

"Excuse me. This is a private conversation."

I was ready to explode. "Quit it, you two. This has gone too far. I can't take it anymore. Stop the bickering. We have a serious situation here. I don't even know what is happening anymore, and yet I have to keep making you behave, as if you were children."

Rikke sat up despite my attempt to protest.

"I'm sorry, Pia. For everything. I will behave. All this has affected me too." She lay back on my lap and wrapped her arms around my hips.

I caressed her spiky hair. "You're a handful sometimes."

A few minutes later, I started recognizing the familiar surroundings that led to Moorsgrange, and soon the manor was peeking at us from behind the tall trees around it. The taxi driver stopped right in front of the main entrance of the hotel, and Dr. Guedes and I helped Rikke out.

At the front desk, Emily was too busy to notice us supporting Rikke up the steps.

"Where are we going?" Dr. Guedes asked.

"We are staying on the second floor."

In the room, I fluffed a pillow and instinctively asked Rikke to lie down on the daybed. As soon as she had made herself comfortable there, I experienced that same sensation of having taken care of someone in that spot many times before. Only this time I was sure the person was her.

"I am losing my mind." I said to Rikke as I treated the bump on her head.

"It seems like a collective hallucination." Rikke retorted, clearly understanding.

"If it is, I'm immune." Dr. Guedes was taking Rikke's pulse and looking at her watch, and I wondered whether the reading would be accurate given Rikke's thinly veiled yet controlled anger. She wasn't immune at all. In fact, I had started to notice the way she stared at Rikke and me, and as difficult as it way to admit it, maybe Rikke had a point in disliking her. The doctor didn't appreciate being on the outside peeking in. "I think it was only a scare. I don't see reason for greater concern." Dr. Guedes professed her diagnosis. "I'd still advise you not to fall asleep for a few hours and to let me know if you feel nauseous, drowsy or if you have a severe headache. Okay?"

Rikke nodded.

"I'll see if they have a room here so I can keep an eye on you overnight. If they do, I'll get my things brought from town."

At that point, I was afraid to look at Rikke,

anticipating the displeasure that I would find stamped on her face if I did.

"Thank you, Dr. Guedes. I would like to rest now. Maybe if you go to the front desk, they will help you with a room?" Rikke was controlling herself, I could tell, to sound more pleasant that I ever imagined she would with the doctor. When I looked at her, curious for an explanation, she simply mouthed a silent "Go!"

I accompanied Dr. Guides to the first floor and helped her get settled. When I came back, Rikke was sitting up in bed.

"Pia," she said without delay, "I think it's time for those letters now."

Chapter 22

Rikke

As we stepped from the museum, the cement sidewalk under me turned to cobblestone and dirt, the blue sky turned dark and gray, torrential water fell from the sky, and I felt lost, confused, and overwhelmed with emotion, and I was who I had been while being who I am. I knew this viscerally, even as I struggled in the experience. It was as if an older me showed up in the backseat of my driving test when I was sixteen, but was so confused about arriving there, they grabbed the wheel, and ran us off the road. I turned and turned, trying to find my way, longing for Pia, but my chest was tight, and my coughing made me double over. My hair hung over my eyes, wet and heavy, and my clothing felt soggy and leaden. In all of this, I lost my way and ran into the pole.

When I woke, the street I knew returned, with Pia and Dr. Guedes. I had a headache. Otherwise, I was fine, but seeing Pia's emotional state, I thought it best to do what she wanted me to do, and for some reason I was not yet able to articulate, I was okay with my arch-nemesis returning with us to Moorsgrange. I believe Pia noted my quiet with alarm, but I was really processing what I'd experienced. Once we returned to the room, and I allowed Pia to fuss over me with the doctor, I wanted nothing else but to look at those letters we found.

Pia brought them to me on the bed. She was frazzled, tired, and I'd never seen her look so distraught. What she experienced finding me in the street had shaken her even more than my flight to England. Before I opened the box, I hugged her, with every bit of me, and said, "I'm not dead. I'm fine. I ran into a pole." This made her laugh and I laughed too, kissing her earnestly.

"This is crazy, Rikke. Why is the Doctor here? Why is she staying here? Why did I agree to that? This has to stop. Let's go home"

"We will," I said, new certainty flooding me. "I think we're almost there." I felt so calm, and I was exactly where I wanted to be, with Pia, on a bed in an old manor in North Yorkshire, England, while the wind howled outside the windows and heavy rain began to fall. I closed my eyes and took in the sounds. The manor absorbed the storm's energy, almost like it was alive and experienced, and as we would find later, tired and worn out. Moorsgrange saw centuries of birth and death, children and the aged, and as she grew old with the Earth, I believe it was she who summoned me back. She was also ready to move on.

I unwrapped the letters in the box and placed them on the bed. The paper was yellowed and brittle and I touched the top one tentatively, unfolding it. At first, I strained to read, the ink blurred with time, but then the words on the page became fresh and clear, and instead of sitting on the bed reading them, I was at a small desk writing them. Time didn't just slip away. I jumped through it. Ink stained my fingers and hand, and my back ached from coughing, so I sat hunched over, writing to Rory.

Rory,

My love. I count the days until I return to you. We will meet in the Church near the village after sunset on Wednesday. Everything is arranged. I have received many offers to play through the country, Europe, and America. I imagine us on a ship, bound for Manhattan. Perhaps we will love the new country and stay.

A man named Christian, who has travelled to America five times, told me there are stories of the air in the West curing my ailment. It is hot there, dry, and it rains only twice a year. The dirt is red and large plants grow with spikes on them. He says you can stand on a mountain and see until the horizon stretches to the other side of the world. It's the desert, like in the heart of Africa. Perhaps we can travel there, and I will finally be freed from the demon in my chest. Maybe we will love it so much we will stay and build a cottage you decorate with blue, and I will play piano for the church in town, and you can be town nurse, and we will never be apart again. I will even learn to cook, so when you are tired after nursing, you can come home to food waiting for you. Can you imagine such a life together?

I thought today about the way you hold your spoon when you eat and wanted to cry because I miss you so much. Do you remember when we were children and we found that baby bunny behind the garden shed? You fed it for weeks and somehow kept it alive. You cried so hard when we had to let it go. I wonder what happened to that rabbit. I hope it lived a long, happy life and had lots of children.

My mind wanders from thing to thing, though you can probably tell. I am tired and it is hard to focus. The concert this afternoon went very well, and I am glad to make these acquaintances, to know that we can care for ourselves, away from Moorsgrange, yet I am eager to return to you, your care, food, and treatments.

This letter is short, but know it is not because my love is waning. Just my stamina. I will see you soon when we are to be married.

Love forever,
Jules

When I finished reading, I raised my eyes, not expecting to see Pia, but a small room, above a town with carriages running over cobblestone roads. Pia was breathing so hard she was almost gasping. She took the letter from my hands, sat it in her lap, and ran her finger down it, touching it lightly. Big tears ran down her face and she wiped them before they dropped on the letter. She folded it and put it back on top of the pile of letters, then wrapped them back up in the cloth, put them in box, and sat it on the end table.

"I'm not finished," I said.

"No. This is finished. It's done. I don't want to read anymore," she said. She went to her bag and began putting her clothes and toiletries in it, shoving them in haphazardly. I watched for a moment then tried to stand. I felt a little off balance and Pia saw me stumble. She gasped and came toward me. I sought to reassure her.

"I'm fine. My foot is asleep." But then I was me, but I wasn't. My feet dragged underneath me, and strong arms grasped on both sides under my armpits, and I was no longer in the room, but in the hallway being moved into the room. Through my shoes I felt the dip in the wood, right where the door closed. I looked up and saw Pia, standing by her bag, her tears gone, replaced by intense shock. Water dripped into my eyes, and I couldn't feel my legs. I had jumped in time again.

Then, I saw Rory running toward me with blankets, calling out orders to everyone, demanding the fire be brought up to its full strength.

I couldn't understand why Rory was there, when she'd sent Doctor Cain to tell me she was not marrying me. I wanted to ask her why she should care at all for me, given her choice, but I could not find words. The room faded from fully formed to black nothing. I moved from my body and watched as Rory screamed, shaking my shoulders, begging me to wake up. I felt the pull of her energy, saw the glow of her essence, and returned, tried to open my eyes. I wanted to ask her why she didn't come to the church. I struggled to open my eyes and did, for a moment, and she saw, stopped drying my hair with the towel, and held my face in her hands. I felt her touch and shivered. I was naked under the piles of blankets and still damp.

"Jules. Why were you in the village? What happened?" I wanted to answer her, but I couldn't keep my eyes open, and they closed again. "Jules," she cried out. "Please open your eyes. Please don't go." Then I was above my body again and Doctor Cain came in, water dripping down his suit and pooling at his feet, and his face was ashen, strained. His eyes were red, and his hands trembled.

"What happened?" he asked, and I looked from him to Rory.

"I don't know," Rory cried, arms around my body, holding me up, though I was no longer in there. "I found him by the butcher shop when I came out tonight." Doctor Cain pulled me from her arms and felt my neck, shook his head with a slow movement before moving away from the bed to stand awkwardly by the door.

"No. I can't. Jules, no!" Over and over again she cried, and then I was back, and Pia's arms were around me, and the blood returned to my foot, and I met her eyes, and I knew she'd been there with me. I also knew what happened.

"It was him. Her. Oh, who the hell ever," I said, and fury raged inside me like I'd never felt before. I wasn't scared of Pia's abandonment, and my feelings about Martín seemed as childish as they were, and now made perfect sense. Pia would never discard me, not follow me, not tell me the truth. She'd followed me to England, and Dr. Guedes had followed her. Rory hadn't sent the Dr. Cain to Jules in the church. If she'd had doubts, she'd have talked to me about them herself. My head whirled from the back and forth, between Rory and Jules, Pia and me, and as each new layer of information revealed itself, I felt more and more whole. It was as if I'd left pieces of myself, scattered through time, and as I collected them, I repaired the fractured parts of me.

I saw Jules standing by the end of the bed, but then, he was me and I was him. He wasn't outside me; he was part of me. We are all more than we know ourselves to be. The product of countless lives lived here and elsewhere, our consciousness limited by what we understand of third-dimensional time and the language we have to describe it. Jules was not a ghost. He was a projection of the pieces of my soul I'd left behind in Moorsgrange.

Pia was confused and yelled at me in exasperation. "Who? What is going on."

I was enraged and threw open the door to our bedroom. I raced down the stairs and heard Pia behind, calling my name. I wasn't sure if she was saying Jules or Rikke, but it no longer mattered. I moved through Moorsgrange like the Master of the house and upon seeing Dr. Guedes standing outside the library door, looking in, I raced to her, grabbed her by the shoulders, and slammed her into the wall. The books behind us rattled and some fell to the ground.

"You lied to me," I raged and let go of her shoulders with another shove. "You sent me to that church, knowing Pia wouldn't be there. You led me to my death. For what? Did you think she'd love you?"

"Rikke, don't do it," Pia said when she saw me, fists curled, in front of Doctor Guedes. "What? Doctor Cain?" Pia asked in a whisper, looking from me to Doctor Guedes. She covered her mouth, realization dawning. "He sent you to the church?"

I turned away from Doctor Guedes and moved toward Pia. "He came to me, when I got home, said you wanted to meet on Tuesday, not Wednesday, but when I got there, you weren't there. He was. He said you wanted to be with him, not me."

Pia shook her head and moved toward me, arms around my neck, one hand in my hair, as she held me close. "I would never, Rikke. I would never." I nodded and let go of a breath I'd held for almost two hundred years and about three incarnations. What had happened had interrupted our progress together, scarred us both and sent our souls careening, until somehow, someway, we found each other again. I closed my eyes and held onto Pia, the doctor forgotten, the storm outside raging. Thunder exploded in the sky, so loud and strong the portraits on the walls shook.

Pia held me even tighter and whispered, "You're always running off."

"Not anymore. I promise." Pia took a deep breath, her stomach firm against mine. Then, my attention returned to the doctor.

Her hands hung at her side. She was pale and shaken, shoulders hunched, and I knew she remembered too.

Pia tugged at my arm, as if to remind me to control myself. "It would be best if you don't come back to Sedona. I think you have some stuff to work out."

She started to speak but I held up my hand. "She's mine. Leave us alone."

The Doctor walked by us, up the stairs, heavy with guilt. I'd noticed it the moment I saw her. She carried the weight of her transgression on her shoulders, in the dark tendrils of grief tangled around her legs when she walked. How she'd reconcile what she did was not my concern, and my rage was still intact, but recoiled, like a cobra resting. When wronged once, our soul builds armor to be certain it doesn't happen again, and it would take time for me to dismantle the rage and replace it with quiet strength like Pia's. But I had time now, and I had Pia.

I turned to Pia and smiled, the promise of a new beginning rising inside me, and I saw it in her eyes too. "I want to go home," Pia said again, and I agreed with a wide grin.

I took her hand, and we walked up the stairs

241

together, slowly, our pace even and measured, moving toward the bedroom. Flashes of our time together at Moorsgrange overcame me and I pulled her close, knowing it was happening to her too. We were children running together in the wide-open fields, and I turned to face her. We held hands, and spun in circles until we fell down, overcome with vertigo. Pia caught me as I fell from a tree that I climbed to impress her, and we fell in a tangled pile of arms and legs. Then, I let Pia dress me, and we giggled at our reflection in the dull mirror. We snuggled together under a tree behind her father's cottage and held a baby rabbit in our hands, coaxing it to eat. We snuck down the backstairs into Cook's kitchen and she gave us rolls and cheese, wrapped up in cloth, and we took to our secret hiding room, where we fed each other and made up stories about pirates on ships.

As we moved to the bedroom door, Pia turned to me, her panic and alarm gone, eyes peaceful and calm and looked at me with so much love I felt infinitely powerful basking in the warmth of her adoration. She didn't say anything because we'd run out of words to describe what we'd experienced. We opened the door and Pia walked toward her bag with a small laugh as she looked at the mess she'd made earlier. I joined her and together we began straightening our belongings, sorting them into their appropriate places.

"I suppose we have to wait until morning to get out of here," I said.

"No," Pia said, strong and declarative. "I'm done. Let's call a car, get a train, whatever. I want to go back to London, and I want to go home."

"Your wish, love" I said, and I took out my phone

to begin searching for options.

"We can stay the night in London," Pia said. scrolled through our travels options on my phone, and as I was ready to book our late-night ride, at a premium rate Pia never needed to see or worry about, screams filled the silence of manor.

I yanked open the door and looked out in the hallway. The other guests were spilling into the hallway, dragging their bags behind them, pushing forward haphazardly.

I grabbed the arm of the young historian we had talked to the night before. "What's going on?"

He pointed behind him, pulled away from me, kept running to the stairs. "Fire! There is a fire!"

That's when I looked up and saw a wall of red flame race across the ceiling and black smoke erupt from a door at the end of hallway. It was moving right toward me and after a moment of paralysis, I snapped into movement.

I raced to Pia. "Grab your purse. There's a fire!" I took her hand, and we ran down the hallway taking the steps two at a time, coughing as we took in too much smoke. We were the last guests down the stairs. Pia held my hand so tightly it hurt, and she only lessened her grasp as we pushed through the front entrance doors. Emily stood on the grass, on the phone with emergency, holding a clipboard with a list of rooms. We stood next to her, disbelieving.

"It doesn't stop," Pia said, exasperated.

I agreed and watched as flames leapt across the roof of Moorsgrange, and danced down each side, licking their way across the planter boxes on each guest window. Pia tugged my arm and I turned to her.

"Rikke, the doctor isn't out here."

"Maybe she left," I said, mesmerized by the flames.

"The doctor we booked a room for. Is she still here?" Pia asked Emily.

"We need to take roll. Can you help?" Emily asked, voice shaky.

Pia took the clipboard, called out room numbers, and ticked off each response. I watched her with admiration. She was so bossy, competent, and responsible. I loved her, but then I realized the doctor was absent. Every guest was accounted for but Dr. Guedes.

I looked at the burning manor. I was going to run into another burning building to save someone who killed me in a past life and stalked my ladylove across the ocean. Pia was right. This was all insane. We'd slipped into a cosmic stream of events no rational mind would believe. Pia handed the clipboard back to Emily and walked toward me.

"No. We will wait for the fire department. You are not going in there to get her. She killed you," Pia said. The other guests looked at us but kept their distance. I began slowly moving back toward Moorsgrange. Pia grabbed my arm. "No. I will not lose you again."

"I think she came here for redemption," I said.

"Really?" Pia asked, angrier than I'd ever seen her. I held up my hands, a momentary surrender in attempt to calm her. "This is ridiculous. I'm a game piece on someone's playing board. Oh, you want to be happy and be in love, chase her around the world! Trip and slip around in time. Discover your ER doctor murdered her in a past life. Have hallucinations. If there is a God, they can forget it. I'm done. We're going home."

"What if this is part of our redemption too? The final arc of the story that brought us here?"

"Since when are you some new age guru? This started with that psychic in Sedona. I'm probably still there," Pia said.

I kissed her.

"I'll be right back," I said and took off running. Doctor Guedes was Doctor Cain, and I was Jules, and Pia was Rory, and I had this overwhelming feeling it would all keep happening until I got it right.

"Stop running off. You promised," Pia called out after me. So, I stopped and turned back to Pia and held out my hand. She ran to me. We made it through the front doors of Moorsgrange, through the lobby, when Pia yelled. The smoke was thick, and the fire burned strong, and I could see very little, but somehow, she'd seen Dr. Guedes's shoes. She'd obviously fallen coming down the stairs. I thought about how damp and cold I was when I sat in front of that butcher shop, crying for Rory, and how much my chest hurt when I was placed in bed. I thought about Rory's tears as I died in her arms and I thought about leaving Dr. Guedes right where she was, my momentary forgiveness and higher awareness replaced with vengeance and pain.

But then I saw Pia, my beautiful friend and lover, who I'd been looking for ever since. Her dark hair fell into her eyes as she bent over Dr. Guedes, feeling for a pulse. Pia motioned me forward, and together we lifted her from the burning manor, making it out the front door as the fire raced down the stairs and chased us out into the night. We stumbled and some of the other guests ran to help us. Pia and I collapsed to the ground together, away from Emily and the other guests, who were now caring for Dr. Guedes.

Pia scooted next to me, and I curled up in her arms on the lawn of Moorsgrange. Together, we watched it burn. Jules's letters to Rory were gone, but so was the despair, sickness, and pain that bound them together. Pia and I let it all go. Someone eventually put a blanket around our shoulders, but we stayed where we were until the sun rose, and with it, blue sky, chasing away the dark. I heard someone say, in the crowd of people gathered, "It was lightening. Can you imagine?"

Chapter 23

Rory

When I left Moorsgrange on that fateful day, I knew in my heart I would never return. There would never be anything there for me again, and the pain of staying in the place without Jules was unthinkable. I would miss the roses and the cottage, but in time they would be stored away in some corner of my memory from where I could retrieve them when the longing became too intense. To live the fantasy of Moorsgrange in my head was a much more welcome prospect than living the rough reality of Moorsgrange in the real world.

I cried all the way to London, sitting in that lonely hackney. But all the while, I was also devising a plan. I was going to Paris, I would find a room, in a decrepit part of town, and I would dedicate my life to easing the pain of those who lived on the margins, forgotten by society and state. It wasn't simply an altruistic decision. Taking care of others gave me the respite I needed from my own suffering and my own emotions. It was almost a selfish thing to do.

Why Paris? I reckoned I was drawn to the night life, to the music, to a sense of nostalgia but wonderment at the same time. In Paris, luxury and decadence were part of the same tale. It was the city where artists went to tell their stories, be it through prose, canvases, or dance. A place where people did not hide being sad, or lost, or vulnerable. I certainly was all three of them.

Among the prostitutes, the painters, the writers, and the workers, I found new purpose. I took care of them, and they paid what they could. Sometimes it was only a coin, hard earned but passed to me with gratitude, for I treated them the same way I would have a king. At other times, if they had won at cards or had sold a new piece or had seen a rich client who suddenly got generous, they paid me more. Share the wealth, they would say. And it wasn't simply money; bread was payment, a bottle of wine was payment, and sometimes there was no payment at all other than a chat by the fire.

When sadness threatened to overtake all of us, there would be music and drink all night, and we would numb our sorrows with cheap wine that was always good and sing until our voices were hoarse. We would all then sleep a big part of the day and start all over again when night came. Eventually, the unhappiness would be chased away, and we could go back to our routines, working day in and day out, pretending to conform to the rules of the well-to-do.

I lived like that for many years, long enough to see some of my new friends perish in the revolution of 1848 when Louis Philippe was king. I certainly witnessed the living conditions that had led to generalized discontent among the working class: poor crops, hunger, the arrogance and ambition of the powerful. I treated the wounds of those who managed to come home, and I gave soothing potions to calm the nerves of those who stayed behind.

I did not take my father with me to Paris in the end.

I moved him to London, and I visited him when I could, which was rare. But in time, he found a good woman, a widow with kind eyes and a talent for cooking, and he married her. Knowing he was cared for after working so hard was a source of relief to me. Together they opened a little milliner's shop and were content in the placidity of their simple existence. He begged me to come home to London, but England bore no attraction anymore.

I heard the house was closed after all that happened. Some staff were relocated to London, where the lady of the manor, Mrs. Emsworth, chose to live, in simpler yet still elegant quarters. At that point, I lost touch with Cook and had no more news.

As I had promised when I left Moorsgrange, I never married. My heart belonged to Jules. Sometimes, when the ache of his absence was too great, I wrote him letters that I would then throw in the river, while I harbored the fantasy that they would sail directly to him, wherever he might be. I read voraciously and found in love stories ways to console my broken heart. I ended up writing a couple, under a pseudonym. They sold well in England, and the money helped further my practice, buy supplies, and treat those who could not afford medicine.

In time, I took a special liking to delivering babies, and people came from the other *arrondissements* specially to have their babies born in my surgery. There were also a few French girls who ended up named Rory in my honor, and I took that homage and commitment very seriously.

The years have passed, and I have been blessed with wonderful friendships. I guess they are a big part of what has been reserved for me in this life. In my old age, I have been supported and surrounded by children whom I brought into this world—their spouses, and their own sons and daughters. I never made much money, I never owned property, but my heart has been patched in surprising ways, and I am grateful.

Treating others became my obsession and my distraction, I know. It could have been worse. It could have been drink, or men, or any number of unhealthy pastimes. And if that meant ignoring my own personal life, I was willing to pay the price. I dedicated my whole existence to Jules and the caring of the ill, and I could not wait for the day, for this I had come to believe with all my heart, when I would see him again.

Chapter 24

Pia

It should have happened one hundred and seventy-nine years ago. Our wedding should have taken place in December of 1840, in a small country church in Yorkshire. We got to visit it before we left England, and I wept, sitting in a pew, feeling Jules's desperation and Rory's helplessness but also their devotion to each other. Rikke held my hand and told me everything was going to be all right. In the days that followed, and despite my initial protests, we worked hard to learn what we could about them, their love, which was our love, and the life that had brought them together only to separate them in the end.

The pain of their wedding's collapse reverberated in the universe for all these years because the suffering of one person is the pain of us all. We are not meant to live in separation. Maybe the day we realize all of that, we will have fewer wars, fewer disagreements, and we will look at other people and see our own humanity in their eyes, no matter how superficially different from us we think they are.

As it is, Rikke and I were separated for far too long. Some couples have to delay their vows because of money, or work. Others want to wait until they are older, or more certain. We had to wait for another lifetime. We had to first become the people whose love could break the cycle of loss we had been in, and when we did, finally nothing could keep us apart.

We arrived home with renewed hope for the future. I looked at Phoenix below us in all its dusty, arid glory and felt happier than I ever remember feeling. I could not wait to reach Sedona, our final destination, where we were meant to be all along. And we knew exactly what had to happen next.

Dr. Guedes would not be there. She had asked for a transfer to a Tucson hospital, and, through an email from one of the nurses, I discovered with relief that she had not even stopped to collect her things, having asked that they be shipped to a new address. I felt sorry for her. She was lonely and on a trajectory that could only lead to heartache. Silently, I did wish her well. When you're happy, you want everyone else to be too.

I have come to the top of Wilson Mountain, overlooking Oak Creek Canyon, because this glorious geography mirrors what I feel inside: that life is full of wonderful possibility, that the outside world with its peaks and valleys, and waterfalls and flowers, is a reflection of our thoughts, dreams and hearts. That when you wish for something to the point of vibrating in tandem with it, you get it. It may take almost two-hundred years, but you get it.

It is September of 2019. Below me is a vast expanse of red soil and dark green trees in one of the most beautiful places on earth. As I climbed, I shed all of my previous beliefs about the nature of things. Many were not my own anyway. They had been solidified by years of social expectations and empty platitudes that try to convince that if you follow the ways of the world as dictated by others, you will be safe. But it is all an illusion. So is control. I have not fully given up all control yet, but I am on my way. Today is a new step in that direction.

There is nowhere else I'd rather be than here, breathing in this air, looking at this canyon, becoming who I have always been. But I am not alone. Rikke is here with me, and this is the spot we chose to seal our future together and make good of a past that was beautiful but also haunting and sad.

James is here too, to officiate. He got ordained especially for the occasion, and Orlando came as well, to carry our rings in a pouch attached to his collar. The rings were my idea. Mine has a brilliant moonstone, once believed to form from frozen moonlight. Rikke has a citrine ring, whose stone is said, appropriately, to have been gifted by the sun itself. The sun and the moon, yin and yang, two parts of the same story, that's what we have always been.

Rikke made a special contribution to the wedding too. She salvaged several pages of Jules's compositions from the museum and got permission to make copies. She recorded one, dedicated to Rory, to play during the ceremony. Then she whispered to me "I wrote this piece of music for you. It's my masterpiece, but you can be sure that others will come. I intend for you to be my inspiration for many years."

I let tears run freely down my face. The wind will dry them in due time. Many things happen in due time so long as we allow them to. As I hold Rikke's hands, Jules and Rory can finally get their wedding too. I put roses in my hair for Rory, and Rikke wears one in her lapel for Jules. We know they loved the roses in Moorsgrange. Since we came back, my episodes have completely stopped as I had expected, and as scary as they once were, I have learned to be grateful for the insight they provided.

We are going to live in the cottage. It seems that my love for those cozy houses transcends time. I plan on making room for changes so that Rikke can feel it is her home too. A piano is on its way, and we will build an annex for a music room where she can compose and teach.

We say our vows. James is beaming at us. The ones I love most in the world are here. Rikke goes first. "You are my music, my muse, and my reason for being. In you, I find what was hidden in me. I will honor and take care of you. It is what is meant to be."

I go next. "I met you once in fear. Yes, I met you in love as well, but primarily in fear. Fear for your health, fear of your not being there. Fear of suffering— mine and yours. This time, I meet you in joy. I will honor and take care of you. It is what is meant to be."

We stay at the mountain while the sun goes down. James and Orlando leave after we eat strawberry cake with a sip of Champagne. Rikke and I seem unable to leave. It doesn't matter. Rikke brought the car, and it will be waiting for us when we are ready. We are suspended in a dream, only it's real this time.

We lie on a blanket we always carry in the trunk. We look at the stars for a long while. Coyotes sing somewhere in the valley, and their music reverberates against the endless mountains.

Endless. It is all endless.

Authors' Notes

We had a wonderful time in the worlds of Pia, Rikke, Rory and Jules. These are characters who have spoken to us, requested their stories told, and who became friends as we followed them around in their adventures.

Creating their universe took some research. The nature of tuberculosis or consumption in the nineteenth century was one such element. Another was the music of Frédéric Chopin (1810-1849), who inspired us to create Jules as a character.

Throughout the story, we placed little details of life in the 1840s. The development of new medical techniques, such as the sutures that Rory teaches Dr. Cain is one example.

We learned the expression "Violins with wings" to refer to cicadas from Dr. Gene Hall in an article found here, https://uanews.arizona.edu/story/7-things-you-didnt-know-about-cicadas

Rikke serenades Pia with the wonderful ballad *Total Eclipse of the Heart*. It was written/produced by Jim Steinman made famous by Bonnie Tyler.

We've written a story about the world as we think it should be. Love is love and eclipses gender, class, time, space, and even death.

Thank you for connecting to this story. We hope you had as much fun reading it as we did writing it!

A word about the author…

Patricia Friedrich writes Women's Fiction as herself and historical romance as Eliza Emmett. She is a scholar and professor. Her stories are often about the journeys of women as they make sense of family, love, and their vocations. There is always a bit of mystery too. Find her on Instagram @patricia.friedrich.author, on https://www.tiktok.com/@morebooksfordessert, and on Facebook
https://www.facebook.com/ElizaEmmettAuthor/
or
https://www.facebook.com/patriciafriedrich2015

Jen Jensen lives in Phoenix, Arizona with her wife and a pack of rescued senior dogs. She works as a technical consultant and author. Find her on Substack: https://jenjensen.substack.com
You can also visit her at www.jenjensen.org or follow her on TikTok: @lifephilos

Thank you for purchasing
this publication of The Wild Rose Press, Inc.

For questions or more information
contact us at
info@thewildrosepress.com.

The Wild Rose Press, Inc.
www.thewildrosepress.com